Away From You

KAY LANGDALE

Away From You

HODDER &
STOUGHTON

First published in Great Britain in 2014 by Hodder & Stoughton
An Hachette UK company

I

Copyright © Kay Langdale 2014

The right of Kay Langdale to be identified as the Author
of the Work has been asserted by her in accordance with the
Copyright, Designs and Patents Act 1988.

A CIP catalogue record for this title is available from the British Library

Hardback ISBN 978 1 444 78473 2
eBook ISBN 978 1 444 78472 5

Set in Plantin Light by Palimpsest Book Production Limited,
Falkirk, Stirlingshire

Printed and bound by CPI Group (UK) Ltd, Croydon CR0 4YY

Hodder & Stoughton policy is to use papers that are
natural, renewable and recyclable products and made
from wood grown in sustainable forests. The logging
and manufacturing processes are expected to conform to
the environmental regulations of the country of origin.

Hodder & Stoughton Ltd
338 Euston Road
London NW1 3BH

www.hodder.co.uk

For P.J.G.; always out there.

Some days, although we cannot pray, a prayer
utters itself. So, a woman will lift
her head from the sieve of her hands and stare
at the minims sung by a tree, a sudden gift.
              From '*Prayer*', by Carol Ann Duffy

I

Monica Watson put her espresso down on the desk. Nobody could fault her workspace. She was working towards paperless, and was almost there. Her inbox, instead of her in-tray, was now peppered with utility bills and requests for meter reads. Her glass desk, her silver MacBook Air and her (almost redundant) pewter pen holder stood testament to the fact that she was a woman with a tidy mind. She drummed her fingers impatiently and stared at the phone. Force of will, evidently, could not cause it to ring.

At university, fifteen years previously, she'd read Social Sciences, and which was the case study that had imprinted itself most firmly in her brain? Cargo Cults. Polynesian tribes cleared spaces in the jungle for airstrips; bald, bare swathes of land which would beckon a plane from the sky. *Create the landing strip*, her tutor had said with conviction, *and the planes will come*. For Monica, it still seemed a winning thought. She nudged her iPhone, lining it up with her MacBook. If she concentrated hard enough, perhaps she could reconfigure her desk as a Polynesian landing strip. This was surely the desk of a woman who would shortly be offered a major freelance role on an exciting film.

Daniel, her husband of ten years, had seemed less taken with the notion of Cargo Cults than she had been. She put this down to two possibilities. The first was that – from the off – he'd seemed amused by much of what captured her imagination. His eyes would twinkle at her and she would know she was being somehow indulged. The second was that he was a consultant orthopaedic surgeon, specialising in abnormalities of the spine; perhaps, as a doctor, you had to believe there were more meticulous, logical steps which facilitated getting from A to B. When she'd explained that the planes had actually arrived, he'd looked surprised but then said that it was just like newts, which seemed to Monica to be distinctly less amazing. He explained that his mother had dug a pond in the garden of his childhood home. (Monica's mind had snagged on this image as if it were a bramble. Her formidable mother-in-law would have, no question, actually taken a shovel and dug the entire thing out herself. *I can only disappoint you*, Monica had said to Daniel, on another occasion when his mother had deboned a raw chicken before stuffing it with almond pesto and Parma ham. Daniel had just laughed.) She'd refocused her attention. The house was miles away from any water. Two years later, Greater *and* Lesser Crested newts. Same thing, he'd added bafflingly.

Sometimes, at the end of one of their conversations, she wondered if Daniel could only just restrain himself from executing a little victorious fencing gesture with an imaginary épée, or perhaps a triumphant shout of huzzah! It would be entirely without malice; more in the spirit of gleeful competition. 'You are still, and always will be, the most interesting woman in the room,' he'd written to her in his tenth wedding anniversary card. Sometimes, she wondered if it had been a wife he wanted or a sparring partner. It was important to be light on her feet. Anyway, the newts hadn't cut it for her; she'd told him that. An amphibious creature, exhausted from hauling itself through ditches and possibly only finding the pond through luck, didn't evoke the same exhilaration as a small plane deliberately swooping and scything through a cloudless blue sky, and then puttering to a halt beside a sleek-leaved palm tree.

It was already eleven o'clock. Ruby had left for school two and a half hours ago. Since her recent ninth birthday she'd insisted on walking the short distance alone. Monica had dropped Luca at the nursery by nine fifteen, and jogged home pushing the Bugaboo. Her endeavour couldn't be faulted. Perhaps she was turning into one of those girls at school whose report cards said *Tries hard*, or, *Can always be counted on to give of her best*. Did anyone look at Ruby and think she was just a try-harder? It was as unbearable as it was unlikely. Hadn't her own mother pronounced Ruby, at three, to be as sharp as a wagonload of monkeys? Ruby, overhearing, had asked what monkeys would be doing in a wagon. The apple hadn't fallen far from the tree: Daniel's logic again. It was like a crochet hook which pulled up short anything that was overly whimsical or fantastical. Some days, Monica wondered whether that didn't include her. She repeatedly resolved to check her tendency to exaggerate, to embellish, but with little success. Sometimes she caught Ruby listening to her with her eyebrow minutely raised. It would be some time, thank goodness, before Luca could be similarly evaluative.

Monica looked down at her feet, flexed her toes, and circled her ankles. Maybe she could become one of those people who set their phone to beep on the hour and then did a sequence of Pilates exercises at their desk. She reminded herself that it wouldn't be necessary to limit herself to a few barely discernible shoulder rolls or discreet calf flexes. Much as she didn't like to dwell on it, rather than being in a smart office, she was at home in the boxroom. There was, in fact, nothing or no one to stop her leaping up and executing flamboyant star jumps in the buff. Maybe then the phone would start into sound; that might be enough to shock it out of its muteness.

At the foot of her desk, she caught sight of a small orange and black striped wooden tiger. It was Luca's, for slotting through the correctly shaped space in a barred cage. There were also a giraffe, a lion, a rhino and a zebra. *HOW much?* Daniel had asked, when she'd told him how much she'd paid an artisanal carpenter.

'But it's beautifully made, and will teach him shape recognition, dexterity and sequencing; they're necessary life skills,' she'd protested.

'Not exactly sequencing,' Daniel had countered; 'in real life, that kind of zoo-keeping would result in a bloodbath.'

Monica stood up and looked out over the garden. The woman next door, Patty, was mulching her herbaceous borders. Patty worked part time now, and her youngest child had recently left to go to university. 'Look at the *Viburnum bodnantense*. See how the *Chionodoxa forbesii* is coming through,' she'd call through the open French doors to Richard, her husband. Monica was pretty sure Patty hadn't known all the Latin names of plants when they'd first moved in eight years ago. Perhaps she'd been fastidiously learning them as her children fledged. Maybe that was what happened: the brain cleared spaces. Cognitive processes which had memorised term dates, the best place to buy hockey sticks, or the name of a driving instructor, gave way to great tracts of availability. Maybe the Latin names of plants swiftly blew in, or the ability to count cards at bridge. Nature abhors a vacuum, Monica reminded herself. That was probably something to hold fast to when you woke up one morning astonished to find your children gone. She tried to summon up Luca, straight-backed, aged twenty, carrying a large holdall. Inconceivable. He was eighteen months old. He hadn't even got a full set of teeth.

She'd watched Patty on the day she'd returned from dropping off her fourth child at college, in early October. Patty had got out of the empty car and stood in the driveway looking forlornly and fixedly at her upturned palms, as if her children might have mysteriously evaporated from her hands. Monica had turned from the window and scooped Ruby and Luca up and kissed them extravagantly. It was unthinkable that they would drive cars, have sex, go to university.

Now, Patty caught sight of her and threw her a straight-armed wave. Monica waved hesitantly back. *Now I look like I have no work to do*, she thought ruefully, before adding, *which I haven't*. It was important, she reminded herself, even if only professionally, not to exaggerate, embellish, or beat about the bush. When she did get an amazing freelance role on a film that became an unexpected critical success, her peers would appreciate her insistence on straight-talking. In an industry full of hype and insincerity, it was a valuable quality.

She took a step backwards and doubled over in pain as she trod on the edge of the wooden tiger, catching the soft part of her foot. *Shit!* she said, picking it up and flipping it onto the armchair by her desk. What had been the advice of the CEO of Facebook to all women co-workers? *Lean in*, she'd said, *lean in* so that your workspace is moulded around the needs of your home life. Monica recovered her stance. On days like this, leaning in seemed perilously close to falling right over. Possibly, spectacularly, right on her arse.

When the phone started ringing shrilly, she'd only just regained her balance.

2

Rose Hallett put her hand on Ursula's and said, *I'm sorry, my dear, there's no changing Jane's view on this. It seems the cloakroom shower with the flip seat was only the start. You know how it often is with eldest children – bossy from the off. It's just something of a surprise when one finds it directed at oneself. Geoffrey can't quite grasp it at all. 'Tell me again, whose idea is this?' he keeps saying.*

Ursula allowed herself to smile, and looked down at Rose's hand, placed gently on hers. She'd been working as Rose's and Geoffrey's housekeeper for more than ten years, the three of them moving around each other softly in this huge house like a small shoal of camouflaged fish. When she began work for them, aged forty, surely her hands hadn't borne any resemblance to Rose's? Now, the veins which snaked beneath Rose's tissue-thin skin seemed to broaden out and continue into tributaries and off-shoots which weaved across Ursula's own. Was she catching Rose up? Surely not? She balled up her fingers and restored the density of her flesh. It was not productive to think of what lay beneath. Neurons, tendons, the whiteness of bone, the deep pulse of the heart. Something roared and shifted deep within Ursula's ear.

I'd hate you to think . . . Rose murmured, then stopped. Ursula looked at the pale, tea-rose pink of her employer's lips. Tea-rose-tinted Rose. She noticed, not for the first time, the milky whiteness in her employer's eye. Her hand, now outstretched, shook with the faintest of tremors. Of course Rose and Geoffrey were increasingly frail, of course their offspring would think that this house was too big for them. It made sense for them to move into the annexe of Jane's home. She was a GP and could provide proper care as they became increasingly vulnerable. Look how slowly Geoffrey now came down the staircase. (Ursula twisted her neck to watch his careful, painstaking progress.) No more stairs to climb; she could see that might turn out to be what he would call *a blessed relief*.

It's not, it's not, Rose began again, *that you haven't cared for us, and for the house, beautifully. So beautifully. I sometimes feel the timbers creak with your care. If I could, if there was somewhere else I could suggest you move on to, some way of making it seem less as if we were . . . showing you the door. Especially after all these years. . .*

Rose faltered again, and a tear spilled down her powdered cheek.

'It's fine, it's absolutely the right thing to do,' Ursula said reassuringly. 'There's no need to explain, to justify.' She swept out her arm in an uncharacteristic arc. 'Caring for you, for all of this . . .' She fell silent, nodding perhaps a little too vigorously, biting at the inside of her cheek. There was no danger of crying. Tears were not a risk.

Later, kneeling, she folded clothing into the large oak chest in Rose's bedroom. She placed her hand on the broad, curlicued width of the drawer, dipped forward and inhaled the familiar scent of lilies of the valley. She stood, hung up one of Geoffrey's jackets and turned the key dextrously in the wardrobe door. She plumped the pillows on the bed and retied the thick, plaited cord which held the curtains. Walking down the stairs, she allowed her fingers to sweep along the grooves of the banister. All the years of coaxing it to a soft gleam, the scent of lavender wax deep in her nails. When she'd first arrived it was scuffed bare; it was the boys' fault, Rose said, the long-ago boys. Years of sliding down it, hurling trunks down it; nobody had ever stayed long enough to restore it to its original glory. Until Ursula, Ursula who had quietly, steadily, steadfastly cajoled the old house back.

It will be sold, I think, Rose had said, *that's the plan. Perhaps there will be a house full of children again, my sewing room reclaimed as the nursery.*

Did people have nurseries nowadays? Ursula doubted it. More likely it would become a home cinema, or a gym. The old pendant lights would be stripped out. They'd have no place.

She shook her head. It was unthinkable. She loved the house just as it was. Its stillness, the thick green pools of shadow in the stair-well, the lemon light of the morning room, the wheeze of the old oil-fired Aga when the wind blew from the southwest. If she closed her eyes she could see the cracks and the pitting in the flagstones of the hallway. She had learned this house with her body; committed it to sensory memory on her knees, with her knuckles, with the misting of her breath as she cleaned the leaded windows, or with a determined scrunch of her eyes as she rubbed at a stubborn mark on the enamel roll-topped bath. She would not stay even if new people wanted her to.

Standing before the linen cupboard, she minutely adjusted the winter flannelette sheets, smoothing the soft pile of the fabric. What had Gideon said, that first weekend, lying in the inky black-ness of a Venice November night, the Grand Canal sinuous like liquorice just beyond their window? *You will sleep in Egyptian cotton linen from now on.* In retrospect, it sounded like a command. She hadn't seen it as that, then; too busy being captivated.

He'd been wrong about the bed linen anyway. She'd spent more time laundering flannelette sheets than lying in Egyptian ones. And, given a chance to choose fabric, she would choose a hair shirt, and to go with it perhaps an implement which would flay her skin raw; allow her to open it up, precisely, neatly, like the scored crackling on a shoulder of pork. She closed the linen cupboard door softly.

The kettle whistled on the Aga downstairs. The sound of it punctuated Ursula's working hours, and the strike of the grandfather clock in the hallway, and the old shop bell which rang out from the walled garden gate. She straightened her spine. Change. Stared at clear-eyed and impassively, it would pass.

Entering her own home, later that evening, she stood in her kitchen and allowed its neutrality to absorb her. She stood very still, concentrating on the in and out of her breath, until she achieved a semblance of invisibility, of corresponding blandness. Was it possible to will the heart to slow?

The precise, impersonal sparseness of her kitchen made it difficult to gauge whether anyone actually lived there at all. No tea caddy on the side, no mail stuffed behind a sugar bowl, no discarded shoes, or bowl of fruit gently, undemandingly softening. Ursula lived in a three-bedroom semi-detached house, but there were rooms she chose never to enter. Her steps were mechanical, familiar, executing well-trodden routes. At night she moved upstairs or to the bathroom without requiring a light.

She opened the post. An envelope from her electricity supplier contained a fridge magnet shaped like a bee. Fat and yellow-striped, it balanced on the tip of her index finger. She stroked its enamel smoothness softly, but did not glance at the fridge. Returning it to its envelope, she placed it swiftly in the bin.

She decided to make a soft-boiled egg. Her hands moved with economical precision. She watched the egg judder in the rolling boil of the water.

She would have to start looking for a new job.

Somewhere between her shoulder blades a muscle flexed with tension, and she felt a corresponding shiver of blood. She scooped the egg from the saucepan with a spoon. What had she learned as a child? To puncture the empty shell so that the witches could not sail out to sea? Ursula had no fear of witches. Some days, she suspected, she feared nothing at all.

3

Cartwheels. Were cartwheels appropriate? Were they even possible?

There was probably insufficient floor space, and a thirty-seven-year-old woman, semi-spontaneously hurling herself into a cartwheel, might feel a little less exuberant rocking up at Accident and Emergency with a fractured wrist. That was a possible outcome.

Maybe Monica could throw the window wide open instead; whoop joyfully and uninhibitedly at the flawless blue sky. She could give thanks, if not to God, to positive thinking. Cargo Cult faith had come through. Her whoop, however, might give Patty a start. It could shock her into a fall; perhaps injuring herself on one of the ornate metal stakes grouped in her flowerbed. She checked herself. The whoop was probably best avoided. The downside was too great.

Was it motherhood, Monica wondered, which recalibrated the mind, ensuring that any spontaneous action should first be subject to a risk assessment?

The phone call had been from Gus, with whom she'd worked when Ruby was about two. It had been on a period drama, something that had been shown on the BBC. Now, he'd contacted Monica because he had a role for an assistant producer on a film that was to start shooting in three weeks' time. Monica sensed that she was not the first person he'd asked.

Twelve weeks' work, he said, *fourteen at the most. The crew's all set to go, and we've lucked out with a couple of members of the cast. Sundance Festival calibre. I'm telling you, Monica, chances like this don't come around very often.*

She hadn't missed a beat.

That's brilliant; sounds fantastic. Of course I'm interested, send me the script. Hey, I don't even need to read it, count me in anyway. (How bad could a script be, she thought, and no less career suicide than sitting at her tidy but empty desk watching her neighbour gardening.)

The best part, he concluded, *I probably should have opened with this, but I know from when we worked together last time you made the whole life/work balance thing seem effortless. The best part is that it's being shot just outside LA. Three months on the West Coast. You get to do some Hollywood dreaming.*

Had she said *Yay!* again? She feared she had. Retrospectively, she might justify it under gamely entering into the spirit of the conversation; the spirit of a long-awaited conversation which had progressed so peachily until geography reared its head. Had she, in fact, allowed the phone call to end *without* saying, 'I'm sorry, just elaborate on that a little more. The film's being shot in LA. Just to clarify, you want me to relocate to LA for three months?'

She had.

She'd said *yay!* and promised Gus she'd confirm within forty-eight hours. *There are a couple of other projects I need to square the circle with,* she'd added. *Projects?* Was that an acceptable way to refer to one's children? Her initial euphoria evaporated and she poked herself with her pen in mute fury. The cartwheel would have been ill-considered. The joy of being offered a job was small beer when the feasibility of actually accepting it was next to nil.

Monica folded herself down onto the floor, and sat propped up by the wardrobe. *Lean in?* More like crumple. What permutation of leaning in was covered by temporarily moving to another continent? She caught sight of herself in the mirror of the slightly ajar door and felt a whoosh of heat. What did she look like? A woman approaching forty with the shards of her career in her lap, catapulted into a frenzy of longing at the thought of how she might strive to have it all? Did Daniel have it all? Probably. He had the stellar career, the family, the cosy home to return to daily. Anyone with a scrap of sense (and now she swallowed an unfamiliar pulse of bitterness) would know that within a marriage there could never be enough 'having it all' to go round.

4

Ever since Ruby had returned from school her mother had been acting a little strange. Strange perhaps wasn't the right word. *Strange* was more like the man who ran through Sainsbury's, his hair all wild and white, shouting 'batten down the hatches', which Mummy said meant he thought he was in a submarine. This puzzled Ruby. How could he account for there being so much food? *Strange* also described the woman – a real grown-up woman – who always pushed a dolly in a pushchair. Sometimes she held a carton of actual milk to its mouth. Once, by the postbox, Ruby had watched her carefully. *My babba,* she'd crooned, and moved the pushchair forward and back with her foot. The doll's big blinky eyes had fallen shut with a click. All that counted as strange, Ruby concluded, shifting her weight on the kitchen chair. All her mother was actually doing was pretending to listen to her. *What did you do at school today*? she'd asked, reaching into the fridge to get out some apple juice, and cutting a piece of brownie and putting it on Ruby's favourite plate, which was decorated with dancing mice. Ruby had given the same answer three times, just to check.

Mmm, that's nice, Mummy said, when Ruby repeated that school lunch was inedible. In-*edible,* she said, with extra emphasis. If Daddy had been home, he would have said that was not strictly accurate. If it were actually inedible, lunch would have to have been impossible to chew and swallow, like the tyre from a tractor, or a thick woolly hat. Daddy would have teased her until she found the right word. He'd have kept thinking up more things that were impossible to eat, until she found a truthful word to describe her school lunch. Ruby was momentarily distracted by what that might be. Lumpy? Slimy? Mummy whacked the fridge door shut with the palm of her hand and Ruby brought her mind back to the kitchen. Now, Mummy whacked the top of the brownie tin closed; she was even whacking her own forehead, sitting at the table and using the heel of her hand to make quick beats just above her eyebrows, as if her head were a soft-skinned drum.

Ruby chewed her brownie thoughtfully. Sometimes Mummy was like this. It was as if she was fizzing; fizzing and crackling.

'Is it time to fetch Luca?' she asked.

One of the reasons Luca went to the nursery all day was so that Mummy had more time to think about work. Daddy had explained this. Daddy never talked about his work because of patient confidentiality. That meant not telling what people had wrong with them. Fixing them was secret. Mummy's work, meanwhile, when she got some, was in film, which she said was basically telling stories. Mummy said what she and Daddy did were basically opposite.

Often, she and Mummy were the last to turn up at the nursery. Ruby wasn't sure whether this was because Mummy had actually been thinking about work. The women in charge would be a little bit grumpy, busy spraying the changing mats with Dettox and cleaning the whiteboards that listed which child had done what when. While Mummy apologised, Ruby read Luca's notes. 'Luca has eaten his lunch with a good appetite' or, 'Luca has played with the building bricks'. Some days, however, it mostly seemed a list of when his nappy had been changed. Then, Ruby would give him an extra big kiss on his fat cheek, because she felt bad that that was all they had to report for a whole day. Luca was more interesting than that. He was easy to make laugh, and danced at the drop of a hat.

Mummy was apologising now. She said she'd lost track of the time. That might be another inaccurate thing, like lunch being inedible. Did time leave tracks? Ruby imagined minutes leaving tiny mice paw prints and weeks leaving huge great treads. Mummy finished apologising and was now zipping up Luca's jacket. Luca sucked noisily at his thumb. Ruby looked forward to when he could tell them his news himself. Maybe his lunch would be inedible too, but also not actually. Daddy would have a conniption if they were both so inaccurate. *Conniption*: her Auntie Cassie had taught her that word. Actually, Daddy was probably the person least likely in the world to have a conniption. Ruby felt sure of that, but she liked Auntie Cassie's words anyway. They flew around like fireworks. Once, when Auntie Cassie said something over supper, Daddy had turned to Ruby and said, *It will be my lifetime's achievement if you don't grow up to exaggerate like your mother or your aunt.*

At supper time, when Ruby had finished putting together a jigsaw puzzle with Luca (*I have mostly done it*, she told him, because it was important he understood who did what), Mummy came in from the kitchen and kissed them both and said, 'Are you having fun?' Ruby nodded. Mummy didn't look like she was having fun. Not the best fun, anyway. Maybe it was because she still had the chicken stew to sort out. She always cut up Luca's food really neatly, blowing and blowing on it so that it wasn't too hot. If Ruby had a whiteboard in the kitchen, like at the nursery, she'd write on it: *Luca helped with a jigsaw puzzle happily, and then waited nicely while his chicken stew was cut and cooled down.* That sounded busier than a list of nappy changes.

5

It had been a long and complicated day. The curve of the last child's spine Daniel had operated on was more complex than the scans showed; the compression of the thorax and the impact on the lung capacity a little more worrying. He'd modified where he'd inserted the dual growth rods, amended the calculation for the foundation sites. His instincts were usually correct. He could make more adjustments at a later stage if further scans showed they were required. The child's torso on the operating table bore all the characteristic hallmarks of idiopathic scoliosis: uneven shoulders and hips, the protrusion of one shoulder blade. Hump-backed, hunch-backed, whatever the lay term, it signified serious internal dysfunction. Cardiopulmonary consequences – he always dwelt on those in pre-operative conversations with procedure-shy parents. *No room for the lungs to grow,* he'd say with careful deliberation. Underlining the increasing inability to breathe was usually the clincher for signing the permission form.

Archaeologists had found Richard III's skeleton recently. *Can you confirm he had scoliosis?* a journalist had e-mailed to ask him. Daniel had concluded that in all probability he had. There was pathos, he felt, in the skeleton found beneath a car park, twisted and contorted just like the scans he looked at every day. If Richard III had indeed fought bravely at Bosworth, it would have required exceptional physical resilience. Why, yes, he'd told the journalist, it looks like an abnormal lateral and rotational curvature of the spine. Swinging a heavy sword would have been a task indeed.

It was pleasing to think it would be correctable now. Shakespeare, Daniel thought with satisfaction, might have had to fish around for some alternative descriptors to make the King memorable if his spine were actually straight in the coronal plane. He loved it when progress threw down such definitive markers.

Daniel changed out of his scrubs, and stood at the basin washing his hands. He'd long ago realised that, once you were a surgeon, the possibility of ever casually doing this evaporated. Now, whether it was before or after an operation, sitting down to eat supper, or simply returning from the supermarket, he followed the same methodical, oddly soothing, completely meticulous routine. Hadn't he been taught it, like a drill, as a medical student? He focused on the backs of his hands, on the creases of skin between his knuckles, and turned off the tap with a practised biff of his elbow.

He stretched out his spine. His neck felt stiff, his shoulders a little tight. There was an irony, he thought, in spending one's days mostly correcting spinal deformities, slightly hunched over an operating table, working deftly and precisely until each of his own vertebrae felt taut with stress.

When his own children had been born, he'd paid little attention to Apgar scores, or to the pink tint of their flesh. As soon as he'd been able, he'd smoothed his thumb gently down the length of their backs, checking that the spinous processes were correctly aligned in the coronal plane. A further quick check of the pelvis to rule out clickety hips. 'Aren't you meant to be changing a nappy?' Monica had asked. She'd been sitting bolt upright in bed, putting Vaseline on her lips. The effort of labour had seemingly left no trace.

When he applied sun cream to his children now (Ruby fidgeting, squirming, keen to be free) he'd check again, subtly, that their spines were as they should be. It pleased him to imagine his children's lungs, roomily and breezily expanding in their thoracic cavities. The spine, he'd told Monica, starts to develop three weeks into gestation. She hadn't looked particularly impressed. She'd preferred a sketch he'd drawn her, at eight weeks, showing a foetus curved like a tiny seahorse, the size of her fingernail.

It was hard to put into words, even for Monica, his fascination with bone; as a child stock still before the fragile carcass of a sparrow, as a teenager rapt before the skeleton hanging in the corner of the biology lab. Bone was triply impressive; it held the body upright, leveraged muscles and tendons, and cradled, at its core, the marrow which made blood. People imagined it to be brittle; something which cracked, shattered, or snapped. The opposite could be true. Had he not seen operations where bone removed from the femur was reshaped to transplant into the jaw of a patient, where it would fuse and regrow? Or, where the plates of an infant's skull were removed and replaced, but this time with more room for the brain to develop? He had stapled, hinged and nailed bone with ice-cooled metal clips, which then moulded into optimum shape when thawed by the bone's natural warmth. *Bone is impressive*, he said to Ruby when she was younger. He looked forward to sharing with her a more complex appraisal. Monica laughed and said, *Lucky Rubes*.

Getting into his car, he switched on his phone, and saw he had a text from his wife. *Need to talk to you tonight*. That sounded ominous. Monica was restless, unsettled. Since Luca's birth, he felt like a man who had somehow failed to come up with the right answer; failed to produce a solution, with a flourish, like flowers from his sleeve. Full-time nursery for Luca had been a concerted attempt but Monica still seemed to be yearning for something just beyond her reach. It hadn't always been the case.

When he'd first met her, she'd been twenty-six, and he was thirty-seven, and he felt he had barely raised his head from his

operating table for a decade. He'd been dazzled by her gorgeous-
ness, her long dark hair, her full mouth, her eyes which were
limpid green in early morning light. She was long limbed. He
had struggled not to say, the first time she lay naked before him,
Do you know what exceptionally long femurs you have? That
wouldn't have made it into a handbook on how to woo a woman
effectively. When he knew her better, if he had said it, she'd have
laughed and said, *Do tell me more.* 'Hardly the loyal little wife,'
his mother had said, but the way she'd said it made Daniel suspect
that she thought it was a good thing. That first morning, Monica
had stood in his bedroom, wrapped in a white towel, her vertebrae
rippling sinuously as she leaned to smooth moisturiser into her
legs, and he imagined the three-dimensionality of her; the foal-
leggedness of her bones, the weft and weave of her muscles, the
sparking of her synapses and nerve endings. And she turned to
him and smiled and it was as if all his studied reserve, application and diligence, all his carefulness, went *whoosh!* down a lift
shaft. So this, he thought, lying mesmerised in bed, this is falling
in love.

He'd had opportunities since – what consultant didn't – in
hospitals full of nurses, female junior doctors, even, on one occasion, the very grateful, glossy mother of a patient who had offered
herself to him, pragmatically, unabashedly, with admirable oppor-
tunistic speed. And yet, he had never been tempted; not when
Monica practically growled with ongoing fury in the last month
of her unexpected pregnancy with Luca, or even now, when he
sensed in her a restlessness, a rustling, subtle dissatisfaction at
what had appeared to have become her lot. Now, driving home,
he wondered what she had to tell him.

As he came into the house, Monica shushed him from the top
of the stairs. Luca was almost asleep in her arms; she was tiptoeing
with him towards the open door of his bedroom. Was it that time
already? How many evenings was he supposed to aim to be home

for Luca's bath? Evidently tonight was not going to be one of them. He peered down the hallway. Ruby looked up from a sticker book and gave him a wave.

And so I am home, Daniel thought, putting his bag down in the hallway. He would look at its contents later; he had a paper he'd been asked to review by a colleague.

How are you, Little, how was your day? he said to Ruby, lifting her into his arms. He'd called her Little since she was about two; no doubt she'd be calling him out on it soon. It wouldn't be accurate for long. He kissed the scramble of curls on her neck.

His children's physical wholeness, the fact that their bodies were unfettered by drip lines, clamps, catheters, cannulas, or the eye-rolling floppiness of a post-anaesthesia drowse, seemed to him to be worthy, each and every day, of heartfelt thanks.

6

'I'd like to make it work.'

Monica sounded childlike; or like someone faced with something mechanical, which, if focused on with enough application, enough fastidiousness, might just click and whirr into life.

Daniel looked at his hands. Something physical to tackle would be a relief. He could use his hands. Cut. Reshape. Fix. Make good. But in fact what was before him – before *them*, he reminded himself – was something far more amorphous, far more complex. How to make Monica happy. Was that what it was? Perhaps, more accurately, how not to make Monica feel professionally short-changed by motherhood. That sounded trickier. She sat next to him on the sofa, her face imploring.

'It's not that I don't love the children, don't love being with them, taking care of them, but I've tried and I can't only do that – I don't mean to diminish it – I mean, I can't do *just* that, just that thing alone. This job is a chance, a huge chance for me . . . if we could only, if we could just make it work . . .'

She stopped. Her finger and thumb rolled and tugged at a pill of wool on her sweater. He resisted leaning over to remove it.

'I know it's asking a lot,' she continued. 'I know it's disruptive, I know it will have all kinds of impacts . . .'

'In the same way that not trying, not going, would have.'

She nodded at his prescience.

'Is that awful to admit?'

'No. We both know that not going, not trying, will most likely end up being worse for the whole family than you taking three months out now. Bitterness. Resentment. You could probably count on mustering some of that.' He imagined her burning blue, like a coil of magnesium, Ruby and Luca powdered with the smouldering ash. 'We just need to think about the best possible way of making it work with the least emotionally negative impact.'

'I couldn't take them with me. I've thought through every permutation of how that might work and it would just be unbelievably expensive and much more disruptive. I'll have to work such long hours, and nothing, no one, will be familiar. But if I could find someone for here, someone to help you, someone who could top and tail your day, do everything in the house, have supper ready when you get home . . .'

'It's sounding like an upgrade already.'

'Ha ha. Obviously, it may well be, but it's not you I'm concerned about. I'm less worried about Ruby than Luca; I could explain to Ruby. I can Skype her, write to her. Luca – I don't know – he might feel confused. Or maybe as soon as I get back he'll forget that I ever went.'

'If he has attachment issues in his twenties, and a protracted fear of abandonment, it will obviously be your fault.' He smiled wryly. 'As opposed to the feelings of guilt that will be his demons if he clocks that maybe you sacrificed all your best chances for him.'

Monica smiled. Daniel continued.

'At least if he's here, he'll have me, and Ruby, and our parents, and Cassie, and the staff at the nursery. Perhaps we should try to see it as an exercise in short-term damage limitation for the kids and long-term damage limitation for you.'

'But what about us in all of that?'

'We were okay when I did that six months' stint in Watford; remember all those miserable Saturdays when I was supposed to come home and then couldn't, and when every on-call weekend fell when we had something planned?'

'Miserable is the word.'

'But we didn't have the children then, and our expectations were different. I think if we don't try . . .'

'Why are you being so good, so reasonable, so supportive about this? Most men would just say it's ridiculously selfish of me.'

'That's what I'm thinking obviously . . .'

She cuffed his arm with her fist.

'But I mean it, why are you being so nice about it?'

'Because, Mon, I can see your point. Because I can see why you feel this job might work as a tipping point for you. And because I don't think that just because we have a family, some doors should automatically be closed to you.'

'God, you're perfect.'

'No, just mindful of how much credit this will give me in the bank. Come my midlife crisis, I'll be living it large.'

'Darling, be serious, do you know what you are agreeing to?'

'Credit me with some insight. I realised within minutes of you telling me about the job what I'd signed up for. It's obvious you really want this; who am I to say that you can't have it? Frankly, I'd be more troubled about how to deal with you feeling resentful and short-changed.'

She kissed him full on the mouth.

Later, in the bathroom, Daniel flossed his teeth. He could hear Monica brushing her hair at the dressing table, the long smooth strokes of the bristles. If he closed his eyes, he could see the exact tilt of her neck.

He flossed precisely around a crown. Dental hygienists had ridiculously high expectations of a surgeon.

Monica going. Was his support a leap of faith? He swooshed vigorously with mouthwash.

He was actually a man with no choice. Beneath his conciliatory approach, he could see the bald truth of that. Some men's wives just walked out of the door and made an unscripted bolt for the blue. This, in contrast, was a joint decision. Surely, surely he could hold it together as a single parent for three months?

Later, when he slept, Monica lay beside him, and ran her fingertip along the length of his middle finger to the scoop of his wrist bone. He had beautiful hands; lean and long, his nails precisely cut. When they'd first met, he'd passed her a glass of wine, and out of nowhere she'd wished – with a heat that pinked the skin at the nape of her neck – that his hands were touching her, placed softly on the arch of her back, the inside of her thigh, his fingertip perhaps tracing the length of her collarbone. She had blushed as she had taken the glass, and avoided meeting his eye. She'd learned later that a capable surgeon was described as having 'good hands'. One of his colleagues had said to her, *And this man, my dear, does not just have good hands, he has the very best.* And Monica had known it from the instant he had passed her a glass of Pinot Grigio. And she had known, in agreeing to marry him, that she would always be in his good hands. Kept safe. Now, she found herself holding his hand tighter. Three months, surely, was no time at all?

Be careful what you wish for, you might just get it, a small voice chimed in her head.

Monica adjusted her pillow. Daniel aside, what would she say to Ruby?

7

'Going away. Away where?' Ruby asked.

She was sitting cross-legged on the sofa.

'To America.'

'America? Whatever for?'

It was a familiar phrase of Cassie's. *Whatever for? Why ever not? What on earth?* Her sister-in-law's mouth was peppered with surprise.

'Because I've been offered a really great job, just for a little while, just from April to July and then I'll be home again, super-quick.'

'But why does it have to be in America?'

'Because that's where the film is being made.'

'But why can't you work on a film that is being made in England?'

'I would love to, darling, but other films, made in England, haven't offered me a job.'

'Did you ask?'

'I did ask. All the time. I've been asking for months. I've tried my hardest, I promise you.'

'But what about Luca? He can't sleep at the nursery.'

'No, nobody's going to have to sleep anywhere but in their own bed. I'm going to find someone great to help Daddy, as well as both your grannies, and Cassie, and they will all help to take care of you and Luca and keep you happy and safe until I come home.'

Ruby tugged at her nail with her teeth.

'What will Luca think? He doesn't know about jobs.'

'I'm hoping he will be happy with you and Daddy, and that he'll be sitting right next to you when I Skype, and when I phone, and he'll see me blowing you a million kisses every time we'll speak, and he'll keep being reminded of me and that I love you both very, very much.'

'I won't forget you. Not at all.'

'I'm counting on that.'

'Is a job important?'

'Sometimes. Not as important as you, not as important as being healthy, or being safe. Not as important as those things. But part of me, outside of me being your mummy, is about being good at my job, and earning money, which helps me to look after you, now and in the future. Even though I'll be far away and it might look as if I'm not looking after you at all, I am.'

'So going away is actually looking after us?'

'Does that sound crazy?'

'Little bit.'

'But it's true. And when you grow up to be a mummy, I want you to be able to choose, to choose to care for your children, and work at your job, in the best way you can.'

'Will you miss my birthday?'

'Nope.'

'Christmas?'

'No.'

'Luca's birthday?'

'No.'

'Good, because who would make his cake?'

Later, as she made supper, Monica wondered if, in the mind of a child, everything boiled down to this grounded pragmatism. The unwieldy, unruly, ongoing heartstorm that was motherhood could be reduced to a Malteser cake studded with wonky candles.

Ruby had looked at her reflectively when they finished talking, watching her move around the kitchen. Her watchful child. What had Daniel called her? A 'noticer'. That would be correct. Ruby noticed everything. She was observant beyond her years. Monica didn't want to dwell on how she might interpret what she saw.

I am not abandoning my children, she said to herself firmly. *I am just trying to take advantage of professional opportunity.*

In her yoga class, they had a mantra which went, *Peace begins with me.* You were meant to tap each finger in turn with your thumb as you said it. Monica gave it a go. Peace hardly swept over her; if anything she felt a little more agitated.

Could unrest, she wondered, also begin with her? Was she unleashing it, skittering, scattering, recklessly into all of their lives?

8

Monica looked at her watch, and waited for the doorbell to ring.

The woman at the domestic staff recruitment agency said she had three possible candidates. She had arranged interviews, an hour apart, for this morning. Daniel had left for work and wished Monica luck. She wasn't quite sure how to interpret that. He'd said it almost breezily, which seemed out of keeping with its importance.

Yesterday, she'd phoned Gus and accepted the job, saying it was provisional on her sorting out her childcare arrangements. *Good work, atta girl,* he'd said, and Monica resisted retorting that she wasn't, in fact, a girl, but rather a woman who was having to try twice as hard to achieve what would be much more smoothly feasible if she were a man. Atta girl indeed.

She put the kettle on to boil and switched on the Nespresso machine so that they would be quicker to heat up when she offered the first candidate a drink. It would leave her less time standing lamely by the kitchen counter, tapping the coffee pod on the side or looking self-consciously at a tea bag at the bottom of a mug. She poured some milk into a small jug. Hell, why was she doing that? She wasn't meant to be the one making a good impression. She checked the sugar spoon in the bowl was clean. If it wasn't, it would be down to her. Daniel would never use it to stir coffee and then put it back; he was far too fastidious. She practically had to stop him counting cutlery in and out of the dishwater, just as his surgical team did with implements before and after an op.

If she thought about it, and she rarely did, what Daniel did on a daily basis was magnificent. When he came home each night, she asked him how his day had been, and he said, *Too short*, or, *A shocker*, or lamented that new cost-cuts meant there was no toner in the photocopier and his secretary hadn't been able to print off aftercare sheets. She pictured him, clean and austere in his scrubs. How skilled he was. Once, with him on a beach, she'd seen a cormorant alone on a rock, and she'd wanted to say to him, so nearly said to him, *Daniel, see, it looks like you*, but she wasn't sure what she meant by it, and the bird was so solitary, so stern, so marked against the shoreline, and he'd suddenly seemed vulnerable to her in a way that was surprising. He'd followed her gaze to the horizon, and she'd bent and kissed his fingertips to conceal that her eyes were misting with tears.

Once, he'd said, *I would tell you, if I could tell you*, and she had decided it was a declaration of heartfelt love, just slightly tangential. Now, standing in her kitchen with three CVs in front of her, what she was proposing to do suddenly seemed absurd, ridiculous. It could jeopardise everything she had. That's what her friend Harriet said when Monica had phoned her to discuss it. *Hey, go ahead, Mon*, she'd laughed, *leave your gorgeous husband, your perfect children, your lovely home, and you go and nail your colours to your career mast. Would you like me to step into your shoes?* Monica wasn't entirely sure Harriet was joking. She was a jaundiced internet dater, and highly successful in the City.

Monica reminded herself that nobody had it all. Sometimes, when she listened to women on the radio, working mothers, non-working mothers, part-time working mothers, all arguing their corner and fighting their agendas, she wondered why the sister-hood couldn't cut each other a little slack; maybe show a little kindness, and recognise that everyone was trying to do the best all-round job they possibly could. Wasn't that what she was trying to do?

She picked up the CVs irritably, and read through them again. All she had to do, she thought with a sudden rush of nervous energy, was find the right person to fill her shoes. Not in every aspect, she corrected herself as the doorbell rang. It would be good if none of the candidates was exceptionally pretty. She shrank from the thought; that wasn't exactly in the spirit of the sisterhood. Pragmatic though. If the successful candidate was beautiful, might she end up in Daniel's bed? She flinched at the thought of his hands touching another woman. That was only okay if they were either unconscious or wearing latex gloves and handing him a fresh scalpel.

9

Vicky Travis sat before Monica, chewing gum. Monica tried not to notice but it was horribly compelling. She was twenty-three, with dip-dyed hair, a small tattoo just below her right ear and what looked like a habit of biting her nails. Monica reminded herself it was shallow to make a judgement based on appearances. Vicky could be really kind-hearted, and she had an open, friendly face. The gum made a swoop from the left to the right of her mouth.

Monica cast her eyes upward, feeling like an irritated, twitchy schoolmistress. If she let this woman look after her children, would she return and find Ruby chewing gum too? This probably counted as sweating the small stuff. She tried to concentrate on the CV. Vicky had worked in a hotel as a chambermaid, in a small cafe as cook, at a nursery for six months, and then recently as a nanny for a family. Did that cover all the bases?

'How did you find working in the hotel?' she asked as an opening gambit. The girl smiled.

'It was okay. You're sort of on show all the time, you know, the front-of-house managers insist on everything being smiley and super-polite. People can be real slobs too; I got fed up of picking up after them, stuff they wouldn't have done in their own homes.'

'I see. And the cafe?'

'I liked that; mostly making paninis, and salads, and pizzas. I got good at all kinds of coffees. Takings were down, though; people don't have the cash to go out for lunch as much. They had to let me go – it says that on my reference, it wasn't anything I did.'

'Okay. And the nursery and the nannying. Have you liked that better?'

'S'been great. The kids are really cute, and getting paid to watch *In the Night Garden* seems like a good deal. I like taking them to the park. I keep a careful eye, but I'm not overprotective.'

Monica thought of a young nanny she'd watched collecting a child from Luca's nursery. She'd let the two year old skip ahead, alongside the busy road. The child was clearly out of reach; Monica had resisted catching the girl up and saying, *You're not keeping her safe – if she was yours you'd be holding on tight.*

Monica tried to envisage Vicky in the park. Perhaps she'd sit daydreaming on the roundabout while Luca toddled in front of a child on a swing. Monica would be asleep, on California time, while Vicky ineptly held her cardigan to his gashed, gaping fore-head. A stranger would have to drive her to A & E. Monica's heart started racing.

'Can you drive?' she asked weakly.

'No, not yet. It's expensive to learn, but I'm planning to. My boyfriend's maybe getting a car. In my current job, he sometimes comes round, gives me a hand with the kids.'

Was police-checking a boyfriend excessive? Vicky's chewing gum seemed to achieve a figure of eight. Perhaps she was one of those women who could tie cherry stalks into knots with the tip of her tongue. Monica had seen it in a film once, it was remarkably deft. She was starting to feel a little bit sick.

'You've got a lovely home,' Vicky said, casting a glance round the kitchen. 'What sort of hours does your husband work?'

'Oh, he's a surgeon, so hospital hours, unless there's an emer-gency and he has to go back in to see a patient. Doesn't happen often. Sometimes ward rounds at weekends, or he needs to check on someone in intensive care.'

'Sweet.'

Sweet? Monica looked back down at the CV.

'I think that's probably about everything. Thank you for coming. I've got two other people to see, so I'll be back in touch with the agency later on today.'

'S'okay. I'll wait to hear.'

Having shown her out of the door, Monica stood with her palms flat on the kitchen counter. It was evidently going to take more than luck. Also, maybe an overhaul of her own attitude. Vicky had been polite, nice. Monica recognised her readiness to judge her harshly. Perhaps she should just telephone Gus now. Over and out, she might say.

Ema Mslovich sat neatly in front of her. No gum-chewing with this one, Monica comforted herself. Ema's forehead gleamed pristinely, her hair pulled back tightly into a neat plait. Her hands were clasped purposefully on the table in front of her.

'And you are from . . . ?'

'Serbia. I have been in the UK now for six years.'

'And how's that been for you?'

'Very happy. Very good. I am here with my boyfriend. He works in construction. Better work for less money than most English builders charge.'

'Oh, okay. And I see you've worked mostly as a cleaner, you have less experience in childcare.'

'If a house is clean, it mostly means a child has everything they need to play safely. I will keep your house clean. Your children will be safe. You will have peace of mind.'

It sounded like a command. Where might watching *In the Night Garden* come in; or any chatting with Ruby when she came home from school? Vicky would do that. Was baking cupcakes allowed?

Ema looked around the kitchen.

'Can I see your Hoover, your cleaning utensils, your cleaning products? I like to know that I have the necessary equipment to do the job properly.'

'Of course; the utility room is just off the kitchen, it's just here.'

Ema turned the vacuum cleaner upside down and examined the roller. She tugged at some fluff, and then turned her attention to flexing the handle of the mop.

'You have no steam cleaner?' she asked. 'They are very good for floor tiles, for shower cubicles, for windows, for chrome fixtures in the bathroom. For hygienic clean.'

'No, I have no steam cleaner, although I guess I could buy one.'

'That would be preferable.'

'But the children, I'm picking up that perhaps you are not so much focused on the children.' (Why, Monica wondered, was she suddenly speaking as if English were not her first language either?)

'In my country, you keep a good home, a clean home, the children grow like flowers. You, in this country, you think about it too much.' Ema's expression was pleasant, but her tight smile brooked no disagreement.

'I can see how you might think that. Thank you for coming. I'll be in touch with the agency.'

The third applicant didn't even turn up. Violet Hemingway; fresh from being a chalet girl, fresh from a gap year in South America, fresh from thinking about applying to university. Her references seemed to have been written by her mother.

Monica sat at her desk and called Christine at the agency.

'Surely you've got someone more suitable than either of these two?'

'The problem is, it's short notice. The really good ones work out a period of notice, so you arrange for them to start in three to six months' time. The difficulty for you is that you want someone to start pretty much immediately, which is a problem in itself, and then it's only for three months, so you'll be about to come back when anyone halfway decent is just about able to start.'

'That might explain why the other agency I contacted has drawn a complete blank. You're currently my only hope. Surely there's someone you haven't connected to my spec?'

Christine paused. Monica could hear her tapping on her keyboard.

'There may be someone. Highly unlikely, although she couldn't come more highly recommended. She stipulates she doesn't want childcare, just a housekeeping role, although she used to be a classroom teaching assistant so she must be good with children. She's been working for the same couple for ten years. To be honest she sounds excellent. Awesome reference.'

'Can you set me up a meeting with her? Surely I can interview her?'

'Not if she knows you want childcare too.'

'Maybe I could broach that during the interview, if she seems suitable, if we get on. There can't be a huge number of jobs out there. If you think her reference is so great, why can't we give it a go?'

'Because it'll probably be a waste of your time and hers, although she lives quite close to you, so that might swing it in your favour.'

'Can't you try?'

Later, after Christine had called back, she texted Daniel. *First two a disaster. Third one didn't even turn up. One new one to try; she's called Ursula Condot. Wish me luck.*

It struck her afterwards that he had already. That was where her day had started.

It wasn't exactly Cargo Cult thinking.

IO

Ursula sat at her dressing table and looked at herself in the mirror. She brushed her hair – which she wore in a smooth, jaw-length bob – and applied a little moisturiser. She had eschewed cosmetics long ago. She fastened the strap of her watch, and ran her fingertips along the length of her cheekbones. They remained resolutely high, even though the flesh around her jaw, her mouth, had softened a little. Her face, she felt, reflected an air of surprise. Perhaps, more accurately, one of unexpected ambush. Her grey eyes looked dark; some days, darker. The skin beneath them retained a bruised, blue quality. She rubbed a little Carmex into her pale lips, and pressed them softly together.

This would be only the third job interview she had ever attended. Was that ridiculous, aged forty-nine, to have only three times presented herself for selection?

The second interview had been with Rose, who had interviewed her, characteristically, in the garden, early in July. There had been a riffling breeze, and the petals of the almost-spent iceberg roses were caught on its breath so that she and Rose talked in a soft drizzle of white petals, like two slightly stiff, recalcitrant brides. Rose had made scones, and rhubarb jam, and Geoffrey, in navy blue corduroys, waved cheerily from the herbaceous border, soil ridged to his knees. When Rose offered her the job, Ursula had not been sure who had in fact been in greater need: Rose, whose arthritis meant she could no longer manage, or Ursula, who wanted to crawl into the aesthetic gentleness of their life as if beneath a thick paisley quilt. Rose and Geoffrey, she reflected, had been like a life raft for her. They gave no sign of guessing.

Her first interview had been altogether different, many years earlier. It had been for a secretarial job at an advertising agency. How young she had been. How untested. She'd stood by the water fountain in reception, wearing a navy blue dress. Her shoes were making themselves felt on her smallest toes. Ursula Condot. She disliked repeating her name to people; it felt like it ended too abruptly. Two generations previously she would have been Ursula Condotti. That had more swing. Her paternal grandfather had lopped off the last two letters in an effort to anglicise himself when he migrated after the war. It was, Ursula felt, emblematic of a kind of self-willed, timid shrinking.

Her mother had called her Ursula because she'd read *Women in Love* when she was pregnant. 'Ursula and Gudrun,' she'd said, 'I thought both names so elegant. And they wore red and blue coloured tights. I saw you as a lovely young woman in beautiful coloured tights.'

Now, at her dressing table, Ursula smoothed her fingers along her slightly stout calves. Another maternal expectation unfulfilled. At least she hadn't christened her Gudrun. It was always important to count saving graces.

When she'd been called in to the interview, she kept her eyes downcast. It was his shoes she saw first; they were very polished, expensive. She guessed he would smell of cologne, and inhaled deeply. He did. She raised her eyes, and tried not to blush. He was handsome. That would be the correct, traditional, word to describe him.

'Ursula Condot,' he said abruptly. 'So you are Ursula Condot. Am I correct in assuming Condot was something more Italianate previously?'

She nodded. 'Condotti.'

'I wonder,' he continued, 'what Hollywood would have made of Gina Lollobrigida as Gina Lowbridge?'

He looked at her fixedly. She had the most curious feeling, mutely standing there, of being competently X-rayed, her navy blue dress suddenly translucent, her skin no longer attached to her muscles or her bones, but adrift somehow, awry, like seaweed caught in the suck and blow of the tide.

'They named a lettuce after her,' he continued, flicking through her CV. 'A lettuce after Gina Lollobrigida. After she'd made the film *The Most Beautiful Woman in the World*. They called the lettuce Lollo. It was meant to look like the curls of her hair. She pulled off playing the most beautiful woman in the world, and what came next, a lettuce.'

Had she been meant to laugh? She felt steeped in uncertainty. A fox in a henhouse; why had that image come into her mind? A wild, wily, potent fox, intent on wreaking havoc and dodging and dancing around her prim, pinched, hapless feet.

'You're blushing,' he said. 'That won't do. I would have thought Gina Lollobrigida was pretty harmless territory. You should know from the off that I can't be doing with thin skins. Too time-consuming, too needy, and dependent on too much oxygen. Skin like rhino hide, Signorina Condotti. If you are to be given this job, that would be the ticket.'

She'd nodded.

'Like rhino hide. I understand.'

As if she possibly could.

She stood up from the dressing table and picked up her notebook.

Monica. She was to be interviewed by a woman called Monica. It would be better not to recollect a flurry of iceberg rose petals, and rhubarb jam. And better, always better, not to recollect the day when she'd first met Gideon.

11

Monica had once, many years previously, in an attempt at creative accomplishment, joined an evening class throwing pottery. She had soon learned she had no hitherto undiscovered talent to speak of. Now, sitting opposite Ursula Condot, she was unexpectedly reminded of the spinning clay, and the way it stubbornly bore no trace of her touch. Ursula's face had the same alabaster smoothness. Monica watched for revealing expression. It seemed mostly still, her top lip a little taut as she wrote details in her notebook with a calligraphy pen. Her writing spread from beneath her fingers like an architectural construction. Monica made a self-deprecating remark about her cooking. Did Ursula smile? If she had, it was certainly so fleeting as to be missable. The effect, Monica reasoned, could be construed as unexpectedly soothing. Perhaps the woman had a preternatural calm. That might not be a bad thing. And not showing emotion, Monica reminded herself, was not the same as not feeling it. There was nothing to suggest that Ursula Condot was not an entirely decent, compassionate woman. Her reference positively glowed; Rose Hallett obviously considered her something of an angel. Monica was reminded of a church she and Daniel had visited once in Suffolk. High in the roof, along the central beam, were wooden angels, their oaky wings spread wide. Poised and tranquil, they seemed gracefully on the qui vive, all set to swoop in and rescue, which had been a comforting thought.

Monica refocused on Ursula's face before her. Ursula was

listening carefully. She leaned slightly forward, as if giving her ears extra purchase on Monica's words. Her head was tilted a little to one side.

'Were Mr and Mrs Hallett frail?' Monica asked. 'Did they require any personal care?'

'No, not on an ongoing basis, although when they were ill – once with flu, once with norovirus, and Geoffrey after his hip replacement – then I attended to them. Why,' she asked after a slight pause, 'is your husband sick?'

'No, no, not at all,' Monica said hastily. 'I'm just trying to get an impression of what your daily work entails. Is there anything you'd like to ask me?'

'It would be helpful to know some of your daily routines, your needs. It's helpful to know expectations at the outset and then I can tell you if I can meet them.'

She spoke with what seemed a quiet confidence, her pen poised to note down Monica's answers.

Monica took a deep breath. She thought of the slightly haphazard chaos that passed for her domestic routine. Would it be smoothed into order by the competent hands of the woman before her? Ironed bed linen? Daniel would be in seventh heaven, although admittedly alone. She composed herself. How was she going to bring up the children?

Ursula continued.

'I'm not clear – the agency didn't clarify – as to where you will be; whether you will be working in your home, or whether you and your husband both work away from the home.'

'My husband is a surgeon. He will be here at the beginning and end of each weekday. But I . . . I've been offered a job in America, in California, for about three months, and then hope-fully something else here when I return. So I would not be here, no, I would not be here.'

'So I would be working just for your husband?'

'Not exactly. That's the thing; not exactly.'

Ursula's face, Monica thought, was momentarily discomfited. She looked around the kitchen. Monica followed her gaze. She saw Ursula register, for the first time, the Tommy Tippee beaker on the crockery shelf, Ruby's drawing stuck to the fridge, Luca's Tripp Trapp high chair tucked behind the door to the pantry.

'You have children? You have a family?'

It sounded both like a question and a bald affirmation.

Monica nodded, biting her lip. Was she on the verge of apologising?

Ursula closed her notebook gently.

'Then I'm afraid there's been some mistake, something the agency didn't communicate or hadn't noted. I have no children and think I'm a little old to work with them. I'm too used to working for elderly adults. It's a different rhythm, I'm sure you can understand. It is my preference, my strong preference, not to work in a house with children.'

She looked as if she were readying herself to stand up and leave.

'No,' Monica said, throwing reserve to the wind. 'No, please don't go, please hear me out. You sound fantastic. You look really capable and competent, and in fact the answer to my wildest dreams. I'm sorry I wasn't upfront about the children. I have two: Ruby is nine and Luca is eighteen months. The agency told me about your preference. I persuaded them to let me see you; it's my fault. You just sounded so perfect. You have no idea how ghastly the other applicants have been. And Christine said you were CRB checked; that it wasn't that you couldn't take care of children, weren't allowed to take care of children or anything like that, but just that you preferred not to, you simply preferred not to.'

She raised her palms to her beseechingly.

'Please, don't rule me out; don't rule us out. They're lovely children, Daniel is a great dad, it's just for a short while, during which you could be looking for something else, a job with no children, to move on to afterwards. I'm sorry for not being upfront, you just sound – and you look – as if I could trust you to take care of my children, of my family, of my home. I could go and do this preposterous, probably ridiculous thing of trying to better my career prospects by taking a job that is wholly inconvenient, probably ludicrous, certainly not financially rewarding, but which if I don't try will swill around my skull until it drives me insane. And so I need to go, even if I come bolting home with my tail between my legs – but in which case I'd still pay you for the whole contract.'

She put her head in her hands

'And, now, goodness knows what you think of me. I'm supposed to be interviewing you in the calm rational manner of a professional woman, and I've blurted all this stuff out and you can see how desperate I am, and how guilty and selfish I feel, and that's probably just motivated you further to stand up and leave, and I'm sorry I've wasted your time; I'm sorry I wasn't truthful at the outset.'

Ursula looked at her steadily.

'Work is the only dignity,' she said.

'I'm sorry?'

'In my life. In my life I've found work to be the only dignity. I can understand, sort of understand, why you would want to make the most of the opportunity offered to you.'

Monica looked at her cautiously.

'Does that mean you might be prepared to overlook your own criteria, maybe meet Ruby and Luca, perhaps think whether you might take us on?'

'You're right that it's only for a short while. Mr and Mrs Hallett are moving into their daughter's house immediately; the house will be packed up, ready to be sold. I'd prefer not to be part of that, and Rose – Mrs Hallett – doesn't expect me to be. And I could use this time to find something more long term. To be honest, I need to work too. I have only myself to support, but I can't *not* work for several months without it becoming a problem.'

'We could be a mutual solution; a mutually inconvenient-convenient solution.'

'We could.'

Monica waited for a smile; even a suggestion of a smile. None came. Instead, Ursula's face was grave. *Work is the only dignity.* It was perhaps a maxim hard won.

Monica reached forward and touched her hand. Ursula stiffened at her touch.

'I understand if you want to sleep on it; will you call me in the morning? If you still think it's feasible, I can arrange for you to meet the children tomorrow.'

Ursula nodded.

She wasn't a plain woman, Monica concluded as she closed the door behind her. Animated by a smile, her features might look different again. But she wasn't pretty; and she was slightly older than Daniel. Monica reprimanded herself for even taking that into account. No, she concluded, going back into the kitchen and preparing to text Daniel, Ursula Condot was just a woman whose face, intentionally or not, gave nothing – absolutely nothing – away.

12

Four days later, sitting in her bedroom beside two packed suit-cases, Monica heard Luca stir in his sleep. She went to his room to check on him. He slept on his stomach, with his knees hunched up beneath him. His nappied bottom rose from the mattress like a surfacing dolphin. She patted its wadded roundness, and let her hand rest for a moment. Would he forget her? He lifted his arms so joyfully to her each morning. The thought was unbear-able. Twelve weeks, she told herself, fourteen weeks max.

She went back to her own room and resumed her position on the side of the bed. She looked at her suitcases. It felt oddly formal, unreal almost, to be sitting in her bedroom, waiting for Daniel, who had been delayed at the hospital for what would be their last night together before she caught the plane in the morning. Ursula Condot had said yes. When she phoned to accept, Monica sensed that her affirmative had been hauled up from somewhere buried deep, like an old bucket retrieved from a well, clanging and shud-dering its way up to the light. Daniel had met her; she'd come after school and drunk tea and made conversation with Ruby. Conversation was too broad a word. Ursula had been polite, factual, and scrupulously appropriate. There was nothing to find fault with – perhaps just an absence of evident warmth, a whisper of chill. Monica kissed Ruby's shoulder fiercely when Ursula left. *Do you like her?* she'd asked. *I don't know her yet,* Ruby replied. It was impossible, Monica concluded, for Ruby to intuit quite how much Monica needed her to say yes.

She looked at her watch. Daniel was even later than the late he'd expected. Something must have gone wrong; someone newly admitted, their spine perhaps damaged from a car accident or a fall from a horse, and Daniel would be there, patiently, meticulously, trying to put it back to rights. Cassie had come over in the afternoon. She'd stood dandling Luca, with Ruby sitting cross-legged next to her, while Monica held up clothing she wasn't sure about packing.

I cannot see you in that in California, Cassie said, and shook her head, saying *tsk tsk,* when Monica held up her favourite sweater. *Two warm things, max, for if you end up in San Francisco. It can be like some kind of chilly fog basin in the middle of July.* Monica had allowed herself to be guided, hectored. As she picked up a swimsuit, she found herself inexplicably about to burst into tears. Cassie sensed it and put Luca down.

'Hey Ruby, enough already of the packing show. Why don't you take Luca down to the kitchen and get him a biscuit?'

Ruby had obliged.

Cassie picked up the discarded swimsuit and pressed it into Monica's hands.

'You should be taking that. You might have to spend a week waxing, smoothing and glossing your body in order to be LA-appropriate, but it's worth a try.'

'I'm not taking it. I won't be going swimming, or going to the beach. It can stay here.'

'Okay then, perhaps just put in an itchy old hair shirt rather than entertain the possibility that just randomly early one Sunday morning you might have time for a walk along a beach and a dip under a heavenly blue sky.'

'I'd feel too guilty. Even having it in my case makes me feel guilty. Now, right at this moment, looking at Ruby and Luca and my suitcases just makes me feel sick.'

She'd put the costume back in the drawer.

Cassie took it back out. Her tone was emphatic.

'Monica, you need to wise up. Do you think I ever thought when Felix was Luca's age that Mike would leave me for another woman before Felix was ten, and that I'd be scrambling around trying to hold it financially together while he set up home with Anna and their "oh what a surprise, I must marry her" new baby, trying to avoid paying me a penny? Damn right I didn't. And, unlikely as it seems, don't think it couldn't happen to you. Daniel's my brother, and I know he loves you and he loves the children, and he's honourable and decent and all that blah, but you know Monica, nice men bolt too, nice men are struck by thunderbolts of middle-aged love, and then as a woman, the smarter you are, the more prepared you are, the more employable you are, the better. I'm telling you, it helps. Don't look at the children and the suitcases and feel sick; look at the children and the suitcases and know that you're keeping yourself more employable, and reducing the risk of being financially shafted. Emotional shafting is less easy to guard against, so just keep your eye on the main chance. Follow the money, believe me.'

Cassie's realism was like a sharp, stinging slap. Monica had meekly folded the costume into the case. *Cheers for that*, she'd said, but she meant it. Her sister-in-law's words, she thought, would help her walk away from Daniel and the children at Heathrow in the morning. But now, right now, she wanted Daniel to come home. She wanted him to come home and hug her, and tell her everything was going to be all right. She wanted him to find some words, however not-quite-right, however not-quite-accurate, to tell her that he loved her, that he would hold her in his heart each and every day until she came home, and that their life together would resume and that everything would be all right. A little additional reassurance about unexpected middle-aged thunderbolts of love and unforeseen spousal desertion might be the ticket too. Was that too much to ask?

She stood up and pressed her head to the bedroom door. Was there anything she had forgotten, anything she had not put into place for Ursula? She'd written enough lists, she felt, to facilitate the invasion of a small country. Ursula had asked so many questions. *Does Luca have a favourite cup or plate? How do you chop his fruit? Is he particular about which clothes go next to his skin? What time is Ruby allowed to keep the light on until at bedtime?*

For a woman who was childless, her insight and attention to detail was phenomenal. She was surely leaving her children in good hands. It should be, Monica reminded herself, her heart lifting as Daniel's car drew up, a consolation of sorts. If she repeated it enough, maybe she would feel it to be so.

13

Ursula stood by the open window. The air was cold; it smelt of the possibility of a late frost. A frost in early April would blacken the tulips in Rose's garden. The wisteria would be set back. She imagined Geoffrey examining it, his hands expertly assessing the damage to the shoots, the buds. It was an unexpectedly poignant thought. That would not do. She resolved to untwine her mind from the rhythms and patterns of Rose's and Geoffrey's house. That part of her life was finished, over.

Jane, their daughter, had shaken her hand when she'd left the house for the last time. *Thank you for all you've done*, she'd said a little stiffly, as if Ursula might have paused briefly to give first aid to a stranger.

She opened the window a little wider, standing there, in her nightdress, her knuckles rigid against the hasp. The night air seized her scalp, her clavicle, the inside of her nose. She felt the skin of her breasts draw tight. Her fingertips throbbed with the cold. If she stood there much longer, they would become mottled and blue. The bone-ache, the lung-throb, that came with the night air were curiously comforting. She resisted rubbing her hands on her arms. She pressed her thumbnail into the pad of her numbed index finger. Sensation was diminishing: how simple it was to physically achieve this. She bit at the corner of her lip. She was ready for the morning; as ready as she could expect to be.

All you have to do, she told herself, is go in there tomorrow and housekeep, and make sure the children are safe, and you have to do it from 7.45 a.m. through to 7 p.m., and then Daniel will come home, and you will do it the next day, and the next, and the one after that, until all the days have joined up and Monica comes home.

Rose had asked her to take a piece of furniture, anything she liked from the house. *Please take something,* she'd asked, *as a thank-you, and a keepsake, from Geoffrey and me.* At first she had resisted, *I'm not one for things, for possessions,* she'd said, but then she'd intuited that Rose was in danger of interpreting it as rejection, as offence; perhaps of ill will at the swift nature of her redundancy.

She'd chosen a red and cream toile de jouy cushion, a soft, beaten-up, goose-feather-filled one from a sofa in the morning room, and a wooden-and-string-handled potato peeler which fitted the span of her palm, the length of her fingers, as if bespoke. The cushion she'd hidden away in the cupboard above her wardrobe. The potato peeler she'd allowed in the utensils drawer in her kitchen in the knowledge that she rarely, if ever, peeled potatoes for herself alone. Neither item, she determined, would be permitted to intrude on her thoughts. And as for the image of Geoffrey standing before the frost-hit wisteria, she resolved to pare it away until it was as smooth and benign as his old ivory shoehorn which she had been sensitive enough, although regrettably tempted, not to choose.

14

Back from the airport, Daniel stood in the kitchen with his children feeling somewhat at sea. He'd promised them a late breakfast. Breakfast. That was a good, practical place to start. Anything to banish the sight of Monica walking away, Ruby's small hand gripping his tighter as her mother receded into Departures.

Now, as he strapped Luca into his Tripp Trapp chair, his fingers were uncharacteristically clumsy with his son's legs and the buckle. Monica would be airborne by now. He felt distance and space spooling wide between them. Last night, she had wrapped herself around him as if there was a possibility their bones might spontaneously fuse. He recollected the smell of her skin, the warmth of her mouth and felt the memory of it spinning and falling down into the ocean she was flying over.

'Bacon?' he said to Ruby. 'Eggs fried, poached or scrambled?'

Ruby shrugged.

'I don't mind. Whichever you can cook best.'

Was she doubting his competence?

'I can do all of them, you just test me. I can cook all kinds of eggs.'

He rootled around in a cupboard; which pan did Monica use?

Ruby poked with her fork at the empty plate in front of her.

'I can help if you want. I can crack an egg although sometimes there's shell. In cakes it doesn't matter, it just gets scrunchily small when you put in the flour.'

'Thank you, Little, but you don't need to help. Today you can pretend you are in a hotel. Maybe I can find a napkin, and I can fold it into your lap, just as if you were being served breakfast in a grand hotel.'

'I could have written out a menu if I knew we were going to do that.'

'You still could. Write one later, when I've gone to work, and each weekend morning you can choose something from it and I will cook it like a chef. French toast. Pancakes. Maybe I will find myself a hat – a toque – that's what a chef's hat is called.'

He mimed the tall shape of the toque. Ruby gamely tried to laugh. Luca was starting to grizzle. He jabbed his spoon into the red apple of his cheek and let out a wail. Teeth? Was that a sign of teething? He could ask Cassie, but she'd either have forgotten or tease him about how little he remembered of his general medical training. Perhaps he'd ask his anaesthetist; she had children. He wouldn't ask Monica. Competence, he resolved. Competence would be key – or at least the impression of it – both to his children and to his wife. He cracked the egg into the pan; the overly hot fat smoked and spattered. Luca's grizzle became a full-blown wail. *Mumma, Mumma,* he cried. Ruby looked as if she was trying not to join in.

She reached over and pat-a-caked his hands together. *Mumma's all gone,* she said, *Mumma's all gone.* She manipulated his palms so that they were turned upwards to the ceiling. *All gone,* she said again, Luca now watching her intently. She sounded, Daniel reflected (as he tried to scrape the egg from the pan – evidently he hadn't chosen the one with the non-stick surface still intact), she sounded for all the world as if she were describing milk, or perhaps biscuits, rather than her mother, his wife; all gone.

'I can't say back soon,' Ruby said, looking directly at Daniel, 'because she won't be, will she?'

He was saved from an answer by the sound of the key in the lock. All three of them turned towards the hallway, surprised by the sound. What must they have looked like, Daniel thought later when driving to work: the egg smoking in the pan; Ruby formal, straight backed; and Luca's face crumpling, tears falling, beginning a full-spirited bawl when Ursula walked shyly, hesitantly, into the kitchen, and failed to soothe him because she couldn't morph into his mumma.

15

When the front door closed behind Daddy, Ruby sat a little straighter in her chair. If she pushed her eyes completely to the right she could see Ursula at the sink, without having to turn her head and make it obvious she was staring. It was a little bit sore, and with her left eye she could mostly see her nose, but she could see her washing up the frying pan that Daddy had cooked the eggs in. When she ran the tap onto it, a big *whoof* of steam rose up because the pan was still hot. Ursula fanned the steam away with her hand and didn't say anything. She was wearing an apron. It was plain blue, with a big rectangular pocket. Ursula took a deep breath. Ruby was certain of that because she saw her ribs push against her jumper. She must have taken in a big scoop of the pan steam. Luca was whacking the back of his spoon on his tray. Daddy had Sellotaped a photo of Mummy to it. She was mostly covered in Weetabix now, which Ruby thought probably wasn't part of his plan. She reached over and used her fingertips to wipe Mummy's face. Exactly as she did so, Ursula turned, stretched towards her, and gave her a piece of kitchen roll.

'Here,' she said, 'that might clean it up better.'

Ruby was taken aback by how speedily the paper was given to her. Had Ursula been watching her with sideways eyes too? Surely not, because then she would have been looking at the pantry, or the cupboard where the glasses were stored? She wiped away the Weetabix. Mummy smiled up at her. Ursula, again, was next to her, hand outstretched, ready for the kitchen roll. Ruby looked up, this time with her eyes straight forward. Ah, the window, she realised, she and Luca were reflected in the window. Even with her back turned to them, Ursula could make them out.

'Thank you,' Ruby said, as Ursula put the paper in the bin.

'You're welcome,' Ursula said. 'Would you like anything else to eat or drink?'

'No, thank you,' Ruby replied.

How polite this morning was. How stiff it all seemed. Everything in the kitchen looked all corners and edges. Her eyeballs were uncomfortable from all the secret staring she'd been doing, and she felt as if she should hold her hands very still in front of her on the table. Perhaps Ursula might magic a tiny dustpan and brush from her apron pocket and sweep away all the crumbs, like the waiter in the restaurant for Daddy's birthday. She'd liked his miniature dustpan and brush. She'd imagined a tiny broom, a mop and a feather duster to go with it. Mummy smiled up at her. Ruby resisted tracing around her face with her fingertips. *Twelve weeks, maybe fourteen, minus one morning*, she thought, then Mummy would be home.

Ursula was lifting Luca out of his Tripp Trapp.

'I thought, if it's all right with you, Luca and I might walk to school with you this morning, just so that I know properly where school is. I can walk him to nursery from there, your mummy drew me a little map.

The map was in her apron pocket; she took it out and passed it to her. Ruby stared at the apron pocket. What else might it contain? Clearly not a miniature dustpan and brush, because Ursula was now wiping the table with a J-cloth.

Mummy had drawn the roads which led to the nursery, and then used a neon yellow marker to draw arrows along the best route via school. The drawing was messy and helpful at the same time; she'd marked the postbox in red biro and the zebra crossing with scrawly black zigzags. Ruby handed it back to her.

'I'll just get my book bag. I keep it upstairs,' she said.

'Is now a good time for brushing your teeth?' Ursula asked.

Spitting the toothpaste out into the basin, Ruby reflected that it had been a good way to remind her to clean her teeth. It sounded like a question when Ursula said it, but really it was an instruction. Maybe, she thought, checking her reading book was in her book bag, this was what it was like when your mummy and daddy paid someone to look after you. It was polite and never shouty, but the grown-up was telling you what to do all the same.

When she came downstairs, Ursula was doing up Luca's jacket. She was crouched in front of him, carefully fastening the six buttons. There were no kisses; Mummy obviously hadn't told her about that. When Mummy put on Luca's coat, each time she did up a button, she kissed him on the nose. *Do up a button, and then a kiss for a button nose*, she'd laugh. She did it when he wore his thick winter coat, even if he had a cold and his nose was a bit red and snotty. Now, Luca was just looking at Ursula, as if it was a very curious thing to have his coat done up with absolutely no kisses. Ursula stood up and turned to reach her own jacket from the peg. Ruby ducked down and kissed Luca swiftly, six times, on the nose. 'Jacket kisses,' she said to Ursula, who tilted her head a little to the side, but didn't say anything further. Luca rubbed his nose with the flat of his palm. Maybe six kisses, so speedily, was as unexpected as none.

Ursula locked the door, checked it, and put the key into her handbag. Mummy's key ring was a pair of high-heeled shoes. If they were ever stuck waiting somewhere, she'd make the shoes tap-dance to keep Luca amused. Ursula's was made of black leather. It was completely plain, flat and smooth and about the size of the yellow-wrapped toffee in Quality Street. If they were ever stuck waiting anywhere, it wouldn't be good for entertaining Luca, except perhaps if he stuck his teeth right in it, in which case an actual toffee would have been much better. Ursula fastened her handbag. Everything about her was very neat and tidy. Mummy was always trailing bright coloured scarves behind her as she walked, or stomping along in shoes which were clumpy. She had one pair that were actually silver. All Ursula's things – her clothes, her bag, her shoes – seemed to be different shades of brown, and there was nothing trailing or flapping or jangling at all. She wore flat, round-toed shoes which made no sound on the pavement.

'I don't think it will rain today,' she said, but she ducked her head a little as she glanced up at the sky, as if imaginary raindrops might be pelting her already. Mummy had painted the downstairs loo a colour called 'Mouse's Back'. *Absurd*, said Daddy, but Ruby had loved the name. She'd imagined the soft sheen of a mouse's fur as it scampered right up the loo wall. And as Ursula ducked, despite there being no raindrops, her shoulder blade made her jacket curl over, and Ruby thought *she* was like a mouse, a very neat but timid mouse.

'I think this buckle is done correctly,' Ursula said, checking that Luca was strapped into the Bugaboo. Ruby wasn't sure whether she was talking to herself or to her; she dipped forward and checked the buckle to make sure. When Mummy was running late, it was Ruby's job to do it anyway. Mummy would put on her lipstick, looking in the hall mirror, and flap her hand out to Ruby, and say *Quick quick you buckle him in*. Maybe that was another thing that hadn't made it to the list. She checked the buckle; Ursula had done it right.

'I'm guessing you will be able to show me the way, even though I have Mummy's clever map,' Ursula said.

Ruby nodded. 'We go this way first,' she said, and they set off for school.

Miss Cameron had come out to meet Ursula in the playground. She'd chatted to her a little bit while they all lined up to go in. Everybody stared.

Now, as they got out their maths books, ready to start the first lesson of the day, Claudie Peters, who sat next to her, swung her head round to face her so that her pigtails swished right across Ruby's cheek. Ruby resisted saying Ouch, even though it stung because Claudie's hair bobble had a tiny metal clasp. Ruby was undecided as to whether Claudie's pigtails were actually a secret, spiteful weapon. They both sat on Table One for maths, and Claudie usually increased her determined swishing if Ruby got more answers correct than she did. Claudie looked at her best friend Stella, who sat opposite them, checked that Miss Cameron was busy with Table Four, and then said to Ruby, 'Maybe that was your granny who brought you to school this morning?'

'No. She's called Ursula. She's helping to look after me and Luca while my mummy is away working.'

'Helping because she likes you, that's nice.'

Stella giggled. Claudie gave a little twitch of her nose.

'How long will she be away?' she continued.

'Who?'

'Your mummy. Surely you haven't forgotten about her already? Didn't she only just leave?'

Ruby bit at her lip. Claudie knew the answer to her first question already, because Mummy had told her mummy last week in the playground. '*Oh, I must make sure Ruby comes often to tea,*' Claudie's mother had said, but in a voice which made Ruby think she didn't actually plan on it happening. *I'll text Daniel,* she'd said, *to arrange it. Gosh, he'll have a lot on his plate.* Best go through Ursula, Mummy had said, smiling but not so that her eyes crinkled at the edges. *Like mother, like daughter,* Mummy had said when they walked away, but she hadn't explained it further.

'Twelve weeks,' Ruby said, staring hard at her page.

Claudie's eyes went as round as Chupa Chups.

'Twelve weeks? Wow. My mummy says she'd never leave me for twelve weeks for any job in the world, even if it paid a million, zillion, trillion pounds. She says I'm just too precious.'

The pigtails swished again. The metal clasp caught the very corner of Ruby's eye.

Miss Cameron appeared at the table.

'Careful, Ruby,' she said, 'don't underline your title so fiercely. Look, you've pressed so hard you've made a little hole right through to the next page.'

Ruby smoothed at the page with her fingertips.

Mummy and Daddy said she wasn't allowed to say Damn it. It counted as a cuss word. Cassie said it often, and Granny Bailey too, but Mummy said there were different rules for grown-ups. Saying Damn it, though, Ruby reflected, was not the same as thinking it, which no one could guess anyway, especially if your face looked as if it was concentrating on the sums in the maths book.

Damn it, she thought, *Damn it, damn it damn it.* She carefully drew out a rectangle, measuring the lengths with her ruler.

Was Mummy still on the plane? Probably; it took a long time to fly all the way to the West Coast. She'd bought an eye mask made of soft wool because she said the airline ones were scratchy, and something called *In Transit* which she said she would spritz on her face in order to make sure she arrived looking fresh. She'd spritzed Ruby for good measure, but when Ruby looked in the mirror, she hadn't looked any different. Maybe you had to actually have been on a plane for it to properly work. Ursula would be at home again by now. What would she be doing?

Daddy would most likely be doing an operation, or a ward round, telling the poorly people what would happen to them, and how he was going to fix them up. It was a curious thing, Ruby considered, thinking about grown-ups. They were meant to look after children, be carefully in charge. But sometimes she felt as if she held all the grown-ups she knew suspended in her head in a wide, gauzy net, keeping them safe and sound and out of harm's way.

16

When Ruby came home from school, she pushed against the front door and it didn't open. Mummy always put it on the latch just before Ruby's arrival, and then she could just push against it and let herself in. She pressed on the doorbell. Ursula took a little while to answer. Ruby held her book bag to her chest. Maybe, from now on, when she came home from school, she'd feel like a visitor to her own house.

'I'm sorry,' Ursula said as she opened it. 'I should have put the door on the latch, I lost track of the time. You don't usually ring the bell, do you?'

Ruby thought it would be mean to agree. Instead, she said hello, and stepped lightly past Ursula and into the hallway. Through the door into the sitting room, she noticed the sofa was pulled away from the wall. The Hoover was propped behind it, and on the table beside it was a small pile of things. She turned back to look at Ursula who lifted her palms.

'I'm just hoovering behind the sofa and I found these. Do you recognise any of them? I thought some of them might be precious.'

Ruby's first thought was: why would anyone hoover behind a sofa? No one walked there, so it wouldn't be dirty anyway. Her second, as she fingered and thumbed her way through them, was how many things you could lose without actually knowing it. Things obviously fell away, leaving no trace that you'd ever had them. A doll's shoe, three puzzle pieces, the hat from Monopoly, a Slinky, Luca's wooden giraffe, four marbles, and a tiny wooden dog that collapsed and jumped up when you pressed the base it stood on.

'Luca will be happy about the giraffe,' she said.

She made the dog jump and collapse a few times. Both her and Ursula's eyes seemed to be stuck to it.

'Easily done,' Ursula said. 'We can put whatever you want in the playroom boxes. I'm guessing the doll will be happy to have her shoe back at last.'

Ruby hesitated. Should she tell Ursula that she didn't have that doll any more? She'd given it away, one-shoed, for a stall at the school fete last summer. She hadn't liked it much anyway. If you pressed a button on its tummy, you could pull out a pigtail from the top of its scalp. You were then supposed to comb it into all kinds of hairstyles. The pink comb had broken the second time she'd tried it. Would it be unkind, now, to tell Ursula that the shoe could be just thrown in the bin? Sucking it straight into the Hoover wouldn't have been a loss. Ruby rubbed at her forehead with her palm. Coming home today was much trickier than usual.

If Daddy asked her how it had been, she thought about telling him it was complicated. That word would be accurate. Ruby's day seemed to have had a lot more guessing in it than usual, and a feeling that she had to think about where she placed her feet. Now Ursula was asking if she was hungry, didn't she usually eat something when she came in from school?

Ruby followed her into the kitchen. Ursula had made a cake. This was an unexpected bonus.

'Victoria sponge, with strawberry jam, and just icing sugar on the top. Luca doesn't like butter, does he, so I didn't make buttercream.'

Could grown-ups be nervous? Ruby hadn't thought so before, but Ursula looked a little nervous, pointing towards the cake. If Cassie had made it, she would have said 'Ta-daah!!! See what a cake-baking genius I am.' Except Cassie wouldn't have baked a cake; she'd have bought one in a shop, and when she unwrapped the ribbon from the box, she'd have tied it in Ruby's hair.

'Would you like some juice, or just water?' Ursula asked, cutting a slice and putting it onto a plate.

How strange the kitchen seemed today, Ruby thought. Her voice and Ursula's seemed to echo through it, a little wobbly, as if passing through water. When Ruby pulled out her chair to sit down, the noise it made sounded much louder than usual.

'I'll leave you to eat; I'll just finish hoovering the sitting room.'

Ruby started to eat her slice of cake. It was properly delicious. She looked over her shoulder at Ursula who was visible behind the sofa, her arm moving in smooth measured strokes with the line of the Hoover.

Ruby shifted a little in her seat. She felt as if a camera might be watching her, like the children in the TV ad who were told not to eat the sweets in front of them and then the camera caught them, stuffing their faces and looking guilty. Ruby looked around her again. The kitchen looked exactly the same. How could it feel so different? If she tried to write it like a sum, Ruby thought it would be: Kitchen + Ursula − Mummy. That would be the way to write it in her maths book, but it wouldn't tell how it felt, it would just say how it was, now, when eating the cake seemed to be giving her a lump in her throat and making her want to cry. She swallowed it down hard. Mummy said her sponge cakes were always doomed to be wonky. That was why, Ruby determined, she was in California helping to make a film, which she could do, without anything going wonky at all, and with Ruby and Luca still being precious even though she wasn't with them.

She finished her cake, and walked slowly up the stairs. Ursula had rolled up the rug by the fireplace, and was hoovering beneath that. From halfway up the stairs, Ruby didn't think it had revealed any more toys. Ursula might look like a conjurer otherwise, with things springing up where she touched. Ruby went into her room and sat down at her desk. Twelve weeks, minus almost one day, or eleven weeks plus six days and one sleep, and then Mummy would be home. Then, the house would stop feeling like one enormous tank, like at the London Aquarium, with she and Ursula stepping through thick warm water, each word they spoke followed by streams of bubbles coming from out of their mouths.

Ruby took out a piece of paper from her desk, and used her ruler to measure out twelve boxes. In each box, she ruled seven lines, and the letter which started each day of the week. Today was a Wednesday. It felt odd not to be starting each week with Monday, but she decided if it was to be a proper calendar, it needed to be accurate. In turquoise crayon, and capital letters, she titled it: THIS IS WHEN MUMMY IS COMING HOME. She folded it very small, and put it in a keepsake box by her bed with the crayon. If she left it out on her desk, Daddy would see it when he kissed her good night. *What a lot he'll have on his plate*, Claudie's mother had said. Mopey calendars wouldn't help, so probably best tucked away.

Ursula appeared at the doorway of her room. How silently she walked, thought Ruby. It was hard not to be surprised. If she wore bracelets, like Mummy, which jangled together, it would be easier to hear her coming.

'I think it's time to fetch Luca,' Ursula said. 'Are you all set?'

Walking down the road together, Ruby felt as if her tongue had gone to sleep in her mouth. All the things she would have chatted to Mummy about didn't seem to make it from her thoughts to her lips. Just ahead of them, halfway up the hill, was a very old woman in a thick winter coat and a headscarf even though it was April. Her body was bent and stooped over, and in her hand was a big fat walking stick. She'd spied something on the pavement, something silver and glittery, and she'd halted and stooped a little more, which was a very slow process. She was using the end of her stick to tap and turn over what glittered, as if she, with great luck, had stumbled on valuable treasure. Ruby wanted to call out to her, *It's just the ring pull from a Coke can,* so that the old lady would stop bending and bending when surely in a moment she would topple right over onto the pavement. And the second thing Ruby would have done, had she been walking with Mummy, was to try and guess what the old lady thought she might have spied – a diamond earring, a precious coin, a tiny engraved christening bracelet just like Luca's? But saying anything to Ursula would have seemed too chatty, too many words bubbling out onto the pavement, and Ursula might just stand surrounded by them rather than answering. Once, the washing machine door seal had broken, and all the soap-sudsy water flowed right out, all around Mummy's ankles, so that she was stranded in a sea of it all. How that looked would be how chatting to Ursula about the old lady would feel. Now, they overtook her, the lady straightening up, flipping the ring pull away into the gutter with the very tip of her stick, and nobody said anything at all. Ruby glanced at Ursula's watch. They were half an hour earlier than she usually was with Mummy. There'd be no Dettox, no explaining, no huffing and puffing from the childminders. Ursula listened patiently while they read out all the things Luca had done which were written on the whiteboard. It seemed silly, Ruby thought, when grown-ups could obviously read it for themselves. Perhaps they only did it to double prove it had happened. Usually, when she and Mummy came, most of the writing was rubbed off. Luca's words were often in a sea of white space. *Thank you, See you tomorrow,* Ursula was saying. The ladies were nodding politely. Ursula wasn't wasting any words.

For supper time, Ursula had made a beef stew. She cut Luca's meat up into small pieces – Ruby was glad that was on the list – but then she put the bowl up high, out of reach, on top of the microwave, to let it cool for itself. She lifted Luca into his chair, and he looked up at the steam curling up and away from the top of the microwave, and he reached out his hands, and Ursula used the moment, swiftly, to wipe them properly clean. She served out some food to Ruby, and asked her if she needed any help with anything, and Ruby shook her head and said No, thank you. Ursula turned to the sink, and started washing up the casserole dish until Luca's bowl had stopped steaming, and then she sat and helped him to eat, giving him one spoon for himself, and keeping one for herself to feed him a proper spoonful with less mess, and that wasn't on the list either, but Ruby thought it was a good idea. Usually Mummy fed Luca without giving him a spoon, and he kept whacking it away so it got quickly messy. But with the beef stew, he ate almost nearly all of it, and Ursula's face kept very still as she did it, unlike Mummy whose mouth made the shapes for taking it from the spoon, and chewing and swallowing, as if she were in fact eating invisible food. But Ursula's face didn't move at all, and Mummy's was smiling, unsmeared, from beside Luca's bowl. Ruby decided not to look at Mummy. This day had been just one out of the twelve weeks with seven days in each of them, and it seemed as if the hours in this day had stretched and kinked way out of shape so that they added up to a day which had been longer than any day previously, and that was not a comforting thought.

I am precious, she said to herself, brushing her teeth after her shower. She heard Daddy come in, and Ursula, leaving, calling *Goodnight* up the stairs.

Daddy came up the stairs three at a time and gave her a huge hug and kiss to greet her.

'So, Little,' he said, 'how was day one?'

Ruby was tempted to say very very long, and then she thought about saying it was complicated, and telling him about the no-button kisses, and the Mouse's Back, and the doll's shoe, and the old lady with her fat walking stick, and all the silvery streams of silence, and Ursula's face which didn't smile much, or move even at all when she fed Luca. Then she thought about what Claudie's mother had said about Daddy having a lot on his plate, and about all the patients who needed fixing, and of Mummy, who maybe actually right now was spritzing *In Transit* on her face so that she looked daisy fresh when she landed, and she thought of them both in the gauzy net she held in her head, and she smiled up at Daddy and said, 'Ursula's not the most smiley but today was fine. Luca ate all his supper.' And as she went to sleep, Ruby reflected that what she said was completely true, and that missing stuff out did not properly count as not answering the question.

17

Monica had set up her computer on the hotel room dressing table and was sitting cross-legged on the bed, her suitcase half unpacked.

'I'm wide awake,' she said, peering into the computer camera lens. 'In fact, rejig that, I'm wired awake. I just had two espressos from room service, and I think that'll set me up until I can legitimately go to bed.'

'What time is it there?'

She leaned over and grabbed the bedside clock.

'I haven't reset my watch yet. See how I'm missing all the things you usually do for me. It's three in the afternoon.'

'It's eleven here. I'm guessing by seven p.m. your time you won't still be bouncing off the walls.'

'No, more likely driving myself crazy trying to reset my watch.' (And now, she had begun fiddling with the mechanism.) 'Why can I never pull this damn thing out to adjust the time and you can do it even though your fingers are so much bigger than mine? Looks like I'm going to spend my whole time in California subtracting eight hours from whatever my watch says.'

'That'll be good for your maths; or at least subtraction by eight.'

'I think I already have that covered.'

She grabbed a pillow, and held it to her chest.

'God, Daniel, I can hardly believe I'm here. I'm so excited. I had a quick meeting with Gus in the lobby; everybody is checked in here for two days before all the house rentals chime in. I've got a tiny place with Amy, one of the costume designers. Gus says you can hear the sea, but the electricity trips at night if you have both the fridge and the air con on, so you have to choose.'

'Sounds like an acceptable trade-off.'

'I don't know – let's see when I get there. I'm also living next door to one of the make-up artists; I might return home much more soignée.'

'I look forward to it, although quite crumpled would also be fine.'

She blew him a kiss.

'Is everything okay; are the children okay? Are they missing me?'

'What do you want me to tell you?'

'You're right; no correct or helpful answer possible.'

'We are doing fine; we are all doing fine. We talk about you a lot. We've taped your photo to Luca's Tripp Trapp. I'm not sure about soignée, you could be mostly repeatedly smeared with food.'

'Gorgeous; that sounds gorgeous. And Ursula. How is Ursula doing?'

'Ursula is so quiet about the place – even on the small margins of time that we overlap, she's quite easy to miss.'

'That's a bit unkind.'

'But she is though, Mon. I swear she's got some magic trick of vaporising from a room rather than walking out of it. I turn round and – *kssst!* – she's disappeared. She's a big fan of her lists too; there are lists reminding her of things everywhere. I don't know whether she intends them to be a permanent fixture. It's a bit like living in a home with someone with dementia. Maybe that was how she organised it with the old people she lived with before. She seems to have done some kind of audit so that when you come back every cupboard will contain exactly what was in it when you left.'

'I think that sounds like she's making a real effort to keep things recognisable and ordered for the children, I bet the notes disappear in a few days. And you, by the way, might benefit from reading a few of them, since I'm not sure you know what's in half of the cupboards. Has Ruby said anything about her?'

'Rubes says she's not the most smiley. I told her that wasn't the worst thing. At least she's not scowling. I told Ruby to keep a watch out, and tell me when she first scores a smile. My money is on Little.'

'It would be. I hope she's not stern with them, though, that wouldn't be great. Especially for Luca; it's mostly good to spend your time beaming like a crazed loon around anyone under three.'

'Okay, I'll up my beaming. Consider me as on it. And, by the way, I don't think Ursula's face is mean, or stern. She doesn't look unkind. She's innocuous, I think, pale as milk. I don't even think she could be pretty, doesn't look like she could ever have been pretty. There's a blankness, a lack of spontaneity, I guess that's what I mean.'

'Music to my ears, darling husband, even though it's wrong to admit it. I want her to be your helpmate, not someone you think of as sparkling and pretty.'

'Mission accomplished. You have nothing to worry about there.'

Monica beamed.

In the morning, when Ursula arrived, Daniel felt a little uncomfortable. Was it fully fledged guilt, he wondered, or a small niggle of bad conscience? He watched as she carefully hung up her coat and tucked her handbag out of the way. She consulted one of her lists, and started to make Ruby's packed lunch.

'Tomatoes,' she said to Ruby, 'okay as long as they are sliced in circles, not cut into quarters?'

Ruby nodded, chewing her cereal.

'And,' (and here Ursula consulted another of her lists), 'it's spellings today, so you need to remember to take your blue book and put it in your book bag.'

'I've already done it,' said Ruby, wiping the milk from her lips with the back of her hand.

Ursula tore off some kitchen roll and passed it to her.

Daniel, waiting for the coffee machine to warm up, winced a little. He had been disrespectful about Ursula in his conversation with Monica. Not hugely, not overtly rudely, but if Ursula had overheard what he'd said, it would probably have been hurtful. Why had he been so set on saying what he thought Monica wanted to hear? He saw her again, dressed in her white vest, her jeans, so excited, babbling almost, sitting on her vast hotel bed. Had he been trying to impress her with his incisiveness, his wit? Was that what it had been? He felt a little ashamed now, watching Ursula move about the kitchen, not just doing a good job of attending to his children, but conscientiously going about it in a way that made it evident she was trying to do the very best she could do. Damn it, he had laughed at the woman for the way she left a room discreetly.

'Ursula,' he said, 'I know we are only on day two, but I just wanted to say what a great start I think you've made. I'm really appreciative of all your efforts. Thank you.' His voice sounded a little forced.

Ursula looked up from Ruby's Tupperware and nodded. She didn't look at all gratified by his praise. Daniel carried his coffee to the car. Maybe from now on he was destined to get it wrong on a daily basis with both the women in his life.

18

Ruby crossed off the fourth day of week one on her calendar. Downstairs, she could hear Ursula talking to Luca, changing his nappy on their return from the nursery.

'What shall you do now?' Ursula said. 'How about some Play-Doh? Would you like to play pat-a-cake with some Play-Doh?'

When Ruby went downstairs, Luca was sitting at the kitchen table, and Ursula had put out four balls of coloured dough. She gave him a little rolling pin and some cookie cutters from the baking cupboard.

'Are you going to make us some biscuits?' Ursula asked, and she rolled out a piece of dough and cut two neat biscuit shapes. 'Here, now you do it, you have a turn. Can you make us a biscuit? I think Ruby might like a blue one.'

'Bit bit,' said Luca.

'I think he's saying biscuit,' Ruby said helpfully, and then to Luca, 'Are you making us bit-bits?'

Luca squidged the dough in his hands and tried to roll it with the pin. The dough was too high on one side and the cookie cutter wouldn't balance.

'Press and roll with the pin like this,' said Ursula, miming with her hands.

Ruby looked between Ursula and Luca; Luca, face upturned, watched Ursula's mime but was unable to imitate it.

'Like this,' Ursula said, pushing her flat hands forward again, 'with the pin, and then press' (and here she flattened the palm of one hand on the back of the other), 'and press down.'

'Like this, Luca,' Ruby added, putting his hands flat to the pin, and her own on top. 'Like this, see, rolly rolly, it's all going flat, and then look . . .'

She picked up the cookie cutter and put it onto the dough, and placed Luca's hands flat to it, and again her own on top of his. 'And pre-sss,' she said, 'press, Luca! Look you've made a bit-bit.' She tapped the Play-Doh from the cutter.

She glanced up at Ursula, who was now taking something from the fridge. Luca was successfully cutting out more shapes.

'Don't eat it,' Ruby said to Luca, nudging the Play-Doh from his lips. 'It's not for actual eating, just playing with. You're not supposed to like the taste. And it's supper time soon.'

'I think people add salt to it, to put babies off eating it,' Ursula said suddenly, turning from the fridge with a fish pie in her hands. 'But salt is so bad for babies, I'm not sure that's such a good idea.'

Luca began to flip the dough onto the floor.

'I think you've had enough of that. Maybe you'd like to do some running around?' Ursula said. 'Ruby, I tidied the playroom today and I saw a big bottle of bubbles. Might you blow some for him just outside the door here and he can run and try and catch them?'

Ursula lifted him down from his chair and Ruby took him by the hand to the paving by the kitchen door.

'Just wait for a minute,' she said, 'Ursula is finding the bubbles.'

Ruby blew huge strings of vast sheeny bubbles, rainbow-tinged and wobbly, which were floating beyond the drainpipe and up to the top of the window, and Luca was running and clapping and popping them with his hands, and laughing so much that Ruby thought it might be his best game ever. Through the open door she caught sight of Ursula standing by the kitchen table.

She was peeling a carrot, and the carrot skin was dangling in a long thread almost to the table, and Ursula was looking at Luca, or perhaps at something a little way past him. Ruby turned her head to see if maybe it was the neighbour's cat, or maybe one of Patty's best flowers, poking over the fence, but there was nothing special beyond Luca at all. She turned back to Ursula, who had not moved. If it had been a game of musical statues, Ursula would definitely have won. She stood at the table, so completely, completely still, her face, her mouth, her hands all as if carved from stone. She wasn't even blinking. And then, suddenly – could Ursula see that Ruby was staring? – she pulled herself up a little taller, gave a little shudder as if to shake something from her shoulders, and she carried on peeling the carrot, the skin snaking into a soft curl on the table, and Luca squealed and clapped and ran around some more, and then it got a little bit dark, and Ursula called them both in.

When Luca was in the bath, Daddy phoned to say he had been held up and that he would be home in forty-five minutes. Ruby went upstairs and told Ursula, who took Luca out of the bath and laid him on the floor to dry him. She put on his nappy and pyjamas, cleverly, almost without lifting him from the floor, and then she took him to his bedroom, put him into his cot and started his favourite lullaby tape. And while he lay and chit-chattered a little, and did his best to join in with the singing, Ursula drew the curtains quietly, and tidied away some things on his floor, and opened his cupboard doors, and refolded some of his sweaters, and untwisted the strings of one of the fishes that hung from his mobile; and all the while she didn't speak, and Luca was watching her, his body all the time getting more still and sleepy, and then Ursula went and stood by the cot, and said, 'Night night little one.' She hesitated, and Ruby wondered if she might perhaps kiss him goodnight, but she didn't. Instead she leaned over and just smoothed the hair away from his forehead, and Luca's eyes were almost closed – he must have been tired from running after all the bubbles – and Ursula stood for a moment, and then turned to come out of the room, and Ruby scooted downstairs thinking that perhaps what she'd been doing was spying.

In the sitting room she turned on the television and stretched herself out onto the sofa hurriedly. Ursula came into the room and said with a little shrug of her shoulders, 'I don't want to start anything else in case it wakes Luca. Shall I sit with you for a little while until Daddy gets home?'

'Sure.'

'I'll just get something from my basket.'

She went to the hallway and came back with a ball of wool and two needles, then sat down and started to knit, the needles click-clicking and the wool falling in a soft pleat of blueness across her lap.

'What are you making?' Ruby asked.

'Nothing, I'm afraid. I just like my hands to be busy. Sometimes I get to the end of a ball, and then I unravel it and start all over again. At lunch time, often, I sit for a coffee and my sandwich and I do a few rows.'

'Will you show me how? Soon, in Design and Technology, we're going to have to make something. I could knit a scarf, something easy, if you would show me how to do it.'

'Watch carefully; see how my hands push this needle behind this one, and then loop the wool around it, and then flick the loop off; see; see how it makes a stitch?'

She leaned over to the sofa and passed the needles to Ruby. 'You try; it doesn't matter if you make a mistake, or if you drop a stitch, it's easy to sort out.'

Ruby took the needles in her hand. They felt stiff and complicated.

'Push the needle in your right hand behind the one in your

left,' said Ursula, 'and then, that's it, wrap the wool around the right-hand needle.'

She was miming again, Ruby noted, just like with the Play-Doh. The loop of wool fell from her fingers.

'Try again, if you want to,' Ursula said, with no hint of impatience.

Flicking the loop off was impossible. The needles just scritch-scratched together, and the loop of the stitch stayed on the right one as if glued.

Ruby looked up at Ursula.

'Will you come and sit next to me, and do what I did for Luca with the Play-Doh? Will you put your hands over mine and show me how to do it because I can't do it just from your words.'

Ursula hesitated, and then sat beside Ruby. Slowly, very slowly, she put her hands over Ruby's and guided her through one, two, three, four stitches. Then she took her hands away and Ruby did one stitch all by herself, and then another, and Ursula said, 'There, you did it, clever girl.'

She moved from the sofa back to the chair and, as she did so, Ruby noticed she very quickly smoothed her palms against her skirt, as if the touch of Ruby's skin might need wiping away. Just as she sat down, Ruby heard Daddy's key in the door. He came in, saying, 'Ursula, I'm really sorry I'm so late, one of my patients had unexpected complications.' Ursula stood up and said, 'It's fine; Monica explained it was to be expected.' She reached out for the knitting, and quickly put it in her basket in the hallway and was suddenly gone.

'It's fish pie for supper,' Ruby said to Daddy, who was now washing his hands. 'It's got three kinds of fish in, and some cheese in the sauce.'

'Perfect. How was your day? How are you getting on with Ursula?'

'She was showing me how to knit, after she put Luca to bed.'

'That's great. I'll put in an order for a jumper for Christmas. Is that a reasonable expectation?'

'I only managed six stitches, and four of those she helped me with. And Daddy . . .'

'I'm so hungry, let me just put this in the microwave. It looks delicious. I'll tell Mummy when I Skype her later that we're certainly not going to starve. Is there anything you want me to tell her or ask her? She'll want to know all your news.'

Ruby sat for a moment, and wondered about what else she had been going to say about Ursula, but Daddy was getting out a knife and fork and filling a glass with water, and she thought it was probably better to think about something for him to tell Mummy when he Skyped her later.

Afterwards, in bed, she thought about it some more. If she'd carried on talking about Ursula she would have said that she was kind, and really good at thinking of things for Luca to do, but that it was a curious thing, because Ursula seemed not to want her hands to touch either of them, unless it was necessary. She uses her words, Ruby would have said, when her hands could do whatever it was much more quickly. Maybe, Ruby thought, turning onto her side and snuggling down further beneath the duvet, some grown-ups preferred that. And she decided not to picture again the way Ursula touched her hands to her skirt as if to wipe all trace of Ruby's skin away, as if it was not a nice thing to touch somebody when there wasn't actually a necessary reason to do so.

19

On Friday night, having completed her first full week at Daniel's, Ursula sat in a taupe linen chair in her living room. Living Room. That was a term that was better not scrutinised. Did she live in hers? As little as possible.

Memories surfaced sometimes. Ambushed her, to be more accurate. They reared up unexpectedly when she was putting diesel in her car, loading washing into the machine; sometimes as she stood brushing her teeth, her face soaped clean. Then, she felt at her most exposed, wrapped in a towel, her feet damp on the tiled floor. Tonight, there was no such subtlety. Tonight, for reasons she couldn't explain, the beginnings came stampeding back. All that dazzle. All his beauty. As she sat in her chair, it nudged and elbowed its way into her skull. 'Here I am again,' the memory said, with the lewd, cocky swagger of a drunk, 'what shall you do with me now?'

And so back, again, again, always back again, to herself, aged twenty-three, in the summer of 1986, her blue dress, her neat shoes, and a curious compliancy – was that how best to see it? If she could call out to her younger self, what would she shout – Run! Run for your life? Doubtless she would not have listened. Gideon wore cufflinks, didn't fiddle with anything as he talked. He made every man she'd known previously seem like a boy. Urbane? Suave? She'd learned new words in order to think about him. She'd been so flattered. Was it the fault of her vanity then; was that the flaw in herself she could blame? It was hard not to be harsh on her soft-skinned, twenty-three-year-old self. Did she need to apportion blame? Evidently so. Evidently still so.

Gideon had said, the first time, 'This is what's going to happen', as if that were the accepted form when asking someone out for a drink. She had been taken aback by his confidence. Perhaps she could attribute her acquiescence to that. He met her, the next evening, in a wine bar off Marylebone High Street. The room was long and thin, and she'd had to turn sideways to make her way through the tables. She approached him feeling like a raggedy clawed crab, her coat draped over her arm, held close to avoid other people.

'True to your roots, Condotti, I've ordered you a peach Bellini,' he said. He turned to the waiter and ordered himself a gimlet. The waiter asked whether he wanted it with vodka or gin. Gimlet. She'd never heard of such a drink. She imagined it written on the small white coaster between them. Gimlet-eyed. Wasn't that an expression? She wasn't sure what it meant. It sounded like something from a witchy incantation: eye of newt, leg of toad. The gimlet was served with a thick wedge of lime. She imagined it must have tasted sharp and clean. The peach Bellini was floral, sweet, verging on sickly. Her lips felt sticky with it, and as if she might inadvertently trap whichever words came out of her mouth. She tried, subtly, to lick her lips clean. His eyes focused, briefly, clearly, on the tip of her tongue edging her lower lip. In the low light of the room, they looked as black as ink. He paused – for the fraction of a second – and she looked down at her hands, mortified that he might think she was trying to look seductive. Should she try to explain, should she stutter, that the Bellini was syrupy? No, she should not. She pressed her lips together. Perhaps now she looked prim. He resumed what he was saying.

When they left for the restaurant, she picked her way through the chairs. It felt necessary to step carefully. He had placed his hand on the small of her back and she was uncertain as to whether she was being steered or supported. It felt important, suddenly, to watch exactly where she put her feet. The floor was solid, evidently, there were no steps, no fissures, but it felt as if there could be, or perhaps a great swoop of sinking sand, ready to swallow her legs. Stepping out onto the pavement was an unexpected relief.

They went to a Thai restaurant, and he ordered pad thai for them both. It was the first time she'd eaten Thai food. The waiter knew him by name. Gideon asked her about Italy, about whether her family had gone there much when she was a child. She could only summon up three memories, which seemed as sparse and bald as tiny pebbles in her pocket. Should she tell him about the priest, stooped like a small black crow saying Easter Mass so slowly in Latin, six tiny-boned nuns in the front pew, and it all taking so long that she'd thought time had truly, actually stopped? Or the April it was so cold that, for the first time in anyone's memory, the olive trees did not fruit? Or the kind of pasta made by her grandmother, which translated as little ears? She had offered none of them up; in retrospect she couldn't understand why she might have contemplated doing so. Had she said anything at all, that night? Perhaps she'd sat in sticky-lipped silence and listened while he told her of his extensive travels in Umbria, in Tuscany. Under the table, she counted on her fingers to make sure that she had calculated their age difference correctly. Nine years apart. That, and it seemed, a wealth of cosmopolitan experience.

After the pad thai, he took her to another restaurant for dessert. This, he'd told her, is the best crème brûlée you will have eaten in your life. The secret, he said, is the quality of the egg yolks in the custard, and the heat of the grill. He cracked the surface of it with the heel of a teaspoon and the caramel shattered like glass. He held the spoon to her mouth, and she felt herself move forward to taste it like a trusting fledgling. That wouldn't be the right image though, she knew that now. That was a benefit of thinking it over and over. Fledglings were ready to fly, were on the verge of assuming an independent life. She, on the contrary, was flying straight to him.

It was raining when he drove her to her flat in Camden, and he walked her to her door with what felt like old-fashioned courtesy, producing a large umbrella which kept her dry as she fumbled, self-consciously, for her keys. He gave no indication of wishing to be invited in.

When the doorbell rang half an hour later, she had already changed into her striped cotton pyjamas. His hair was soaking wet, and she was momentarily distracted by this. Had he not driven away in his car? Had he walked on somewhere else, but not taken his huge umbrella? She looked for it in his hand, and forgot that she was wearing pyjamas more fitting for a boy.

'Tomorrow,' he said, 'I'll pick you up at ten tomorrow morning. We can go to a great restaurant I know on the coast. Serves seafood that has to be eaten to be believed.'

He scrutinised her pyjamas, and, reaching forward, carefully adjusted the collar where it had turned in on itself. His thumb brushed her collarbone so gently she wasn't sure if she'd actually been touched. 'If this is what passes for nightwear,' he said softly, 'there needs to be an upgrade before I start lobbying to stay the night.'

She'd blushed, there on the doorstep, the gutter overflowing from the sharp heaviness of the rain, and his hair all wet, and a puddle pooled right by the step. The blush went right to her scalp, she could feel it prickling and steeping, and he said, 'You are blushing, Signorina Condotti, that won't do either.'

The oysters were unbelievable, fresh and infused with the sea. They also ate lobster, garlicky and pink-shelled from the grill. He touched her hand as he passed her a menu, and she found herself looking at her skin to see if it bore any trace. What was she expecting? A pulse of colour? A scribble of heat? The pale outline of his fingertips? She wanted him to touch her again. She knew that, sitting there, the lobster cracked open before them. She tried to banish the thought. What was he talking about? He was showing her some platform, staked out in the estuary, where the fishermen gutted their fish. He pointed to the row of crab pots. Yes, she found herself saying, yes, I can see them.

When she came home from work on Tuesday, there was a parcel in the hallway. When she unwrapped it – the box had had a thick, soft ribbon – it contained a nightgown made of the slipperiest oyster-coloured silk. The accompanying card was written in the bold blue ink of the fountain pen that was familiar on his desk. Take this, it said, as serving notice of intent.

What time was it now? It was too dark to see her wristwatch clearly. While she had been sitting there, nightfall had nuzzled and scooched its way into the room, so that now she was surrounded by a soft fuzz of grey shadow. She rubbed her arms. It had also become chilly. She reached over and turned on the lamp. Eight thirty. She hadn't eaten, but didn't feel hungry. What was that poem – she recalled a poem; 'In my beginning was my end'. Was that it? How odd that it should come to her now. That was the benefit of reconsidering; turning it over and over in her mind. Now, all these years later, finally she knew what she would have called out to her younger self, on that day, returning from the coast, full of lobster and sunshine and skin-rushes when she looked at him. 'In this beginning is your end', she would have said, and thereby squared the circle with a woman, aged almost fifty, sitting alone in a living room which was not.

20

Claudie peered over to Ruby's spelling sheet.

'Have you got the same ones as me?'

'Yes.'

'Don't forget that we have a test tomorrow. Miss Cameron says whoever gets everything right can pin their sheet to the top of the spelling tree.'

Ruby put the sheet in her book bag.

'Mummy says,' Claudie continued, 'that when I get home tonight we can have a proper spelling bee, and go over and over the words until I have them so right I can't get them wrong. What will you do to learn yours, with your mummy not there; will the Ursula person help you?'

'If I asked her to, I expect so. If I need help, which I might not.'

'She might be busy doing other things though, mightn't she? My mummy says she's your housekeeper as well. She might be too busy doing jobs so she can't help you with your spelling. Maybe. That's why we have Philomena. She does all the cleaning so that my mummy can just look after me. My mummy says too many people who go to work mix up housework and childcare when they are very different things. I might invite Stella to my spelling bee, but she doesn't have the same spellings as us. Mummy wouldn't mind though; she'd test Stella on hers as well.'

Claudie swished her pigtails.

When she came through the door after school, Ruby felt a

little bit sick. Ursula would be busy with Luca for a while yet – fetching him, sorting him out after the nursery. She might not even know the best way to go about learning spellings. She came into the kitchen and Ursula was holding something out to her.

'Look what came in the post,' she said, 'a postcard especially and just for you.'

Ruby took it from her, and looked at the front. It was a picture of white letters spelling *HOLLYWOOD*, which were up in the hills outside of Los Angeles. She knew this because she read it in small, italic letters in the bottom corner of the card. Mummy had drawn a small stick figure of herself in front of the letters, and on the back of the card she'd written *I am here and thinking of you and sending Hollywood hills of love.*

'Isn't that nice?' Ursula said. 'Mummy must have found that postcard almost as soon as she got there and posted it straight to you.'

Ruby nodded. It was nice, but perhaps not as nice as having a mummy who'd do your own spelling bee so that your sheet was the one that was pinned to the top of the tree.

'I've got some spellings to practise for my homework,' she said. 'I'll just go up to my room and start.'

Necessary was a very hard word. She'd copied it out three times, and kept getting muddled up over how many c's and s's it contained. She screwed up the piece of paper she was writing on and threw it against her bedroom wall. The Hollywood post-card stared at her from her desk. It suddenly looked like it was mocking; mocking her spelling practice, and the c's and s's in necessary. Claudie no doubt would now be whizzing through her spelling bee and getting everything right. Ruby felt a flash of hotness, and found herself reaching out and tearing the postcard quickly and precisely into very small pieces, so that the white letters became a scribble of snowy whiteness, and Mummy's stick arms and legs were a jumble of not belonging together, and the biro writing on the back was just beetle legs of blue pen strokes. Immediately after she'd ripped it up, she felt a little bit better; less angry, anyway, with Mummy for not being there, and with Claudie for being so spiteful. And then, as quickly, she felt like she wanted to cry, Mummy's happy postcard was in a little heap in front of her. Why had she done that? She went over to her bedside table and picked up her keepsake box. She took out the calendar of days and ticked off one more, and then carried the box to her desk and started putting into it all the tiny, soft ripped pieces. As she carried the box back to her bedside table, she realised Ursula was standing in the doorway. She was holding a plate, and a mug. Ruby didn't know how long she had been there.

'I thought spelling-practisers deserved a cupcake and some milk.'

Ursula put the plate down on the desk. She bent down and picked up two scraps of the postcard which had floated down to the carpet. Ruby caught a flash of blue sky, and maybe one corner of the letter H. They nestled in Ursula's palm.

'I think you dropped these,' Ursula said softly. 'I'm sure you wouldn't want to lose them. Are you storing them in that little box? That's a good place for precious things. Here, open the lid and I can put them in for you.'

Ursula came towards her, and Ruby opened the box and held it in front of her. Ursula added the two pieces in and said, 'There, tucked up all safe and sound.'

She stepped back towards the desk, and glanced over the spelling list.

'What a good speller you must be, aged nine, to have all these difficult words.'

'I might not get them all right, though. Claudie probably will. Her mum's doing a spelling bee so that she gets them so right she can't possibly get them wrong. And then it will be her sheet that gets pinned to the top of the spelling tree.'

'I don't know how to begin to put together a spelling bee, or what a spelling tree looks like, but I do know that if you eat your cupcake it might cheer you up a bit, and I can tell you ways of thinking about the spellings which might help them to stick in your head.'

'What kind of ways?'

'Well, let's see,' said Ursula, scanning down the list. 'Necessary. I learned to spell necessary by thinking I had one collar and two shoes. Might that work for you?'

Her mouth full of cupcake, Ruby nodded.

'Now let's think of some others,' said Ursula. 'We can have this sorted in no time.'

Twenty minutes later, marking them against her original sheet, Ruby put a large orange tick next to each of the correct words. All of them were right. Ursula made to leave the room.

'Now I must start cooking supper. Your daddy is finishing work early and he's collecting Luca so we don't have to go to the nursery.'

She went and stood by the door, and at the last moment, turned to look at Ruby. She glanced over to the keepsake box.

'Ruby,' she said, so softly that Ruby had to tilt forwards to properly hear, 'even when mummies are not with their children, can't be with them for all sorts of good reasons, they're still loving you, and rooting for you, and thinking about you, and that's why Mummy sent you that postcard. It took more time to find it, and buy it, and draw on it, and get a stamp and post it than to sort out a few spellings, and what your mummy wrote on that post-card is far more important than knowing how to spell necessary. If anybody at school says any different – maybe Claudie? – they are just plain wrong. Your mummy loves you very much; I know that and I've only been in your house for two weeks. It's right that you've put your postcard in a precious place. And, look at it this way; it wouldn't have fitted in the box in its original size.'

Ruby swallowed, and felt her cheeks pinken. When she looked up, Ursula was gone.

'Do you want to go to the park?' Daddy called up to her as he came through the front door. 'Give me five minutes to change out of my suit and I'll be all set. Ursula says its forty-five minutes to supper. Luca can have a go on the swings – will you come?'

Ruby pulled her school dress off over her head, and put on some shorts and a T-shirt. As she went out of the front door, following Daddy who was carrying Luca, bouncing a football and laughing, she looked down the hallway to Ursula in the kitchen. For a moment, she caught her eye, and then Ursula looked away and turned towards the fridge. Ruby blew her a kiss, but she didn't think she saw it.

Eating supper later, watching Daddy feeding Luca and making so much mess it was funny, Ruby went and sat on his knee. 'What a love huddle we are,' he said, kissing both hers and Luca's heads.

'Ursula was kind today, and very helpful,' Ruby said. 'She helped me to learn my spellings and to look after something properly.'

'Gosh, Little, that sounds like a very formal appraisal. I'll tell Mummy; she'll be glad to hear it.'

'Can I Skype her too? I want to thank her for something.'

When Ruby came running up the driveway from school, she burst into the house to find Ursula hoovering the stairs. She started to speak, but could see that Ursula couldn't hear her. She was tilting her head, Ruby's voice drowned out by the vacuum cleaner, which was at the bottom of the stairs. Ruby ran and switched it off.

'My spelling test,' she said, 'it's pinned to the top of the spelling tree. I got fifteen out of fifteen. I was the only one in my group.'

She jumped to where Ursula was standing, holding the Hoover brush with one hand.

'High five!' Ruby said gleefully, raising her arm.

And, a little slowly, a little uncertainly, Ursula lifted her free hand, and Ruby whacked palm to palm. Ursula said, 'Well done,' and smiled a little bit, but Ruby noticed she then put her hand in her apron pocket, as if to make extra sure she wouldn't have to high-five again.

21

Awake. Monica opened her eyes and listened to the hum of the air conditioning. The fridge was silent; it was an acceptable trade-off. She got out of bed and walked to the kitchen; turned off the air conditioning and flicked the fridge back on. If they only did this at night, the food in there stayed cool. She reached across to the fruit bowl and took two apricots and a handful of almonds. She walked out onto the tiny veranda, which was decked in a scramble of blue morning glory. She breathed in the morning and looked up at the wide expanse of sky. She stretched up her arms and smiled broadly. To begin the day like this still felt like a gift. She heard Amy turn on the radio in her room.

'Are we late?' Amy called.

'Not even a bit. Bags of time.'

Monica settled into the hammock, and began to swing gently. Ruby would still be in school; Daniel would probably be checking all his patients post-theatre. Luca would be doing something that would be written on a whiteboard, and Ursula, what would Ursula be doing, in her home, amongst all Monica's things?

Domestic items, Monica felt, always spoke volumes. They were oddly personal, carrying an imprint of use, of habit. A carving board, an ice-cream scoop, a milk pan, salad servers. All her things would be becoming familiar in Ursula's hands. She tried not to think of them. If dusted forensically, would they still bear a trace of her fingerprints?

She thought again of Daniel, Ruby and Luca. How familiar their images were, but now, in the clear planes of the morning light, they had assumed a separateness, a self-containedness, like an unopened envelope. They were like tiny figures in a souvenir glass orb who, with one shake of her wrist, might be standing in a flurry of snowflakes. She missed them; she reassured herself that she missed them. At night, sometimes stirring in her sleep, her body anticipated Daniel's. She would stretch out her leg, expecting to find his, or reach her palm across the pillow, waiting to touch the thick softness of his hair. The children required more of an overt effort. She would look at the bath and try to envisage Ruby and Luca in it; Luca sitting splashing, Ruby washing her limbs with studied concentration. But somehow she couldn't properly see them, couldn't evoke the smooth density of their limbs. She couldn't imagine them in the mall either, despite it being swarming with children, or in her hire car on the wide freeways, or driving through residential areas, looking at irrigated gardens tended by taciturn Hispanics in the heat. Daniel, Ruby and Luca shimmered beyond her daily life and she felt she had to somehow safeguard them, like a match kept lit in the face of a riffling breeze, so that if she cupped her palm securely enough, all would be well, and they would be safe, and their life together would resume.

Her new routine was all-consuming; she reassured herself that that was why they felt so separate, so mirage-like. The intense focus of work on set, the amiable pleasantries of the daily round. It was enveloping. Surely Californians couldn't mean, with sincerity, what they said to strangers at every available exchange? *Have a great day; it's been fantastic to serve you.* Was fellow-feeling somehow ratcheted up in California? At the heart of it, she suspected, was something which would ring hollow. And yet how comforting it was, how gloriously welcoming, so that Monica felt, as she swung gently in the hammock, the blue of the morning glory framing her peripheral vision, that California was in fact the most perfect place to be. She bit into an apricot. It was exquisitely ripe.

Yesterday, the crew had a prolonged lunch break because the lead actress was giving some promotional interviews for another film. Monica had sat with four other women, eating watermelon beneath some vast Californian pines. The noonday heat was intense, the cicadas were scritch-scratching, and the dusty soil beneath her flip-flops was red and warm. She'd tilted her head back for a moment, squinted up through the branches of the pine tree, allowing the chatter of the other women to bob softly around her. The talk was of lovers, breasts, ageing parents, calories, a particular colour of nail varnish, an abdominal exercise, a recipe with pomegranate seeds. Questions peppered through it. Monica listened, her eyelashes blurring with the needles of the pine tree branches.

'And what about you, Monica?' one of them said.

'What about me?' she'd replied.

'You know, how have you managed all this? You've got kids, haven't you, a husband – is he just holding the fort?'

And as Monica explained the arrangement she and Daniel had reached, she could see from the other women's faces that they were struck by her good fortune. A husband who was prepared to support her in this way; enough money to pay for a full-time housekeeper; an emphasis on what this job might mean to her long term rather than on the specific, insistent need to earn income.

'Jeez, Monica,' said one, 'you've lucked out.'

And now, as she lay there in the hammock, Monica felt sheepish, as if she had not, until the moment beneath the pine tree, actually calibrated how lucky she was. And she'd blushed a little as the women moved on in their chatter, talking of someone's mother who was beginning to show signs of dementia, and of a husband who insisted on separate bank accounts, and a dress put by in a boutique until payday. She *was* incredibly lucky. She hoped now, in recognising it, that she wouldn't jinx her good fortune.

22

Venice. That had been the first time they'd made love. Odd that she should suddenly think of that as she put fresh linen on Daniel and Monica's bed. Daniel and Monica's bed; it felt like that even though Monica was so absent. The marital bed. How solid it seemed; what square-edged certainty and implacability it carried, like one of Moses's tablets brought down from the mountain.

As a young woman, it had seemed to her such a cosy thought; that one would spend all one's adult life sharing a bed with someone much loved. She'd imagined conversations carried out propped up on pillows, or cold feet pressed companionably against warmer ones. The complexity – the inherent emotional minefield – had not been apparent to her then. The trading of sex, who wanted it, who didn't; the tactical withholding of small reproaches, the familiar litanies of complaint, secret sorrows, and most of all the unbearable bone-aching loneliness which could not be assuaged by the person only a pillow's breadth away. How might it be, one night, the sky white with the moon, to lean on one's elbow and say calmly, with poise, 'I should never have married you'? How many wished for that moment of honesty? She smoothed the clean, ironed duvet cover with her hand. Venice.

He had come into her office and said, 'On Friday, bring a small suitcase; be discreet. Passport. Temperature warmer than this but not by much.' Ridiculous. She could not just be told she was going; not even told where. He reappeared around the door-frame. 'Shall I take that as a yes? It felt like a yes.' She nodded. He was impossible. Gloriously impossible.

On Friday, they sat in a restaurant eating a very late lunch overlooking the church of the Santa Maria della Salute. Walking there, they had stopped in another church and he'd shown her a painting – something dark, ochry, religious. 'By Tintoretto's daughter,' he'd said. 'Some say she would have been the better painter, were it not for discrimination, unequal opportunity, lack of a patron.'

She thought the painting forlorn; crimped somehow, perhaps cramped. Maybe that was how Tintoretto's daughter felt. Marietta, was she called? Ursula could just make out the name from her signature. Perhaps Marietta painted in a small attic space, with inadequate light, and eaves which required her to move hesitantly, stooped. More than likely, Marietta was responsible for organising the household too; every time she mixed a colour or picked up a brush, fielding an interruption to a pay a butcher who called, send a maid on an errand, or to tell the cook what to prepare when her father came home for lunch with his patron. Same old, same old, she'd thought, surprised at her cynicism. Gideon had moved on and was looking at an altarpiece.

After lunch they went to the Guggenheim Museum. She was struck by Peggy Guggenheim's bedstead; the headboard made from twisted fingers of iron. Magnificent, Gideon said. Her first thought was how uncomfortable it would be to lean against, but she found herself nodding. It was difficult not to be caught up in the current of his aesthetic certainty.

When they returned to the room, he had lifted her in his arms and laid her gently on the bed. Like a sacrifice, she thought, expecting flames, combustion. She had cried softly, that first time, her skin rising, hotly, to his touch. Over dinner, he poured her a glass of champagne. 'May I congratulate you,' he said softly, 'on fulfilling everything that might be ascribed to the passionate stereotype of your gene pool.'

That night, Ursula thought every part of her had been kissed, made familiar. She lay on his chest and he read to her from *Room with a View*. 'Wrong city,' he said, 'but that's a petty objection.' His voice was deep and resonant, more so with her ear pressed so close to him, her hair streaming out behind his shoulder (how long, how thick it had been then) and the dominant sensation of a blurring of where he stopped and she began. If I died now, she'd thought, an uncharacteristically morbid thought for her, it would be okay. It would definitely be okay, here in this room, with the flock wallpaper, the darkness at the window, the sheets crumpled and warm. Yes, it would be all right, she'd thought, struggling not to drift into sleep, because nothing could be more perfect, or more beautiful than this.

It was difficult not to sit down on Daniel and Monica's bed; not to place her head in her hands, press her closed eyes into blackness. Instead, she looked at the clock on the nightstand. Yes, she would go and fetch Luca. If she walked very slowly, she would arrive at her usual time.

23

Daniel had gone early to a conference in Oxford. He'd left in a rush, and Ursula moved deftly around the kitchen, restoring it to order. She dried Luca's breakfast bowl and wiped his high chair meticulously.

Oxford.

'Have you ever been there?' Daniel had asked, yesterday evening, freshly back from work. He was careful, Ursula noted, never to assume, presume or to second-guess. They moved around each other awkwardly, both physically and verbally. She thought of it sometimes like an elaborate dance. She avoided speech when a gesture would suffice.

'No,' she said, 'I haven't. I have never had reason to go.'

'You should,' Daniel said, 'it's a beautiful city. I did one of my foundation years at the John Radcliffe hospital, which is out of town in Headington. The city itself is mainly three streets: the High, the Broad and St Giles. It's very easy to walk around, and Christ Church meadows, which are behind the college, they're lovely, with the river running through them. And Addison's walk, in Magdalen College – see how I'm warming to my theme. I'm giving you a virtual tour.'

She'd just nodded, quietly busied herself with loading the dishwasher with the children's supper things, and sweeping the floor in smooth, methodical strokes. Daniel had verbally ground to halt. He stood in the kitchen, clearly noticing that his enthusiasm for Oxford, for why she should visit Oxford, was falling on stony ground. He could, she thought, be justified in thinking her cold-hearted, mean as a snake. How unreasonable she was, refusing to give and take just a little. She reminded herself that that way lay ruin, and stiffened her resolve.

Daniel had rustled papers in his briefcase, made a show of scooping up the day's post. The colleague giving the paper, he said, often made a great deal of trumpeting about not very much. Ursula had nodded again. Oxford, and its inherent appeal, were swiftly laid to rest. Ursula moved to the utility room, hung up her apron neatly and began to put on her coat.

Her untruth sat smooth as a butter pat in her mouth.

Oxford. She had been to Oxford. She would not tell Daniel that. *When?* he might ask; *where did you go?*

They'd walked round Christ Church meadow. It had been a Sunday morning, early in June. The air was thick with the peal of bells and the soft lowing of cattle. Gideon was purposeful, brisk. 'Nothing like a visit to my alma mater,' he'd said, 'to remind me quite so effectively of how much I have gained and lost.' She tried to imagine him younger than she was now – eighteen, nineteen? – perhaps carefree on a bicycle, wrapped in a college scarf, holding an armful of books. The image would not hold. Had he always been, she wondered, smooth, impenetrable, as polished as Bakelite?

They'd gone to the cathedral for Matins; Gideon had suggested it. The sunlight streamed fulsomely through the stained-glass windows. She'd noticed, with surprise, that he was word-perfect throughout the service; the liturgy, the Creed, the responses, even the hymns. It sounded, from his lips, like something worn smooth with use.

'I hadn't expected that,' she said, as they hurriedly crossed Tom Quad.

'What?'

'The Creed, the responses, the hymns; that you would be word perfect in them all.'

'Observant,' he said. 'Well noticed, Condotti. My father was a theologian, a dean at Salisbury. I spent a great deal of my childhood squirming in pews. If you prick me, out would come "Nunc Dimittis".'

His tone suggested the subject was now closed.

They'd eaten at a hotel on the High Street, and afterwards they'd walked to Magdalen Bridge where Gideon hired a punt. Less surprisingly, he was very capable at steering it, the punt sliding effortlessly beneath them. Ursula lay back, one arm folded beneath her, her head resting on her rolled-up sweater. The emerald smoothness of the water was visible between her half-closed eyes. She felt drowsy, full of lunch, rocked as if in a watery cradle.

As she looked up, through her eyelashes, perspective made Gideon seem taller, more isolated. She shivered at the unbidden image of him as a ferryman for the dead. As the deep shadow of overhanging trees eclipsed him into darkness, her mouth, her tongue, suddenly felt heavy with grave goods. 'Stop,' she was tempted to say, wanting him to put down the pole and lie with her for a moment, so that she could feel the warmth and strength of his arms, his lips. He would have no time, she guessed, for such unpredictable skittishness. He would not welcome her sharing her unbidden thought. Instead, she raised herself up on her elbow, looked at him more carefully in the adjusted full light of the sun, her other hand creating a sun-visor for her eyes. He became himself again.

'So,' she said archly, playfully, 'Gideon, the priest's son, who knows the liturgy by heart, can sing like someone who was once a choirboy, and can punt like an expert . . .'

How confident she had been. How sure of her attractiveness to him.

'The past's history,' he'd said abruptly, ducking beneath a low-hanging bough. 'The biggest mistake is to think it sheds light on what is to come.'

How right he had been. How possible it was to hear but not listen.

Daniel's kitchen suddenly felt chilly. Ursula retrieved a cardigan from her bag.

Oxford. Why would she ever want to go to Oxford again?

24

Daniel's mother was arriving later in the day. Ursula wondered what she was like. Frank and forthright, she imagined. Perhaps she should clean downstairs again, wipe the curtain rails, pull out the sofas? She'd done it recently – it was unlikely to need doing again. Was Elisabeth Bailey the sort of woman who ran her finger along window ledges, glanced behind the fridge, all the time assessing quite how thoroughly Ursula was doing her job? Perhaps, later, over a glass of wine (Ursula switched this to a gin and tonic, hazarding this might be more Elisabeth's drink), might she rate her to Daniel? Might she describe her as adequate, or would Elisabeth think she was doing a good job? Elisabeth would have no idea what it was taking. The digging deep. The self-steeling. The counting of out-breaths each morning she woke. Perhaps Elisabeth would focus on Ruby and Luca instead; appraise them, at length, and decide if they were flourishing under Ursula's nominal care. What might Ruby say? She could count on her to say she was kind. Ruby had no grounds to think otherwise.

Was it comforting, she wondered, for Daniel to have a parent alive? To feel himself still at the centre of Elisabeth's curiosity and focus, with her aware of his life trajectory? Her own mother had been dead for almost twelve years, her father for five years before that. If not a comfort, it could be construed as a blessing.

She'd taken Gideon to visit her mother, three months into their relationship. The memory of that day came back to her now, freshly minted.

They'd driven up in his car. It was evident, as Gideon made to turn into her mother's small, faux-brick-paved driveway, that the car was too wide to fit. Ursula had blushed a little – how awkward it seemed; Gideon turning the wheel, and clearly registering the plastic pots of busy lizzies, marigolds, pansies, a small concrete dog statue, and a wide-winged copper butterfly atop a metal stem, all of it reducing the available width of her mother's too-small drive.

Her mother, Ava, served them coffee in the best room. All of the cushions were embroidered with bon mots: *Home is where the heart is*, said the one next to Gideon. *Love; Laugh; Dance*, said the footstool in mustard-coloured stitching. Did her mother really believe that? Ursula found it hard to credit. Her two recurrent themes were the arthritis in her knees and her overriding anxiety that Ursula lived alone. 'Can't you work closer to here; away from London?' she repeatedly asked. Ursula was sceptical as to whether Solihull would have yielded as much love, laughter and dancing as her mother might wish for her.

Gideon sat very upright on the sofa, being careful not to dislodge the lace antimacassars. Had he thought, Ursula wondered, as her mother offered him a plate of squares of Battenburg cake, that as he met earlier generations of her family, he might progress towards someone more authentically Italian? Had he imagined Ava serving him a bitter-sweet espresso, a small chocolate and pistachio cantuccino on a saucer beside it, having emerged from the kitchen, aproned, hands floury from making great sheets of pasta? Instead, he was experiencing suburban Solihull, and her mother's love of all things brightly patterned. Ursula looked around the room, at the windowsill where pools of sunlight outwitted the net curtains. Perplexingly – she had never really considered it before – the only painting in the room was of a solitary, antlered stag. It seemed to be beside a Scottish loch and made no connective sense at all. Although, she thought (now with contrition), what might she have expected her mother to choose? The leaning tower of Pisa? St Mark's Square? Her father came from Norwich. Maybe a cathedral would have been more apt, or a flat, salt-marsh landscape redolent of the Fens? The stag looked at her forlornly. He wasn't the only one out of place: Gideon was gamely eating the pink and yellow Battenburg cake. How gaudy, how synthetic, it looked in his hands. She noticed he'd modulated the characteristic sharpness and impatience of his tone. He was answering her mother, who had asked him what line of work he was in.

Not one that would make sense to her, Ursula was confident of that. Her mother's concept of work involved two kinds of jobs: factories and professions, with nothing conceivable in between. Gideon patiently persevered in his explanation. How grateful she'd felt.

When they got up to leave, her mother had, uncharacteristi-cally, placed her hand on Gideon's arm. She'd looked small and round next to his angular leanness. She'd stood on the doorstep and taken in the expanse of his gleaming car, parked out on the road. 'I worry about Ursula,' she'd blurted out, and Gideon had turned to her, given her his most dazzling smile, and said, 'No need for that, Mrs Condot, her wellbeing is my number one priority.' Her mother had looked like someone stood down from years of fraught vigilance, from the need to constantly assess the proximity of danger, of risk. 'Thank you,' she'd said to him, her eyes grateful, beseeching. 'Thank you.'

Ursula couldn't bear to remember it. She picked up the broom and started sweeping vigorously. Elisabeth Bailey wouldn't be able to fault her on that.

25

Elisabeth stood outside the kitchen door, with Ruby crouched by her side.

'But how can a cigarette be electric?' Ruby asked.

'Search me. Turns out it can be, although your father says it's probably no better.'

'But why are we still standing outside, like when you had a real smoke break?'

'All the years of me being banished out here so you wouldn't breathe the smoke. I've got used to it. Standing by this drainpipe is appealingly familiar, even in the winter when the temperature's minus three. Do you think Luca's asleep yet?'

'Probably. Do you know the end glows like a real cigarette?'

'It's about the only similarity, sadly.'

'If I go up and bath now, will you come up to my room and tell me a story about when you were my age in Cyprus?'

'I can't pretend I won't be making half of it up, but yes, scoot. I'll be up there shortly.

Ruby vanished.

Elisabeth listened for the sound of Daniel's voice upstairs. There was an unreal quality to standing by while her son confidently put his children to bed. How things had changed; his own father wouldn't have had a clue how to go about it, and her father – a military man – would have been more comfortable receiving a salute from his offspring than a hug. There was something to be said for contemporary masculinity.

She came back into the kitchen. It was spotless, immaculate. Good old Monica making sure that was taken care of. Ursula had left shortly after she'd arrived. Plain little thing; inoffensive. Timid, even. Monica had probably had an eye to that too. Monica had smarts. Good for her to have pulled this one off. Too many women of her own generation had swallowed the domestic caboodle lock, stock and barrel. Her own mother, an army wife, relocated at the drop of a hat, spending a lifetime filed under the collective title of officers' wives. It produced particular offspring: children, like her, who simply got on with things. She'd lost count of the schools she'd been to. Daniel and Cassie had benefited, no doubt, from an infusion of some military spine; as a mother she'd encouraged them to not stand around bleating. She was proud of the way they'd turned out.

It was hard to recall the detail, the immediacy, of them as children. There were only fourteen months between them; they were often mistaken for twins. Even though Daniel was older, Cassie always got her version of events in first. He'd be considering what he might say and Cassie would blurt and babble it out, leaving him mouthing like a fish. What scrapes they'd got into, Daniel bringing up the rear, mostly trying to fix whatever it was that they'd broken.

Elisabeth went upstairs. Through the half-open door, she could see Daniel rocking Luca to sleep. In her own room, Ruby was sitting up in bed, her arms wrapped around her knees.

'So,' Elisabeth said, 'before I start telling you about snakes, and nights spent sleeping in the back of a jeep while my parents were inside at a dinner party, do you have anything to report?'

Granny Bailey always said it like this, as if Ruby might have a list, pre-prepared, which she could read off, each item in order. Ruby looked at her carefully. Her spine was the straightest ever. Daddy wouldn't ever need to fix that. She said Ruby could think only of her as old when she could no longer climb a tree, or run fast enough to beat a traffic warden about to put a ticket on her car. Now Granny Bailey was sitting on her bed, not smelling of cigarette smoke like she usually did, her hands familiar on the bedspread, with all the brown spots visible from living too much of her life in hot sun.

'Anything to report?' Granny Bailey asked again.

Ruby paused.

What might she say? What would Granny Bailey most like to hear?

'Mummy's working hard, Daddy's working hard, Ursula's working hard,' she ventured.

'Splendid. Good girl. Now, shall I tell you about when I woke up, in the jeep, and looked out of the window, and my parents, and all their friends, had taken off all their dinner party clothes, and were skinny-dipping in the pool?'

Afterwards, as Ruby fell asleep, she could hear Granny Bailey talking to Daddy downstairs, her laughter raspy and throaty. She must have given the right answer.

26

Being alone in someone else's house, Ursula felt, was a particular kind of intrusiveness. Tidying a cupboard, cleaning around a desk, involved a curious intimacy. People's things spoke volumes, even the simplest, most personal things: a toothbrush with the bristles shaped by a particularly vigorous style of brushing; the worn heel of a boot, upturned, revealing an idiosyncratic footfall. It was like scooping up pixels which made up a composite portrait. *Now I have you*, she might think, moving between study, bedroom, kitchen and hallway. Daniel preferred a particular mug, was fastidious about replacing the lid of the toothpaste, clearly removed his shirts over his head without undoing most of the buttons. It was odd to know so much detail, and yet so little about someone. Everything communicates, Ursula reminded herself, now, in Daniel's study, moving with particular care.

Her objective was to restore cleanliness, to wipe keyboards, clean screens, dust the desk surface, but all of it done with her eyes fixed to the middle distance, so that they did not fall upon and instinctively read what lay before her – the titles of papers, the headings of e-mails – or be caught out by family photographs suddenly scrolling on screen, hooking in her peripheral vision so that the image became seen, known.

Methodically, carefully, she moved amongst Daniel's things. She averted her eyes from a framed photograph on the desk of Monica, bikinied on a beach, laughing, smile wide, looking up at whoever – Daniel? – had taken the photograph.

The first time she'd been alone in Gideon's flat she had felt wary, uncertain. He had woken early and left to fly to a meeting in Paris. She had dressed and sat awkwardly on the edge of the bed. She felt hesitant about moving. The morning sun through the window cast her shadow across the bedroom floor. Perhaps she should allow herself to move within its elongated perimeter? Why, she reflected, should she feel so uncertain in his space? It was imposing, certainly; the dark, blocked wood floor, the mahogany wardrobes, the pristine white bed linen. Everything was linear, symmetrical, the drawers opened by touch, without handles. It felt masculine, uncompromising. She shook herself; it was ridiculous to be intimidated by her lover's room, but still she seemed unable to move beyond the bed.

When the key turned in the lock, and the front door opened, she nearly died of fright. She collected herself; it was only his cleaner. When he was dressing earlier, and she was half asleep, she remembered he'd said it was one of the mornings she came.

Ursula stood up from the bed and moved shyly towards the hallway. The woman – small, taut, resolute, with a mouth that brooked no nonsense – was removing her coat, rolling up her shirt sleeves, tying on an apron. Ursula's entrance hardly caused her to miss a beat. Was it a frequent occurrence? At least she had not found her sleeping, naked beneath the sheet.

The woman . . . Maia – now she remembered, he'd said her name was Maia – moved to the cupboard in which all the cleaning products were stored. She reached into it and took out a small wedge of photos, flipped through them before stuffing them, unceremoniously, into her apron pocket.

She watched as Maia opened the dishwasher, ready to unstack it, and took from her apron a photograph of the cupboard in which all the tableware was stored.

'Oh goodness,' Ursula said, as Maia began to stack the crockery identically.

'Can I see,' she'd asked, 'can I see the others?'

Maia sucked on her teeth, but handed them to her.

The bathroom; his razor, his shaving brush and gel, the soap at a particular angle in the soap dish. The shelves in his wardrobe, the sweaters folded neatly in consonant colours; the bureau in the sitting room, a horse's head in bronze, a seventeenth-century writing box; all of it captured precisely for Maia to clean and restore to its exact place.

Ursula drifted from the kitchen. She touched the lip of a bookcase, noted the alphabetical ordering of the authors. She stroked the bronze horse head. What might happen if it gazed more to the left? Her fingers traced the outline of its mane, and nudged it a little.

Maia reappeared with a feather duster and corrected its position.

'His ex-wife,' she said, 'she would mess with the placement. He knew that it was not me. When she left, the photograph of her clothes in the wardrobe, he ripped it into small pieces.'

Ursula tried hard not to display her surprise. A wife? Gideon had been married? How secretive he was.

She went back into the bedroom and opened the left side of the wardrobe. Empty; completely empty. Was that where all her clothes had been stored? There was no trace of her at all, nothing which indicated that a woman might have lived in this space.

Gideon was tired that night when he returned from his meeting.

'Let's just eat in the bistro round the corner,' he'd said, and he ordered them both French onion soup, in the spirit, he said, of a day spent in Paris when all he had seen was the inside of an airport, a plane, a taxi, a meeting room and the same again in reverse.

The soup when it arrived was steaming, the cheese-toasted baguette floating in it like a sodden raft. Ursula made it bob with the rounded back of her spoon.

'I met Maia,' she said, 'I only half remembered she was coming. Thank goodness I was up.'

'I hope she was accommodating.'

'Yes, perfectly. I noticed the photos she works from. The photos that mean everything is precisely as it should be.'

'And . . .'

'Nothing, no nothing.' The words melted away.

Gideon shrugged. 'It is what it is. Saves time all round.'

There was sense in that. She brought the soup spoon to her lips. She dared not bring up his wife. She imagined the photo ripped into a confetti of small, soft pieces. What would he say if she asked him about her? Would 'it was what it was' perhaps cover that too?

She lifted her eyes to him. Tired, his face had a softness it did not usually assume. Now he was asking her about her day. Maybe his photographs did make Maia's job easier, and they had not talked about previous relationships. It would be foolish to expect that, at thirty-two, his past was as bald, as unremarkable, as her own. She leaned forward and kissed him.

Now, at Daniel's desk, she dusted a photo, in a heavy silver frame, of him and Monica on their wedding day. Unusually, she allowed herself to look at it properly. How delighted they looked.

Gideon had asked her to marry him after they had been together for only five months. *You'll marry me, won't you*, he'd said, lifting her onto his lap. Was it a question, or did it carry with it the muscle flex of a command? It was consonant with the tone of much of their early relationship. *This is what's going to happen, I'll take you for dinner, Bring a suitcase on Friday.* How biddable she'd been.

How easy it had been to do things his way. How easy to become one more thing to be precisely, unbendingly, aesthetically arranged.

27

As Daniel pulled into the hospital car park, he reflected that Monica was probably now asleep, air conditioning thrumming, possibly drowning out the noise of the ocean. Might there be a chorus of bullfrogs, cicadas? What would she be wearing; maybe the little blue polka-dot shorts he liked; perhaps the white nightgown he'd bought her last Christmas. Her skin would be tanned all-over honey. Her limbs would be warm, with the softest shimmer of sweat. Skype wouldn't do it justice. She would be asleep on her stomach, her arms crossed beneath her breastbone, her head turned to the right. How many mornings had he left early for work and kissed her goodbye as she lay in their bed like that? He got out of the car and turned towards the department. He missed his wife. He missed making love to his wife. That thought, he resolved, was best parked along with the car.

It had been an unsatisfactory Skype at 6 a.m. They had yet to hit upon the right time for their communication. The eight-hour time difference made it difficult to tap into a consonant mood. This morning he had been on edge, listening for Luca's first cry, mindful that he needed to leave by seven fifteen, and distracted by the thought that he should make at least some effort in getting the children started on breakfast. It wasn't fair for Ursula to arrive and be up against the clock from the off. Monica, meanwhile, had a glass of chardonnay in her hand. She looked warm, relaxed, happy. She was picking at a salad as she spoke. She'd had a great day, she said, a really great day. *Look at this enormous peach*, she'd laughed, holding it up to the computer's camera. *Only in America.*

Now, he imagined her biting into it, the juice sticky on her chin, the taste of it in her mouth. That wasn't helpful either. He'd been abrupt in their conversation, distracted, edgy. Had she sensed that? She had given no clue. He'd wanted to tell her how much he missed her, but when the morning felt ready to spring like a trap, it didn't feel appropriate.

If he called her back this evening, his time, she would be at work. If he waited until midnight, it might just chime with her lunch. Two days ago, she'd kept her ear-piece in while she talked with him. Lying in bed, tired at the end of a taxing day, while she was so clearly caught up with her own, had made him feel superfluous. When the director called for her, she'd said *Hold on*, and answered his question, and Daniel had lain there, feeling awkward, a little sheepish, checking his alarm for the morning, flicking through a novel on the bedside table. It had been unsatisfactory, lying there, pyjama'd in bed, with his wife surrounded by all her upbeat, go-for-it Californian film crew. She peered at him through the fuzz of an overly sunlit screen, and something about it made him feel suddenly older, a little bit left behind. Skyping might just lose its shine. That, or there must be a better time for calling.

He came into his office and scanned down the list for the day. He checked his watch; his ward round would begin shortly. His secretary, Sarah, popped her head around the door.

'Charlie Grace wants to see you; he says it's important.'

Daniel rolled up his sleeves and began washing his hands.

'Can it wait? Did he say what it was about?'

'That would be no, and no again. He said he'd like to see you before you start your round.'

He reached for his jacket. 'This is what happens when you take a perfectly reasonable orthopaedic surgeon and appoint him clinical director. Instead of being perfectly content fixing all the failed hips and knees in the community, he turns into a man obsessed with efficiency, accountability, and general all-round obedience to ridiculous criteria. And saving money becomes his priority, rather than taking care of patients, which is the business I thought we were in.'

'I didn't hear any of that. Should I have been listening? I'll buzz him and tell him you are already down the corridor, shall I?'

'Does he know how many patients are on my list this morning?'

'I'm buzzing . . .'

Daniel mock-saluted her, and left his office.

When he knocked on Charlie's door, he found him in front of his computer with three empty coffee cups next to him.

'Take a seat,' Charlie said.

'Do I really have to? I've got a lot to get sorted this morning.'

'I think it's probably a good idea. It's not particularly good news, my old mucker. At least, not for now.'

Daniel had a theory that when senior colleagues harked back to shared days as junior doctors, or used terminology more suited to black-and-white films, it was usually because it was about to be incumbent upon them to say something that was awkward or difficult. He felt increasingly irritated. The day hadn't got off to a good start.

'This is the thing,' Charlie said, 'the hospital's been doing an audit, an audit of each department, each surgeon, and comparing it to national averages, and—'

'And?'

'And I'm afraid it's not looking good. To be accurate, your statistics aren't looking good.'

'How not looking good?'

'Well, according to the data . . .'

'The data which were most probably put together by someone in the management tier whose knowledge of the complexity of what we do is based on watching *24 Hours in A&E*?'

'It's not helpful, Daniel, to dispute the accuracy or relevance of the information at the outset.'

'The outset of what?'

'Daniel, the national average for post-op neurological complications is two-to-three per cent. Yours is closer to five per cent. I don't imagine you can explain why this is, straight off the bat, nor would I expect you to. In fact, I'd bet you have no idea of your neurological complication rate, as most of these figures are compiled up to six months after surgery when the vast majority of these patients are quite rightly being dealt with in outpatient clinics.'

'I can't tell you that, no, but I can tell you that I know the post-op integrity of the spinal cord of the vast majority of my patients is exactly as it was pre-operatively.'

'You may tell me that, Daniel, in good faith; but the audit may tell a different story, and we just need to check it out.'

'What do you mean, check it out?'

'We need to dig a little deeper; look at the range of operations you are carrying out, whether any of the affected patients had other comorbidities which may have influenced the outcome, and until then . . .'

'Until then?'

'Well, until then, this is – how shall I put it? – serving notice. You can go ahead with your list today, but we may reallocate some operations to other members of the team until we know more.'

'And then?'

'And then, if the figures *are* correct, we'll have to look at some options, maybe some retraining . . .'

'*What?*'

'Daniel, it's a foolish man who baulks at retraining should it be required, and it may well not be. I just want you to be in full possession of the facts so that you are in a position to respond. Let's leave it at that, shall we? I'm sure I don't need to remind you that you've got a list to do now, and getting angry with me is perhaps not the best way of preparing for it.'

'Charlie, you're being a bureaucrat. You know as well as I do that these audit figures can be massaged to show anything.'

'Look, I'll keep you posted, and I'll be discreet, and as few people will know about this as possible. Don't shoot the messenger. Okay?'

'Well, cheers, cheers for that.'

'I'm sorry. I appreciate it's not good news at the best of times, and especially not now, what with you single-handedly manning the domestic front; a lot on your shoulders and all that.'

Later, scrubbing up for theatre, Daniel inwardly fumed. Damn Charlie, his oleaginous manner, his misleading, bald statistics, and his patronising nod to Monica's absence.

At home, the children long asleep, he sat in his favourite chair and flicked through TV channels. He was restless, unsettled. Monica had managed to briefly Skype at the children's bedtime. She was out of the studio, on location, somewhere near Yosemite. She peepo-ed from behind a pine tree for Luca; *I love you, I love you,* she'd said, blowing kisses from both of her hands. Ruby had held Luca's palms, and helped him to blow kisses back.

Ursula had left hours ago. Sometimes, it was hard to track whether she'd gone or was still tidying something, somewhere. She didn't so much leave the house as soundlessly disappear from it. One minute she seemed to be gathering her coat, bag and car keys, and the next, downstairs seemed to echo with a sense of his solitariness.

Monica had asked, *How was your day, darling?*

She evidently wasn't expecting a long answer. When she asked it, she was balancing herself on a large log. Ruby was singing a song about a speckled frog for Luca, who knew some of the words, and Monica was all set to jump off the log on cue. Luca was laughing like a drain. Monica was wearing white cut-off shorts. How long her legs looked.

But what taxed him now was the realisation that even if she had asked him the question without the children there, he wouldn't have told her anything of what Charlie Grace had said about the audit. And his reason for withholding that bore uncomfortable further examination. Was it that he didn't want her to be concerned about his stress levels? Unlikely. She had got used to him handling the demands of his job without recourse to her. She had no lack of compassion for his patients, particularly the children, but her attitude to his job could most accurately be termed blithe. No, he realised, switching off the television and tossing the remote onto the sofa, his disinclination to tell her came down to pride; how ridiculous was that? He did not want to tell his own wife that he was under investigation. It was humiliating, demeaning. Especially now, when he wished to appear the most competent, the most capable, the most effortlessly able to hold the fort for three months.

So, thought Daniel, there was the first casualty of their separation. His career might be on the line, and he didn't want Monica to know.

28

Claudie was so eager to tell Ruby whatever was on the tip of her tongue, it looked as if she might pop.

Miss Cameron was talking, now holding up a permission form to go swimming on a school trip.

'Please ask your parents or carers' (Claudie nudged Ruby sharply in the ribs) 'to sign this, remembering to complete the part about how far you can swim unaided, and please can everybody bring it back to school by Friday. And speaking of Friday, that's the day of our cake sale for our partnership school in South Africa. We're very lucky to have Claudie's mum organising this for us, and she's given me another form for you to take home tonight, asking for help either on the stall after school or earlier in the day, setting up and labelling the cakes. So, two forms to remember, everyone. Poppy is going to hand them round now and can everyone please put them straight into their book bags.'

Claudie turned to Ruby, 'We're making red velvet cupcakes. They're delicious and really pretty. Mummy has bought special cupcake cases from John Lewis which are red with tiny silver hearts, and she's bought white chocolate little hearts to sprinkle on the top. They're going to be beautiful, and probably cost about forty pence each, which means my cakes might make the most money for the children in Africa to buy things for their school with.'

Ruby decided not replying was the best bet.

Claudie tried again.

'Do you know what you're making? Your lady, your helper,

can she bake cakes? Have you talked to her about what you might be making?'

'Not yet, and yes she can, she makes cakes for when I come home from school.'

'I expect that's part of her job, isn't it? Will she use your mum's cookbooks? Does your mum have any? I asked my mummy and she thought your mummy hadn't ever helped on the cake stall before.'

Ruby reflected. Mummy always said she wasn't a baker. *Too much precision involved,* she would laugh; *all that careful weighing and measuring.*

'I'm really looking forward to Friday,' Claudie said. 'The picture of the red velvet cupcakes looks so yummy. I know everyone is going to love them. Maybe your person will help too, you never know. You could say it's part of her job too, and then she'd have to, wouldn't she?'

Poppy gave Ruby the two forms. Claudie's mother had evidently designed the cake sale one herself. There were coloured pictures of all sorts of cakes in the margin, and she'd printed it out in turquoise ink. The first line read: *Greetings, cake-baking parents! Wooden spoons at the ready!* Last year, at Sports Day, Claudie's mum had run beside the whole length of the course, cheering Claudie on. Mummy had watched with Cassie, and Luca in his car seat with a sunshade clipped to it, and they'd brought along some cans of Pimm's and some strawberries. They clapped from the blanket they were sitting on, and then Mummy won the Mother's race running barefoot. Claudie's mum hadn't looked best pleased. Mummy said she must have worn herself out running alongside all of Claudie's races.

When Ruby got home, Ursula was in the kitchen, cleaning the oven. It looked like a difficult job. She didn't think Mummy or Daddy had ever done it. Perhaps that was why. Ursula had news-paper on the floor, and racks from inside the oven soaking in polythene bags filled with foam, and the smell of chemicals made the inside of Ruby's nose wrinkle. She didn't want to say; that would sound unkind when Ursula was doing something so horrible. She tried to press her hand to her nose, but not obviously, so she pretended it was a little bit itchy. Ursula looked up from where she was scrubbing the glass door with a soapy pad.

'Is this bothering you? Sorry. Here, let me open the door and the window. It smells disgusting, doesn't it?'

She was very good at guessing. Ursula didn't usually start conversations, but she always seemed to be listening and watching. When Luca dropped something or needed something, Ursula was right there. Coming home felt less awkward now than it had when Ursula had first started. There just weren't any jokes. Some laughing would have been nice. Granny Bailey said it was important to try not to complain, even inside your own head. *Complainers,* she said, *even ones who hold their tongues, end up with their complaints writ large in the lines of their faces.* Ruby hadn't been sure she didn't mean Granny Watson when she said that.

Ursula had opened the door and window and was wiping her forehead with the back of her wrist.

'I made some flapjacks; they're in the tin on the side. Do you want to help yourself so I can just finish this off?'

Flapjacks were a pretty good substitute for jokes. Ruby held the tin to her chest, and pulled open the lid. They looked goldenly perfect. Maybe she could ask Ursula if she would make more of these. Perhaps with some sprinkles they might even look all right sitting next to Red Velvet cupcakes.

Ruby poured herself some milk and sat down at the table. As she ate her flapjack, Ursula finished cleaning the oven door and racks and then neatly folded away the damp newspaper.

'There, all done,' she said, washing her hands, and then splashing her face with a little water. 'It feels as if gets all on your skin.'

She turned to Ruby. Maybe, Ruby thought, it was because the tap water had been running for so long, and so must have been very cold, but Ursula looked pinker, rosier. She looked less like someone whose face might have just the thinnest covering of pale wax. Ruby had dipped her finger once, in the melt of a candle, and it emerged, smoothly white, making her fingertip a secret.

Ursula dried herself with some kitchen towel, and sat down beside her.

'Time for a cup of tea, I think. Is there anything you have to give me?'

'There's this,' Ruby said, reaching down into her book bag. 'Well, actually, this and this,' she said, making sure she had both sheets in her hand.

Ursula glanced at the swimming permission sheet.

'Daddy really ought to sign this; he knows how far you can swim. And what's this one?' And now, her eyes scanned over the brightly coloured letter.

'That's nice – having a sale to raise money for another school far away. I see one of the mothers is running it; that's very good of her.'

'It's Claudie's mum.'

Ursula looked as if she was taking a moment to remember.

'Ah yes, Claudie. Claudie of the spelling bee. And am I right in guessing Claudie might have told you what she is making already?'

'You are. You completely are. Red velvet cupcakes, in silver and red cases and sprinkled with little white chocolate hearts. Probably forty pence each.'

'Goodness, you have all the details.'

'There's helpers too . . .'

'I'm sorry?'

'On the form, there's a part you can tick if you want to help on the day.'

Ruby looked down at her flapjack crumbs; she couldn't meet

Ursula's gaze. Might she be a helper? That would be one in the eye for Claudie. Ursula stood up from the table, and moved towards the kettle. Her hand was over her lips, and she had her nervous look again. Ruby thought perhaps she shouldn't have asked. Even though she hadn't said it directly, hadn't said those words, she knew she had actually asked her, just without saying it clearly. They both knew it.

'I don't think so,' Ursula said. 'I have Luca to collect, and I imagine these things are usually organised by mothers who all know each other. It wouldn't be the right thing to do, Ruby, but I'll help you make something nice. We can do it tomorrow when you get home from school. I can go out in the morning and get all the ingredients. Is there anything particular you'd like to make, anything you usually make with Mummy?'

Ruby shook her head. She didn't feel like admitting that what they usually made for school cake sales was Rice Krispies in melted chocolate, which mostly ended up not sticking together properly. They'd tried it with mini-marshmallows once and that hadn't worked either.

Ruby chewed at her lip.

'Well, I can think of something,' Ursula said, as the kettle came to the boil. 'In fact, I know something that might be perfect.'

When Ruby came home the following day, Ursula had cleared a space on the kitchen table. She'd bought a whole tray of eggs, and next to them were a bag of red liquorice laces, two tubes of tiny silver balls and two tubs of jelly diamonds. She'd also put out several large baking sheets, and she was trimming greaseproof paper to fit them.

Ruby looked at her quizzically.

'What are we making?'

'Meringue mice. Do you know how to separate egg yolks and whites?'

'Not properly.'

'Okay, well, wash your hands and hold them over this bowl, and then I'll crack the eggs into them one by one. You can let the white run through the cracks in your fingers and pop the yolk in this bowl here. I'll make a lemon tart with the yolks – isn't your aunt Cassie coming for lunch on Sunday?'

Ruby washed her hands quickly, and held them out as Ursula tapped the first egg briskly on the rim of the bowl and said, 'One down, twenty-three to go.'

When she'd helped Ruby to use the electric beaters to whip the egg whites and sugar into white, foamy clouds, Ursula took out a teaspoon and showed her how to put a scoop of meringue mix onto the baking sheet.

'And now for the fun part,' she said. She cut a small length of liquorice and made it into a tail, used two silver balls as beady little eyes, then sliced a jelly triangle in half and put the halves on the top for ears.

'Meringue Mice,' she said to Ruby, 'and I'm guessing at least thirty pence each, and we're going to have so many of them – look at all this mixture.'

When Daddy came home with Luca later, Ruby met him at the door, feeling as if her skin was dusted with sugar and sweet silveriness. Some of her curls were dipped with meringue mix from bending over the tray.

'We've got hundreds of mice,' she said to Daddy, laughing, and for a moment he looked worried, carrying Luca swiftly into the kitchen, and then Luca whooped and clapped his hands at the sight of the kitchen sides, the top of the fridge, the draining board, all covered with scamperings of smooth white mice with bright jelly ears and whippy red tails.

'Who's a star baker?' said Daddy, and bent down to kiss her. He smiled at Ursula, who was standing with a palm full of silver balls, and Ruby was reminded of the film when Nanny McPhee got prettier; but it wasn't that Ursula wasn't getting prettier, she thought, just that she was looking a little more like someone who was pinkly alive, maybe as if she was thawing, like something brought out of the freezer. She had some meringue in her hair, was almost smiling at Luca's excitement, and her cheeks were warm from the oven, all her quiet busy-ness a success.

The next morning, Ursula helped Ruby put all the mice into Tupperwares, stacking them carefully on top of each other with greaseproof paper in between. They surveyed them with satisfaction, and then Ruby looked across at Ursula who was chewing at her lip, and had that same faraway expression as when she had been peeling the carrots. Ruby coughed a little bit, just to remind Ursula that she was there, and Ursula did that same little shake, and seemed to breathe a deep breath before saying, slowly, carefully, and as if it was something that was quite difficult, 'I'll drive you to school. This is far too many to carry, and I can help you take them into your classroom all ready for the sale.'

They carried them in together, and everyone stared when they walked through the door, and Miss Cameron said, 'Gosh, you've been busy,' and then, 'Can I take a peek?' Everyone crowded round as Miss Cameron carefully lifted out a mouse and said, 'Look, class, how perfect, won't these look beautiful on our cake stall!'

And Ruby turned to smile at Ursula, but she had melted away from her shoulder, and from the classroom itself. Through the window she could see her darting across the playground. It had started to drizzle, and Ursula's head was ducked down, her shoulders rounded, and Ruby was reminded again of the Mouse's Back paint, and of the first day Ursula had come to work for them. For a moment, in spite of all the happy flurry of words about the meringue mice, she felt sad for Ursula, walking so hurriedly away, not looking like she had in the kitchen last night, when everything smelled of sugar and was brightly coloured. And she watched until Ursula disappeared from view, and Claudie said, 'So she can bake then,' in a sharp, tight voice.

After the sale at the end of school, Ruby ran all the way home and into the kitchen. 'Every single mouse was sold. Everybody loved them!' she said, and Ursula said, 'I'm very glad to hear it.' Then she raised an eyebrow and asked, 'And the Red Velvet cupcakes, how did they go down?'

'Not so well; some of the mums said they didn't want to buy them because of so much food colouring.'

Ursula turned quickly to the fridge, but Ruby was sure her lips had given a little twitch, as if the possibility of maybe laughing, just a little bit, might not be out of the question.

Ruby stood just beyond her, her arms loose to her sides. She would have liked to give Ursula a hug, but she was pretty sure it wasn't what she would have chosen.

29

Ursula lay back in the bath. Her hair still smelt of sugar. She dipped beneath the water, and smoothed it back from her forehead. Ruby had been so proud of the mice. She'd dashed into the house, bursting to tell. What was it about childhood; the proximity of feelings to the surface of the skin, making them bubble forth? It was short-lived. Adults were more guarded, capable of far more modified, dense-skinned communication.

Gideon had acknowledged his first wife, finally, when they'd started discussing wedding plans. She was the reason the wedding would not take place in a church. 'I am divorced,' he'd said briskly, without emotion. 'Error of judgement. The marriage lasted under a year.'

Had she feigned surprise? How odd that she still could not remember how she had reacted. She lay back further in the bath, letting the water lap around her.

'Your first wife,' she remembered saying, a little falteringly, that night in bed. 'Where is she now?'

'No idea. And no interest in knowing.' He'd scooped her hair in his hands and kissed her extravagantly. It almost sufficed to tamp down her curiosity. How effective he was at making her feel cherished, valued, as if she swept away the woman who preceded her into irrelevance.

'But, your first wife,' she tried again, 'that must have been a difficult experience, so soon after marrying, people's expectations, your own . . .'

She sensed him stiffen, pull away from her a little, and then completely so, stashing the pillow up behind him, leaning up against it, his arm behind his head.

'Does this mean you want to talk about it?'

She'd felt immediately silenced.

Ursula flinched, now, all these years later. How speechless, how vulnerable, he had rendered her. She envisioned herself diminishing daily, folding inwards like a complex piece of origami.

'If you really want to know,' he said, 'she was a nightmare. Total nightmare. The woman had jangling nerve endings where she should have had bone, muscle, skin, possibly even major life organs. She left me for a man she said was "gentle". A gentle man. Although possibly not a gentleman. Who knows, who cares?, frankly I wish him luck placating her. And I,' he said, turning to Ursula and embracing her so that she was totally wrapped within his arms (how glorious it had felt), 'and I have you. Darling you. So new, so untainted, and in that, for me, a form of absolution.'

Absolution. The next morning on the Tube to work, she'd struggled with the idea of herself as a form of absolution. Did absolution imply previous guilt? Was Gideon guilty of anything? Surely not. Untainted; that was the other word he'd used. She supposed she probably was, if that was another way of expressing inexperience. Was his first wife 'tainted'? Did her jangling nerves infect all that they touched? He had not referred to her by name. Ursula resolved it was better to leave it that way; she could put her to one side, think of her as a small scribble of nervousness. Nameless, she would remain faceless. That was probably the best way to go.

That night, she'd arrived back at his flat before him. She'd gone back to her own en route to collect more clothes. How tawdry it seemed; how small, and rag-baggedy, compared to the sweep and scale of Gideon's home. She hadn't been back for ten days, and on that occasion there'd been a power cut. She'd sat cross-legged in the dark, feeling cold and hungry, and eaten a large tomato as if it were an apple, and some tuna straight from the tin with a fork. In the new life that was beckoning her, she couldn't imagine this happening again. On this night, she'd arrived at his flat with her clothes in a holdall. 'I think it's about time you put something in the wardrobe,' he'd said. She tried not to think of the ripped-up photograph as she opened the wardrobe door wide and took in the completely clean, empty space. She reached up to feel the depth of the top shelf. Her hand struck something; she stood on her tiptoes to reach it down. It was a pale blue leather photo album. Dare she?

The tissue between the leaves seemed to roar and rattle at her touch. There was Gideon as a child, sitting on the lap of a woman – his mother presumably – who wore a raspberry silk dress, a pearl brooch pinned to her collar. Gideon faced the camera gravely, seriously. And again, holding his father's hand on the steps of a church, his father in Easter vestments and Gideon clutching a red-foil-covered egg. At school, wielding a cricket bat; one in black tie, presumably at an Oxford ball. And then, more recognisably himself, tanned and smiling broadly on a beach, with a volleyball under his arm; sitting on a pale blue Vespa; and outside in a café, an espresso cup at his lips. And then a whole string of photos, with parts cut away, filleted. Every trace of his first wife eradicated; Ursula saw it immediately. And so, Gideon sat alone on a tartan rug, an expansive mountain behind him, the photo jagged-edged. If she had been sitting next to him, she had been razored away. Gideon had cut away part of his own outstretched leg too; had it been entwined with hers? The damaged photo hinted at a bygone intimacy. Had she lain there, tanned and smiling like him, leaning back on her elbows, her calf resting on his? Another picture showed Gideon holding something in an artisanal shop (was it the writing set now on the bureau?). His fingers had been carefully cut around. Had her hands held it too? It was curious, Ursula thought; the woman's absence made the viewer try to imagine her more. What had she looked like, what had she been wearing? Were they honeymooning? A last photograph showed Gideon alone on a bike, somewhere steep, dry and scrubby. The picture was undamaged. Had she taken it? All that was left of her was her implicit presence, beyond the lens.

Ursula paused. Gideon was nothing if not absolute. She turned to the last page and let out an involuntary gasp. It was a photograph of her. She hardly remembered him taking it.

She was seated in the café opposite the church of Santa Maria della Salute and holding a rose-coloured cup. She was looking straight at him; now she remembered how quickly he had produced the camera. Her gaze was fixed, ardent.

He'd stuck the photo in the very centre of the page; she looked out, earnestly, hopefully, surrounded by blackness.

You are so new, he'd said to her when he'd proposed. She could understand how he felt that, seeing herself at a table in Venice. Absolution indeed.

She'd put the album back, and hung her clothes hurriedly but tidily in the wardrobe. She'd smoothed out the imprint her body had made on the bed. As she did so, she was reminded of the snow angels she used to make in the garden in her childhood, her mother waving from the window, Ursula's woollen mittens smoothing the edges of the wings. Her hand again, then, in Gideon's flat, smoothing away at the ripples in the duvet. There must be no trace of her dallying; why had she felt this?

Now, getting out of the bath, her skin prune-wrinkled from

how long she had lain there, Ursula reflected she had no use for photos now. It had been more than a decade since anyone had taken her picture. She wrapped herself in a towel and peered at herself in the steamed-up mirror. Her face, and skin, certainly bore no trace of newness now.

30

Monica was holding up her iPad. Behind her, on the beach, Daniel could make out some clapboard cottages, clustered together in the sand dunes.

'I was just driving,' Monica was saying, breathlessly, off camera, the breeze from the shoreline whipping away her words. 'I was driving along the Pacific Coast Highway between Laguna and Newport Beach, and look what I found. I stopped for a walk, and this stretch of beach is part of a National Park. Can you believe how pretty this is, how rustic, right off the highway?'

She turned the iPad one hundred and eighty degrees.

'Look, see that seal in the water?'

Daniel could just make out a blurry splash.

'And look at all the ladies doing their morning stroll, white sun-visors on. See what a slice of Californian life I'm showing you, darling.'

Monica's voice was quite loud now. Daniel was mindful of the door of his office standing ajar. Could Sarah hear every word? It wasn't exactly appropriate, at four in the afternoon, to be sitting in his office being Skyped by his wife and given a virtual tour of some beach shacks she was taken with.

'They were built in 1930, as part of some film community project,' Monica was explaining. 'That counts as practically medieval here. Don't you think they're lovely? And the beach is so wild, so unspoilt. If I was working here over the school holidays, I'd try and book one for us. Ruby would love it. Don't you think so?'

'Yes; yes,' Daniel answered. Was he shouting? The iPad wobbled as Monica held her arm outstretched and smoothed back her hair which was blowing across her mouth.

Her mouth looked lovely. Was that inappropriate too; sitting in his office at four in the afternoon, less taken with the heritage cottages and more by his wife's lips? Would they taste of salt spray? He heard Sarah open and close a filing cabinet drawer. She would be preparing after-care packs for the patients who were going home. Now Monica was showing him the shoreline.

'See how beautiful this is; imagine walking along this each morning.'

Daniel wasn't sure this required much imagination from Monica, since she actually *was* walking along it – and he was sitting at work, feeling awkward and, somewhat unexpectedly, a little tetchy. He tried to suppress it.

'It looks great, darling, I'd love to be walking along it too.'

Monica focused the iPad full on her face.

'There's a catch in your voice. Are you cross? Am I being insensitive? The first thing I think of as I walk along here is that I want to share it with you, and then when I do – I can hear it in your tone – you sound off with me. I can tell; I can see it in your expression, too.'

'I'm not being off with you, honestly. And it's great that you are sharing it with me. I'm sorry. It's just time difference, context difference, I've had a difficult morning, there's a whole pile of stuff I need to wrap up before going home.'

'So would you have preferred me not to call?'

Her arms were lengthened now, and she looked smaller on the screen; maybe even a little forlorn, the breeze whipping around her, the expanse of sand, of sky, beyond her. Daniel felt mean.

'Honestly, Mon. I loved it that you called. It's great to hear from you whenever you can. The place looks fantastic. I can see why it's captivated you.' Did he sound insincere? Maybe Sarah would think so. He refocused his attention.

Monica tugged her hair back from her face, tucking it behind her ear. Her tone was crisper, efficient.

'Okay, sorry to have caught you at a busy time. I should be getting on with my day too. I'm supposed to be in Newport by eight thirty scouting a beach café site. I'll try and catch the children at bedtime, but don't promise them as it may not happen if the day gets crazy.'

'Okay.' How flat, how awkward his voice sounded. 'Mon, you look beautiful. It's a perfect context for you.' He threw it in wildly, hoping it would somehow reverse where the conversation seemed to be heading, which was to a place of fractious mutual disappointment. He would have liked to tell her that he couldn't take his eyes off her mouth. Saying that, from his office chair, would have felt inappropriately intimate. Beyond him, he heard Sarah fielding a call.

'I think I have to go, I'm sorry, I think I have to take a call that's coming through.'

Monica smiled and waved, but there was something about it that felt performed, inauthentic. Should he tell her he loved her? Sarah would hear it for sure.

'Love you,' he said, thinking that not saying 'I' made it less serious, more sunny, less private somehow.

'You too.' She looked genuinely remorseful. 'Sorry if my timing was off. I should check before I start enthusing.'

She held the iPad to her face and filmed herself just a fraction longer. Her eyes spoke volumes. It was wordless, but explicit, both of them acknowledging that long-distance conversations between mismatched time zones could be a bitch, and that all the awkward feelings could be instantly assuaged if they were in close proximity.

'Talk when you can,' he said.

She blew him a kiss, which felt genuine, heartfelt, even a little melancholy, and her face faded from the screen.

Daniel pushed his chair back from the desk. Things were never simple. His computer flashed an e-mail from Sarah, with the number of a rep from an instrument and device company who needed to be called back.

'Thanks,' he called through to her, 'I'm onto it.'

She lifted her hand in acknowledgement and continued leafing through the after-care sheets. If she mentioned Monica, it would be obvious she had overheard every word. He couldn't fault her tact. It felt doubly embarrassing, though, knowing she was bound to have heard. Had she sensed the call wasn't exactly a success? How visible his life felt, Daniel thought; how open to scrutiny from Ursula at home and Sarah here. Perhaps that was what he hadn't anticipated in choosing to support his wife working away for three months; that somehow his privacy would be sacrificed as well.

31

Cassie sliced a lemon for her gin and tonic. She didn't use a chopping board, and ignored a pip which skittered along the worktop. She reached into the freezer and took out a handful of ice. A cube bounced across the floor, and she ignored that too. She reached into the cupboard with her available hand and took out a tumbler.

'Are you sure you don't want to join me for one?' she said to Daniel, pouring a stiff slug of gin over the ice and lemon.

'Absolutely sure, no thanks,' he said. Had Cassie always been this noisy in the kitchen? It felt as if she were crashing around in it, with waves of untidiness and stickiness in her wake. Had he just never noticed? Maybe he was becoming used to Ursula, who left no trace of whatever she'd been doing.

Cassie pulled out a stool from under the counter, and sat down.

'I have had the *most* appalling day,' she said, with emphasis. Cassie, Daniel reflected, could be relied on largely to exist in the superlative. 'I've been collecting data for case studies in a women's refuge,' she continued. 'Just when I think there are no more ways men can surprise me with how shittily they can behave, your gender exceeds my expectations and comes up with some great new humiliation. Nothing if not viciously creative.'

'Not every single one of my gender, obviously,' Daniel said mildly.

'True, and you'll be surprised to hear that I am in fact beginning to feel as sorry for the good guys as I do for the women in my case studies, what with all the bastards letting the side down.'

'Letting the side down; that feels familiar right now.'

'Why? What's happened?'

He sketched out his conversation with Charlie.

'You're kidding? It's not some private patient threatening to sue you because the outcome of his prolapsed disc op didn't meet his expectations?'

'I wish it were. No, this is a lot more difficult to challenge. It involves patients six months down the line, post-op, going back about four years. It'll be hard to work through it all, although I've asked for the data and the records and I'm going to damn well try.'

'What does Monica think?'

Daniel didn't meet her eye.

'I said what does Monica . . . oh, wait. I know that expression – you haven't told Monica yet, have you?'

'I haven't had the opportunity.'

'But you spoke to her yesterday. When were you told about it? Wait, wait – let's just remember that I can read you like a book. You're not going to tell her at all, are you?'

'I just haven't found the right moment yet.'

'Daniel, why ever not?'

'Well, for a start, what can she do, apart from worry about it and perhaps dispense sympathy via Skype? Would she be able to take Charlie Grace to task, or give up her big break to come home early and shore me up twenty-four/seven?'

'Obviously neither of the above, but I'd have thought you'd have mentioned it, what with the prospect of your professional reputation being completely destroyed.'

'Don't beat about the bush, Cass, call it as you see it.'

'I'm onto you. You haven't told her because you don't want to look like a lame duck, the beta male who's been left holding the babies while she furthers her career and yours comes crashing down. Am I right? Come on, just a little bit right?'

Always, since they were children, her ability to nail him.

'There may be something in what you say.' He held up his index finger and thumb. 'About a centimetre of truth. Max.'

'And the rest. So you haven't told Monica because you don't want her to think less of you. The pressures on the honourable male, on the good husband and father. There's a paper in that, if I could just tear myself away from the joys of domestic abuse.'

'Always good to know I can provide research material for you. In the knowledge, of course, that from your paradigm, as a man, I'm always going to be on the wrong side anyway.'

'Don't beat yourself up. Anyway, I told you, I'm increasingly lining up for the good guys.'

Daniel crossed the kitchen and opened the cupboard.

'Maybe I will have that drink.'

'Maybe you shouldn't, now that there's the possibility of you compulsively drinking like a miserable lonely bastard and contemplating the ruins of your stellar career.'

'Again, thanks for your tact. Anyway, the findings are at an initial stage. It'll probably turn out that the management consultant read the chart upside down. Believe me, it happens. And maybe I won't have that drink. Ursula made a great clementine cake. I wonder if there's any left?'

He opened the tin, and lifted out the cake on a plate.

Cass laughed.

'Great, so on this trajectory you'll be fat, alcoholic *and* unemployed; it gets better all the time.'

'Sometimes, Cassie, it's unfathomable to me why Mike left you.'

She laughed again.

'Evidently his loss. Anna doesn't have a critical bone in her body, which although spousally a contrast, can't be very challenging. Did you tell Ursula, by the way?'

'Tell Ursula what?'

'About the audit, about the fact that you are under investigation.'

'In as much as I asked her to clear the dining room table, and all the stuff from the sideboard. I want a clean space to lay out all the files and my study isn't big enough. I asked her to keep the children away from it, and underlined patient confidentiality.'

'But you didn't tell her you had your back against the wall.'

'Matter of fact, I sort of did. All the audit charts will be around; she'll see it for herself if she has half a brain, and I think she has considerably more.'

'So you sort of told her.'

'Ish. Why?'

'Just wondering'

'Wondering what?'

'How she responded.'

'She responded how she does to most things: quietly, passively, with a show of minimal to moderate interest and no readable facial expression. Do you want me to go on?'

'I'm also wondering what she thought.'

'About which part of it?'

'The fact that she's been working for you for a few weeks, everything seemingly hunky-dory, and then you come home and offload all this.'

'I think "offload" may be overstating our brief conversation, and anyway, you know what, it didn't cause a ripple. She couldn't have appeared more disinterested, less engaged. It didn't seem – how can I put it? – that serious an issue to her.'

'Which it isn't, obviously, because it isn't her career on the line. Remember, darling, just because someone works for you domestically, it doesn't mean they have to take on board all of your battles with the world. That was kind of cut from the deal with serfdom. What you're actually surprised by – maybe even a little bit aggrieved by – is that she didn't instantly minister to you, and shower you with concern. Take it on the chin, Daniel. She probably saw you as just another needy male bleating for sympathy, and perhaps she's had a fair few of those in her life. She was probably working quite hard to manage walking away without rolling her eyes. One more overly demanding man wanting to be mothered. No thanks.'

Daniel smiled.

'You're terrible. Possibly even cruel. Anyway, whatever Ursula's thinking, I'd have no clue or insight. She's a firmly closed book and, evidently, not particularly troubled by the thought of her employer's career taking a nose-dive. Retraining – I ask you; I can't believe Charlie even suggested it. He knows I've got the best hands in the unit, even if his audit isn't showing it.'

'I'll drink to Charlie's enlightenment.' Cassie raised her glass. 'Are you just going to eat cake, or are we still going to have supper?'

'I think Ursula's made something for us.' He opened the fridge.

'She sounds pretty perfect to me; short on sympathy – which, by the way, you should never make a call on when you don't know where someone's coming from – and long on culinary forethought.'

She went to the cupboard and clattered out some plates and cutlery.

Daniel looked down at his hands and flexed his fingers carefully. It was important to keep faith.

32

Ursula took the blondies out of the oven and touched them lightly to check they were cooked. The white chocolate gleamed. Ruby would like them; she'd whoop when she came through the door. Ursula hesitated for a moment, and tamped down what might have become the smallest pulse of corresponding exuberance. She would not allow herself to imagine or anticipate Ruby's smiling face. No, she would not. She stacked the blondies on a plate, left them on the side, and went upstairs to clean the children's bathroom.

On her wedding day, Ursula remembered as she rinsed the basin, she had looked like something carefully confected: a French macaroon, perhaps, gleaming expensively. *Small and elegant.* Those were the watchwords Gideon had told her were to be at the heart of the wedding. Her mother had taken some reining in. There had been a hat – or was it a fascinator, Ursula puzzled now? It was something extravagant, vastly fronded and feathery, which Ursula knew would not be to Gideon's taste. *No, Mama*, she'd said, nudging her towards something less showy. How mean-hearted, how paltry that now seemed, that she should have explicitly collaborated in not allowing her mother full licence to express her enthusiasm. Could one apologise to the dead? Ursula did so, momentarily pausing as she swooshed Cif around the plughole. What a day the wedding had been. What an exquisite, costly, choreographed day. Despite the forsaken hat, her mother had looked thrilled throughout.

Gideon had booked a small hotel in Belgravia and had chosen the wine and the menu himself. They'd gone to a florist, 'These, sir, and these, sir?' the assistant had asked, proffering Gideon long-stemmed blooms, lilies, roses, delphiniums, complex orchids. 'And for your bouquet, miss?'

'She will have these,' Gideon said, gesturing to sprays of orange blossom, 'hand tied with nude ribbon.'

'How lovely to have a groom who takes such an interest, has such taste.'

Ursula had just nodded. She'd nodded her way through most of it, with the exception of her dress, which she bought with her mother in a shop in Beauchamp Place, her face troubled, insecure without Gideon, wondering whether the cappuccino silk was flattering. She bought taupe satin shoes which made her feet feel like sugared almonds, and lingerie so exquisite that it was difficult to believe it had come from a plain needle and thread.

'You lucky girl, you lucky, lucky girl,' her mother had said, squeezing her hand in her hotel room as she prepared to leave for the register office with Gideon.

She had said the same when Gideon suggested Ursula hand in her notice at the office.

Initially, he said it would be awkward them working for the same company, but when she started to look for another job, he said that she would have enough things to keep her occupied, because he was planning to buy a house in need of refurbishment. It would be the perfect project for her talents.

He bought a small rectory just outside Chalfont St Giles and drove her to see it one Saturday afternoon shortly after their wedding, under the pretext of a day at the races. Before she got out of the car, he wrapped his fine wool scarf around her eyes. 'Three steps forward, wait, I'm opening the gate, now up a step, just one more moment.' He'd taken off the scarf with a flourish, and there it was, her new home. She'd thought at first that he wanted her opinion, but contracts had already been exchanged and completed. *Fait accompli*, he'd said. *How's that for a surprise?*

How lovely, her mother had said, that he should go to such lengths. Ursula had nodded, swallowing her feeling of unease. Seven months after moving to London, it appeared she was already moving away. Her engagement ring winked at her again. Sometimes, it snagged on her clothes, so she had to move her hand with a new, careful precision.

'But what will I do?' she'd said to Gideon, once she'd arranged a little exterior painting and a bathroom refit.

'Look after me. Be happy. Help build our life together.'

It was hard to express exception. Not to take it, thought Ursula, now mopping the bathroom tiled floor. It had been hard *not* to quietly take exception, feeling everything clanging closed so decisively around her.

33

Daniel propped the front door open and carried the boxes, one by one, through to the dining room. He noticed that Ursula swiftly picked Luca up to stop him wandering out onto the driveway or the road.

'That looks like a lot of work,' Ruby said.

'It is, Little, it is.'

He turned to Ursula.

'I'm sorry, I should have asked you earlier, but could you stay for a while longer and put the children to bed? I've got a long night of it.' He gestured to the boxes.

Ursula nodded.

'Bath time,' she said to Luca. 'Ruby, would you like to help me or do you want to watch something on television?'

Daniel laid out all the files, cross-referencing patient data alphabetically and chronologically. He did not hear Ursula come into the room behind him. She cleared her throat, and he turned to find her there.

'Luca's asleep; Ruby's reading and has agreed to turn out her light in fifteen minutes if you are able to take a break to go up and say goodnight.' She proffered a tray. 'The children had this stew this evening. I'm sorry, it's not the most exciting, but Luca can feed himself with it and he counts that as a bonus. I've reheated this; you should probably eat something, at some point.' Her glance took in the volume of papers spread out across the table.

'Thank you, Ursula, that's very kind of you. Stew sounds great, with the added bonus that I can also feed myself, and thank you for putting the children to bed.'

She nodded again, and was gone.

By three o'clock in the morning, he thought he had reread most of the contentious cases. Next to each operation he had a column of alternative information and interpretations to consider. Some of it was blindingly obvious. A child whom the auditor had listed as having subsequent heart problems had not been audited as also having Down's syndrome. Most of the audit's negative findings so far could be traced to a partial or ignorant view of each case. Daniel didn't know whether to feel furious or relieved.

He leaned back in his chair, adrenalin giving way to exhaustion, rubbed his eyes, rolled his shoulders, and put his head on his desk. Surely they would capitulate; accept the contrary evidence he was amassing in the face of their findings. What if they didn't? It was an unbearable thought.

He stood up and walked over to the hearth and picked up a photo of his family. It had been taken at Christmas time. Monica was holding Luca and he'd lifted Ruby up by her waist so that her face was level with his. She was laughing. They were standing in a nearby woodland and there was a soft dusting of snow. It looked so perfect, so idyllic. And yet now, Monica had left to go and work in Los Angeles. What might she be doing now? Possibly eating dinner with someone who was new and exciting, who was not fighting the prospect of professional humiliation, who was not ten years older than she was, and who had not just sat eating microwaved stew on his own. He winced at his unbidden flash of insecurity. That line of thinking, he thought, was probably best not pursued, particularly at three in the morning.

He reached over to his iPad and pressed the Skype tile.

It flashed, *Mon is offline.*

He sighed. He would like to have talked to her, although not about this. He glanced at the spread of files. He would have turned the screen away so that Monica couldn't see. He would have liked to have heard her voice enthusing about something, or laughing, and to have reminded himself that he had a parallel life to this one, which felt solitary, unfairly precarious, and as if a crack had opened beneath his feet in a way that was entirely unexpected and wholly undeserved.

Although it had only been a few minutes, he tried to Skype her again. *Mon is offline* blinked at him impassively. Where was she? It was (he was so tired he had to count back on his fingers) eight thirty in the evening. Maybe she was running on the beach. She'd started to do that – *I'm living the Californian dream,* she'd told him. *There were dolphins just offshore this morning.* Maybe she was eating supper with the crew. To be fair, he reasoned, she would not expect him to be awake. He could text her and tell her that she could Skype if it suited her. He picked up his phone and then placed it back where it had been. What had Cassie said about just one more needy male demanding sympathy? Was it that he was seeking that, even if not overtly? If he spoke to her, if she saw his face, she would intuit something was wrong. My husband, she might say after the call, he's having some problems at work. What a B-team player he'd sound.

He put his head in his hands.

'Shit,' he said softly. 'Shit, shit, shit.'

Had Ursula said his name three times, four, before he stirred? Jesus, he'd fallen asleep where he sat, his head on his folded arms. As he sat up she turned her back to him, and started opening the curtains. How measured she was. What kind of a mess must he appear? At least she afforded him the dignity of not looking, instead busying herself with the tie-back. 'God, what time is it?'

he asked. 'Am I late? I'm due at the hospital for eight. I must have fallen asleep.'

'It's only 6.45, don't worry. I came in early. I thought maybe you'd need a hand with the children as it looked like you were planning to work late. I've already checked upstairs and Luca hasn't stirred yet. If you want to go and take a shower, I can make you some coffee and breakfast. I can put all this back in the boxes if you have to take it back in this morning.'

Daniel stood up.

'That would be great. That's really kind. Thank you. I'm speechless.' He ran his hand through his hair. 'Well, rambling, so obviously not speechless, but more than a little embarrassed. All of this,' he said, suddenly feeling he needed to explain, to justify, 'someone's got the wrong end of the stick; staying up all night has at least given me the ammunition to challenge that.'

Ursula gestured to the papers.

'And if you can't,' she said, 'is it the worst that can happen, the very worst that can happen?'

It was the most direct thing she'd ever said to him, even though it seemed to take the form of a tentative question.

She had a point, Daniel thought, as he soaped himself in the shower, upturning his face to the warmth of the water. What was at stake, he recognised, was that which might be sacrificed on the altar of his ego: his reputation, his peer status, his pride, his self-respect. It seemed a hefty lot to lose. Logically, however, it was clearly not the worst that could happen, but it felt close. Was Ursula herself in any position to know the worst that might happen? Daniel doubted it. Her face was too smooth, too unvanquished for that.

He went into Ruby's room to chide her awake, then scooped up Luca and carried him into the kitchen. Ursula had made poached eggs on toast for him, and boiled eggs with soldiers for the children. When he thanked her for her kindness and for her forethought in coming early, she did not meet his eyes, but went to sort the laundry. She was unreachable, he thought, although evidently kind, and attuned to what was going on around her.

She is oddly remote. He would tell Monica that when next he spoke to her. Oddly remote and impossible to fathom.

He got into the car and made his way to the hospital. He hoped not to see Charlie Grace or any of his cohort. It would be difficult to be civil, especially when it increasingly appeared that their outcomes had been based on inaccurate work.

34

When Ruby had gone to school and she'd taken Luca to nursery, Ursula came back to the house and stood, very still, in the utility room.

Daniel had looked shocking: his eyes red-rimmed, his face careworn. She hadn't expected to find him asleep at the table. She had felt awkward, hesitant, trying to wake him by her presence in the room. She could not have touched him, not even placed her hand on his shoulder to shake him gently awake. What unbearable intimacy. It was hard enough to face him directly.

Is it the worst that can happen? she had asked him. She could hardly believe she had said it. It was not a foolish question, at least not by her own lights, but perhaps insensitive all the same. He had shaken his head, and left the room to shower. She'd tidied the papers, averting her eyes from their details. What horrors might they hold?

Now she placed her hands on the laundry worktop and tried to steady her breathing. Anxiety was infectious; it ran, like water, over every available surface. Now, it flooded through her veins. What was the worst that could happen?

She flexed her fingers and traced around the dial of the washing machine over and over. In her previous house – the one after Chalfont St Giles – she had organised the building of a small extension. She'd called it the laundry, which sounded more grandiose than it was. She'd banked the walls with cupboards, and bought large cream tins which she'd filled with shoe polish, candles and matches, light bulbs, string, rope, parcel tape. Everything she might ever need seemed to be detailed and listed in that room. Another tin contained the instruction manuals for all of the white goods. Sometimes, she just stood in the laundry seeking its order, its reliability, soothed by the soft hum of the tumble dryer, and the coarse feel of the rope in her hands as she hauled the drying racks up to the ceiling.

It was where she would bolt, she had felt, if disaster struck in any shape or form. She would shepherd everyone in there, confidently locating a candle, a match, a hammer, a torch. She'd told Gideon this, when the building work was completed, and he'd laughed, laughed right out loud, and said: *Ursula, the point of a disaster room is that it's meant to be windowless. Yours, need I point out, has a panoramic window out to the hills. Nice thought, but ineptly executed.* It was a fair point, but it hadn't changed how she felt.

The fact that it had faced south, with such an expanse of glass, meant that it was filled with fat slices of sunshine, and that the laundry dried quickly, and she often found herself lifting her eyes to the hills. What was the psalm? *I will lift mine eyes up to the hills/From whence cometh my help.* Or, it turned out, not; not at all. Ironically, her disaster room had had the inverse effect of making disaster seem unlikely. It exuded safety and preparedness. She had once found herself whistling in there, positively jaunty, although that had been long years ago. Now, she placed her lips into the position which might be a starter for whistling. Could she still whistle? Even the thought of it seemed preposterous. She raised her fingers to her lips, and felt her outbreath ripple over them. Not a peep.

She looked around her again. Monica's utility room had no windows at all. Compared to her old laundry, it could be, if the occasion required, much more suited to disaster. Ursula counted her breaths. It would not need to become that. There was absolutely no connection between anticipating disaster and it happening. Furthermore, disaster frequently blew in unannounced, with no correlation whatsoever with one's capacity to endure.

35

Miss Cameron was full of project ideas. Her latest (and now she was holding up a shoe box and peering into it as if there was something she could see which was invisible to the rest of the class) was to make a miniature model of a shop.

'For Design and Technology,' she said, 'and with an eye to Open Afternoon at the end of term. I want you all to make a shop-in-a-box. You can choose whatever kind of shop you'd like – a baker's, a butcher's, a clothes shop, a sports equipment shop – and you can make the insides from lolly sticks, from modelling clay, from scraps of fabric, from toilet rolls, whatever. It's my hope, on Open Day, to put them along the whole of that shelf, like a busy High Street, for all the parents, and carers and families to see.'

Ruby walked home, considering shops. Claudie was going to do a *boulangerie*; she said that she would make éclairs and baguettes and *religieuses au café* from Fimo. Lauren was making miniature footballs in bright colours from screwed-up sweet papers for her sports shop. Ruby scuffed her shoe against a dandelion growing in a crack in the pavement. Her shop was proving tricky to imagine.

When she came in, Ursula was making supper. The house looked so perfectly tidy, so completely clean, that Ruby put her book bag down very neatly.

'How was your day?' asked Ursula.

'Fine. I've got some new homework – a project; I have to make a shop-in-a-box. Any kind of shop, but in a shoe box on its side, with a counter, and a till, and everything tiny. Miss Cameron suggested a butcher's but that would be too hard. I've been thinking all the way home – and I walked slowly – but I don't know what to make.'

Ursula stopped what she was doing and thought for a moment.

'You could do a haberdasher's.'

'I don't know what one of those is.'

'It's a shop which sells fabric, and cottons and sewing things. You could put scraps of material around little rolls of coloured cardboard, and have stacks of those against the sides of the box. It could look really pretty and colourful.'

'Can we go and see a haberdasher's?'

'That would be a sensible place to start. We'll drive to fetch Luca and I'll take you to the one in town. We could buy a few tiny scraps of material and get the things that you'd need, some ribbon, some elastic, some bits and bobs.'

'I'd like that, can we?'

Ruby had never been in Ursula's car before. It was smaller than Daddy's, and not untidy like Mummy's. It was like a car that had just been bought from a garage but without the new smell. Both the passenger and back seats looked as if nobody ever sat in them. Luca's car seat looked strange, strapped in, empty and ready. When Ruby pulled out the seatbelt, it was gleaming black. There was no sign that it was a car which was used every day, except for a pair of sunglasses, which Ursula took out of the glove box and put on before she started driving, and a packet of mints, with the green foil twisted tightly to keep the remaining ones from spilling. It didn't look as if Ursula ate them often. Ruby adjusted her stance to sit a little more tidily and put her hands neatly together in her lap. Ursula adjusted her mirror.

'Your car is very tidy,' Ruby said.

Ursula started the ignition, and kept her eyes looking straight ahead.

'It's only me who goes in it, so it just stays like this.'

The gauzy net in Ruby's mind flapped wide and soft. Mummy was perhaps driving along in her big American car, Daddy was probably in theatre, or standing by a hospital bed surrounded by students who were training to become doctors. She put the images of them carefully in the net. She remembered clearly how the net began. She was about seven, watching Mummy and Daddy getting ready to go out, and she suddenly realised that they had a life beyond her, a life which carried on when she was not with them, as they went about their day. She'd thought of the net as a way of keeping them safe; wherever they went, she could think of them and hold them safe. Perhaps Ursula, and her life in her own house, should also be in it.

Ruby let the soft gauze envelope her. Might her house contain other people, or, like the car, only Ursula? If so, it would be very quiet. Ursula wore no wedding ring. Mummy said she wasn't married. She had no children. She never spoke anybody else's name. Ruby gave a little shiver; it seemed a lonely thought. Ruby looked at her sideways. Perhaps Ursula ate her breakfast every day completely by herself. She imagined her eating cereal, the only sound in the kitchen the clink of the spoon against the bowl. Maybe she listened to the radio, and when she went upstairs to go and clean her teeth, the voice of the announcer carried on talking to the empty room. Mummy hated that. She'd said once it was like dying, and the world carrying on without even missing a beat. Ruby had been careful to switch off the radio when she left a room ever since. But maybe Ursula didn't even listen to the radio. Perhaps she had a big fat marmalade cat which sat on her lap while she buttered toast or waited for the kettle to boil. That was a comforting thought. Maybe her parents were still alive, and she phoned them each morning to ask how they were.

If that was true, maybe they travelled in this car sometimes. She reconsidered the car's interior. It gave no sign of the presence of someone like either of her grannies.

Whenever Mummy gave Granny Bailey a lift, the car was full of the memory of her afterwards. The seatbelt smelt of her perfume, which was sweet and heavy. She left liquorice pastilles, tissues, and sometimes a glove, the finger bunched up where she'd taken it off, or a scarf which had slipped from her neck as she turned to talk to Ruby and Luca in the back. Once she left a bracelet – it was silver with a deep blue stone set in it. She had taken it off, and rubbed her wrist, which she said was sore from perhaps being too old to keep playing tennis. The bracelet stayed in the well between the front seats for weeks, nestled with one of Mummy's lipsticks, some sherbet lemons, a car park ticket, a stick of chewing gum, two hair bobbles and a biro. By comparison, Ursula's mints looked very lonely too. Very lonely and very tightly closed. Maybe her parents could still be alive, but perhaps they didn't like mints and were also super-tidy in cars.

'Are your parents alive?' Ruby asked. It would be better to know.

'No,' Ursula said softly, 'none of my family are alive,' and Ruby felt that possibility flush clean away. She looked down at the rubber mat at her feet; even that had no dirt on it, no gravel or leaves trodden in by someone's shoes. She summoned up, for consolation, the fat marmalade cat.

Ursula was correct that a haberdasher's would make a good shop-in-a-box. Ruby saw that right away, standing inside the doorway and looking at the bright bolts of cloth, the reels of gauzy ribbon, the tins of pins, and cards of white elastic. Ursula explained to the assistant what Ruby had to do, and she said Ruby could choose fabrics to cut a thin strip from. Ursula bought some larger scraps from a basket (*We can cover the shop counter with this one, look it's like oil cloth,* she said), and some narrow ribbon, and then she took Ruby to the stationer's to buy coloured card and glue, and coarse glitter (*we can stick it in clumps and it will look like pins,* she said).

Three nights later, when the shop-in-a-box was finished, Ruby thought it was the most beautiful thing she'd ever made in her life. Now, lying in bed, she turned on her side and looked at it some more. Ursula had shown her how to make rolls from the coloured card, and they'd glued fabric around them and piled them on the shelves they'd made from cutting up a cereal box and folding it at right angles. They'd made a counter, and a tiny till from Plasticine, and Ruby had written a sign in black biro which said *Welcome.* They'd pinned twists of ribbon hanging down behind the counter, and made tins of pins from glitter like Ursula had suggested. Ursula had cut a few little strands of bristle from the outside broom, and they'd stuck them to the floor to make a mat for customers to wipe their feet. They'd made a measuring length from a lolly stick, and Ruby had marked it carefully and evenly with black ink so that a tiny assistant could measure the fabric to sell. Ruby had tried to make tiny scissors and a tiny shop bell, but that hadn't worked out. Ursula said it didn't matter, and that she could add a drawing in black ink of scissors, needles, and a bobbin on the shop sign. It looked very fine. And then, when she came home today, Ursula had put a paper bag in the middle of the chocolate chip cookies she'd made, and when Ruby opened it, there was a figure of a miniature woman, made to go on the top of a cake. Ruby had clapped her hands with pleasure and immediately Blu-tacked the woman next to the till, and now, lying in bed, she patted her softly with her fingertip, checking she was still stuck fast. The woman stood patiently waiting for a customer to arrive.

After Ruby had added the final touches to the shop, she'd crossed her arms on the table, and laid her chin on them. She gazed at the haberdasher's with a smile on her face, liking even its name with its hint of a hurry. She'd become aware that Ursula had stopped sweeping the kitchen floor, and was watching Ruby without saying anything at all, so Ruby had turned to her and said, 'It looks like the most perfect world, doesn't it, with everything exactly as it should be, and where nothing can possibly go wrong and where everything is safe.' Ursula had nodded, but she looked sadder than Ruby had ever seen anybody's face to be, and then she'd started sweeping again, still saying nothing but biting a little at the inside of her lip.

Ruby turned over in her bed so that she wasn't looking at the shop-in-a-box any more. Ursula was probably in her quiet house now. Ruby rearranged her pillow, whacking it with the heel of her hand. Thinking about someone all by themselves was like picking at a splinter in the pad of your finger; it was impossible to leave alone, even though doing it was uncomfortable.

Ursula sat alone in the gauzy net in Ruby's mind. Ruby added the fat marmalade cat to her lap with resolve.

36

At the beginning of the Art lesson, Claudie was sharpening crayons purposefully. She lay down an azure blue one on her paper.

'It's Mother's Day on Sunday,' she said.

'No, it isn't,' said Stella, 'that's already gone. It was in March when it was nearly Easter.'

Claudie looked at her. 'Don't be so silly, Stella,' she said smoothly. 'That was only in England. It's Mother's Day on Sunday in Australia, Canada and America. May the twelfth. I'm right. You can check on any calendar. Why don't we all make a card for our mothers?'

Claudie smiled at all the girls around the table, and started to hand the crayons round. 'Has anyone got a different idea, a better idea?' she said. 'Miss Cameron said we can draw what we want.'

She looked at each girl in turn until her eyes fell on Ruby.

'Oh wait,' she said, 'you won't be able to give your card to your mummy because she's not looking after you at the moment. All the American mothers will have one. Maybe you could post it? Maybe scan it and then e-mail it? Perhaps your helper could help you to do that?'

Ruby tip-tapped her pencil on the desk.

'We don't all have to draw the same thing. I've already decided I'm going to draw a cat.'

'Fine. Draw a cat. Who wants to draw Mother's Day cards with me?'

Coming out of the playground, Ruby kicked a stone hard. It skittered across the tarmac. Claudie was doing it on purpose; repeatedly saying her mum wasn't there, wasn't taking care of her, and didn't love her as much as other mums did. When Claudie had finished drawing her card, she'd written inside it, and read out the words loudly. *Thank you for taking care of me each and every day.* Then she'd put it down on the table and looked calmly at Ruby.

'How's your cat coming along?'

Ruby scribbled hard with her orange crayon.

'Fine, thank you.'

She'd finished the cat's tail. She made it curl around its hip. The cat looked fat and important. If it purred, it would sound like it had a baby rattle deep in its chest. She imagined it stretched out, lazily, in a puddle of sunshine on a warm paving stone. It looked like a very companionable cat. Now, she just had to find some way to give it to Ursula. Maybe Ursula would put it on her fridge, perhaps prop it onto her windowsill. The cat could look contentedly at her when she ate her cereal in her kitchen.

Now, she watched Claudie greeting her mother in the playground. She stood on her tiptoes to kiss her and then smiled across at Ruby and gave a little wave. Ruby tried not to look fierce; she would not give Claudie the satisfaction. She waved back, and Claudie's mother joined in. *There's poor Ruby*, she heard her say. *How wild her curls look. I don't think daddies are very on the ball about haircuts. Can you imagine, Claudie, if Daddy were in charge of your plaits?*

It wasn't bullying; it wasn't exactly bullying, Ruby knew that. She walked home slowly.

Six weeks and four days. That was how long Mummy had been gone. It felt like a very long time. Some days, it felt longer than others, when the day seemed to have a Mummy-shaped space punched through it. Last night, she'd missed her. The feeling pounced on her, just as she got out of the shower; the desire to curl up on Mummy's lap, her hair all wet from the shower, to snuggle into Mummy's neck and maybe talk about nothing at all, just play with the gold locket she wore, smooth it between her finger and thumb, maybe watch something on television, her knees crooked up so that her whole body just touched Mummy, not the sofa. Ursula had left, and Daddy was putting Luca to sleep, and she'd gone into the spare bedroom and stood by Mummy's desk. She'd tried to conjure her up there, tapping away at her computer. It didn't work. The room felt empty and very clean.

She'd heard Daddy coming out of Luca's room and quickly scooted into bed. It felt important that he didn't think she was ever sad about Mummy being away. All the files, all the work he was now bringing home. When he came in to kiss her goodnight, she'd told him about something funny that had happened at school. He'd said, 'So everything's okay, Little?' and she'd smiled and said, 'Of course it is,' because mostly it was. Almost nearly all of the time it was; just not today, now, with Claudie being mean, and Claudie's mother saying her curls looked wild, and suddenly, more than anything, she wanted to go home and have Mummy there, late for something, putting lipstick on in front of the hall mirror. She refocused on the marmalade cat. She would find a way to give it to Ursula. Granny Bailey always said doing a kind thing for someone else could make you feel better.

When she got home, Ursula was out in the garden with Luca.

'I fetched him early,' she said, 'it's such a beautiful afternoon, and I thought it would be nicer for him to be outside in the garden in the sunshine.'

She'd given him a bucket to pick up the windfalls from the

apple tree. As he picked each one up, he said, 'Ap-ul, ap-ul.' He took a bite out of one and wrinkled his nose at the sourness.

'Not in your mouth,' Ursula said, 'only in your bucket.'

Ruby thought Ursula was good at thinking up games for Luca. She seemed like someone who had had a lot of practice at it, which was curious. She gave him bowls of water, and pouring jugs, and let him sit on the kitchen floor and get everything wet and messy before bath time, and then she whizzed round with the mop and everything looked as good as new. Last night, when he was a bit grizzly, she'd quickly sewn two buttons on an old, odd sock and shown him how to make a puppet with his hand. Luca had fallen asleep still wearing it. Daddy said next step ventriloquism, but then he laughed and said actually Luca had to learn to speak for himself first. When Daddy made jokes, Ursula smiled a little bit, but she looked like someone who would like to get out of the room as well. When Daddy came home, she was always quick to leave.

One of Ruby's best things was to lie in bed and hear Mummy and Daddy talking downstairs, their voices a soft murmur, and then one of them would laugh and the sound would bubble up the stairs and make Ruby's bed seem warmer, and cosier, and she'd fall asleep feeling happy, her parents chatting and laughing together downstairs. Thinking of Mummy now made her miss her again. She looked up at Luca; his bucket was almost full.

Ruby chewed at her lip, and plucked a wide blade of grass. She split it with her thumbnail and blew through it, trying to make it whistle. No luck. She looked up and was aware of Ursula watching her from by the washing line.

Ursula came over with the basket and sat down beside her. The laundry smelt of sunshine and fresh air. Ruby felt like pressing her face into it.

'Penny for them,' said Ursula. 'Penny for whatever you're thinking.' She waited for a moment longer, and then got up and walked back into the house. She put the washing in the utility room, ready to be ironed. She came back outside with a bowl of water for Luca.

'Do you want to wash all your apples?' she asked him, putting down the bowl of shallow water and giving him a little nail brush.

Luca started scrubbing at the apples, laughing as they bobbed in the water.

Ruby followed Ursula inside. Ursula was emptying her book bag, putting forms on the table for Daniel to sign. The marmalade cat lay fatly beside them.

Ursula gestured towards it.

'That's a very fine cat. Your mummy would love that. It's a beautiful drawing. Why don't you write something on it and we can post it to her? Unless you want to put it in your bedroom, perhaps on the shelf by your bed? Or Luca could have it in his room. We could put it in a little frame.'

'Would you like it?' Ruby asked. 'I thought maybe you would like it, for your house, for your fridge or something.'

Ursula hesitated, then shook her head. 'No, that's a very sweet thought, but I think it should go to Mummy, or be here. It's a very lovely cat.'

Ruby detected the firmness in her voice. Ursula didn't want the cat. She wasn't being unkind, she just didn't want it. It was only a picture. Maybe she didn't like pictures in her house. Maybe her fridge was completely bare and she liked it that way. Grown-ups sometimes preferred that. Granny Watson said she'd had enough sticky fingers with three children to last a whole lifetime, which was why she preferred to come and visit them. For years, she told Ruby, I longed for a white sofa, and now I've got one it's staying that way. You couldn't argue with that.

Ursula stood in her kitchen, her fingertips pressed to the fridge door. The memory of the marmalade cat held her motionless for a moment. How impossible to think of it stuck there, looking out over the room. She hoped she hadn't hurt Ruby's feelings, but no, bringing the drawing home, she did not want that.

She prepared an omelette, and sat at the table. As she ate, she shifted a little in her chair. How odd it was. The silence in her kitchen seemed thicker, heavier. It was growing edges and elbows. She thought back to the Great House, to its vast pools of quietness. How consonant with her muteness that had been. Now she found her ear habitually half-cocked, listening for Ruby's footsteps down the stairs, for Luca calling to her. *Ursla, Ursla,* he said. It was difficult not to be charmed.

As she got up from the table she automatically scanned the floor around her feet, checking she was not about to step on some Duplo or a toy. She caught herself, and gave a tiny shudder. It was exactly as she'd feared.

37

Monica was twirling a white turban on her fingers merrily as they spoke.

'It's called Kundalini yoga,' she said. 'Amy and I have gone to a couple of classes. See this, look,' (and here she ducked and rummaged around beside her bed), 'I splashed out on a sheepskin mat. It helps create my sacred space, and apparently supports my back better. I'm guessing you might have a view on the second.'

Daniel looked bemused. 'Mostly tosh, I'm guessing,' he said.

'You have to wear all white,' she continued, 'to "expand your autoradiance". For some reason, that helps you to reflect your positive energy out into the world, whereas the turban' – she spun it again – 'holds it in.'

'And the end benefit?' Daniel asked.

'I knew you'd ask that, and see how ready my answer is. The end benefit is a detox of all the stagnant energy and limiting beliefs that we hold in our body.'

'Very Californian,' he said. 'Cast out those limiting beliefs.'

'There's more; you can put crystals on your sheepskin mat, to spread your aura further. And, our teacher says, anything else that is precious to you. I did class this morning with a photo of the three of you tucked under the edge of the mat. I hope you felt all that good karma washing over you.'

'Right, so that's what it was; about three forty-five as I'd finished checking my patients.'

'Curly kale features large, too.'

'I'm sorry?'

'You have to start your day with a green smoothie. Number one virtuous ingredient is curly kale, then ginger, and beetroot. Wheatgrass is so last year.'

'I'm guessing watching Ruby eat Rice Krispies might be a little traumatic on your return.'

'I can't wait to watch Ruby eat Rice Krispies, but for now, God, Daniel, what a ball this all is; so kooky, so different, so energising. I'm missing you all horribly but I'm having such a lovely time too.'

'Must be down to all the autoradiating, and detoxing all of that stagnant energy.'

'But you're all okay, aren't you?' Suddenly her voice was concerned, authentic. 'Everything's okay, isn't it?'

And there was the moment when he might have broached it, might have told her what was wrong, but instead he'd nodded, said breezily, 'Everything's fine,' and the moment was gone, and Monica was on to describing a brunch she'd eaten the day before when she'd had to go to San Francisco. 'French toast,' she said, 'Oh my God, French toast with raspberries to die for.'

When the call ended, she was laughing, and chanting the line which began the Kundalini class. She'd put on her turban, and bowed to him, a deep namaste. Perhaps he should have waved in return, pulled off some kind of gesture to match her exuberance. Instead he'd felt weary, as if he'd been faking his responses. How liberated she seemed. It was churlish, he thought, not to take pleasure in that, but it felt difficult to do when his own shoulders felt so loaded. He'd received notification of the first internal panel hearing. He just had to hope that they would come with an open mind and listen.

38

Ruby came into the kitchen holding two books.

'Are you going out into the garden to read?' Ursula asked.

'I've read all my books, so I have to read these ones again.'

Ursula considered this for a moment.

'Are there not more you can bring home from school?'

'You're only allowed one from the reading scheme box and then one non-fiction. I want to read stories and I've run out of new ones.'

'I guess we could go to the library,' said Ursula. 'Did Mummy or Daddy ever take you there? Do you know if you're registered?'

'I don't think so.'

'If we leave now, we'll have time to go before collecting Luca.'

Ursula hadn't been into the library for years. As she came through the revolving door, the smell of it was unchanged. Did the books still have plastic sleeves to protect the covers? She imagined not. Neither, she thought, would the librarian have a stamp and ink pad, ready to put the return-by date on a ticket which fitted into a pocket stuck to the inside leaf. It would be digitally scanned, recorded, a small light processing all relevant information.

Ruby was running her finger along the spines of the books on the shelves.

'Do you want some help,' Ursula asked her, 'or can you work it out for yourself?'

'I can do it; it's arranged like at school.'

Ruby began making her selection, reading the covers and the inside flaps. Ursula moved to a semi-circle of chairs at the centre of the room. She sat down tentatively and looked around her. A woman with two small children – were they aged three, four? – was helping them to choose books, crouching at their level to show them the pictures. An old man, hunched over a newspaper in the corner, coughing and spluttering, caught her eye. Ursula looked down at her lap. She felt exposed, open to scrutiny, even though there were only half a dozen people present. She had successfully reduced her life to such a small footprint: a weekly shop in the supermarket, always early on a weekend morning; an occasional walk along the towpath; her drive to and from work. Any break from her routine made her feel conspicuous.

On the way in the car, Ruby had asked, clearly, brightly, *If you could choose to be an animal, a creature, any kind, what would you be?* When Ursula had demurred and deflected the question straight back, Ruby, after reflection, chose a dolphin. What Ursula didn't say – claiming when pressed that she'd like to be a horse or maybe a robin – was that she'd have chosen to be a plaice or a lemon sole; a flat fish which swam pressed close to the floor of the ocean, a creature which managed to exist on the margins of life, camouflaged, invisible, bearing witness to what went on, but remaining peripheral.

Now, Ruby came towards her balancing six books precariously under her chin.

'I think that's your allowance,' Ursula said. 'Shall we check them out and go and fetch Luca?'

The librarian began the process of registering Ruby and checking the books out, her voice a little disdainful, a little bored, her questions to Ruby worn threadbare by rote. As she scanned the books, a woman came through the revolving entrance – the speed of the door's mechanism giving the effect of her having tumbled, somewhat unexpectedly, into the room – and looked directly at Ursula. She put her head on one side, raised an eyebrow, stared quite hard, and then said, 'Don't I know you, your face looks familiar. I can't place you, how frustrating . . . do I look familiar to you too?' The woman continued to stare, her palm pressed to her breastbone. Ursula reached for Ruby's books and started to put them in the canvas bag she was carrying, her hands suddenly inept, clumsy, so that two of the books dropped to the floor. Ruby reached down to help pick them up, her head simultaneously turning to take in the woman, and Ursula dropped one of the books again, so Ruby tucked it under her arm.

'No, I'm sure I don't know you,' Ursula said. 'You must be mistaken. You don't look familiar to me at all.'

'Oh, then, I'm sorry, I could have sworn . . . My mistake, obviously,' and she headed over to the fiction section. The librarian gave Ruby her ticket.

'Come on,' Ursula said to Ruby, 'let's go. We mustn't be late for Luca.'

In the car, Ruby watched Ursula from the side of her eyes. She didn't put the key in the ignition. She sat for a moment, with her fingertips pressed to either side of her nose, and she breathed out of her mouth, once, twice, quite loudly. Then, she pressed her hand to where her heart was and looked up at the roof of the car. Ruby wondered when she would speak, but Ursula stayed silent.

Ruby tapped her fingertips softly together. Maybe a question would help.

'Did you know that lady, do you think?' Ruby asked.

'No, not at all. She said she was mistaken, she must have been mistaken, it's such a flustering thing, when somebody thinks they know you. You flip through all the names, all the faces in your head, all the time getting more flustered because you're sure you don't actually know them. You'll see, when you're old like me and you've met too many people.'

Ruby looked at her directly. Ursula's cheeks were red. Along the top of her upper lip was a faint sheen of sweat. She had dropped the books, twice. That was very unusual. Her hands were usually so safe. Now, she wiped her lip with her fingers, put the key in the ignition.

Neither of them spoke as they drove to the nursery.

When Daddy came home, Ruby was sitting on a pile of cushions on the sofa, surrounded by all her books.

'Look, Daddy, Ursula took me to the library, look at everything I've got to read.'

Ursula appeared in the doorway, putting on her coat. Daniel smiled at her.

'That's really kind of you, Ursula, thank you, and a great idea. I don't know why Monica nor I have ever thought about it before. Thank you for sorting out a ticket, and showing Ruby the ropes. You'll have to teach me now, Little.'

'My pleasure,' Ursula said, and reached down to take some torn-up tissue from Luca's hand. It wasn't really her pleasure, thought Ruby, remembering how flustered she'd got, how she was even quieter than usual all the way home.

Daniel spoke again.

'My guess is now that Ruby will be keen to go to the library at weekends. Anything that saves me from mowing the lawn has to have extra plus-points. But I owe you, thank you. If you think of a way for me to repay you, let me know.'

Ruby clapped her hands at the perfectness of an unexpected idea.

'Let's all go somewhere nice and Ursula could come with us. The beach! Daddy why don't you take us to the seaside for the day? We could go on Saturday and Ursula could come too.'

Daniel hesitated.

'Sounds good to me. Ursula, are you game? Do you have plans

already for the weekend, or would you like to redefine what a quiet day at the seaside might entail?'

Ursula was twisting the torn-up tissue in her fingers. Ruby watched her carefully. She looked as if she were thinking very fast.

'I'm sorry, I have plans, and the beach, the seaside . . .' She trailed off. 'I think better to go without me. I don't like the beach. It's a lovely idea though, Ruby, and the weather is meant to be sunny on Saturday.'

'Of course,' said Daniel quickly, 'of course, whatever you'd prefer to do.'

'Yes, then, no thank you, but thank you Ruby for thinking, for inviting me . . .' Ursula seemed to have run out of words.

'I'll just put this in the bin in the kitchen,' she said, holding up the piece of torn tissue, 'and then I'll be going, I should be going, I'll see you tomorrow.'

She left the room.

'Can we still go to the beach?' Ruby asked. 'Even though Ursula doesn't want to come?'

'Why, yes, if you'd like to. Yes, we can do that.'

Ursula didn't want to come.

Ruby brushed her teeth, staring at herself fixedly in the mirror. Ursula didn't want to come to the beach. She didn't know the woman in the library. And she hadn't wanted the drawing of the marmalade cat.

Granny Watson told her once that sometimes grown-ups had a part of them that was broken, and it was difficult for anybody to fix it because not everything could be made right. Mummy was cross, saying, 'Why fill the child's head with all your gloomy nonsense?' and Granny said, 'It's better that she knows it now rather than grow up thinking any different.' Granny Bailey would disagree. She thought everything could be fixed, mostly by deciding it could be and then working very hard. Ursula did that anyway. Not with her teeth gritted, which Granny Bailey said helped, but with her face all smooth.

Ruby spat out the toothpaste and rinsed her mouth with clean water. Grown-ups were actually a mystery. Look how Mummy's job offer had come out of the blue. Ruby had gone to school in the morning and come back to a completely different life. She'd told Luca yesterday that it was best to be very, very watchful. Keeping a close eye on adults might give you a better chance of guessing what they might do next.

It was regrettable, Daniel reflected later, pouring himself a scotch, that Ruby had put Ursula on the spot like that; asking her in front of him, when it was predictable she would most likely not want to come. Had it crossed a line, Ruby inviting her to do something over the weekend? Daniel hoped not. He hoped it was obvious that the offer – and his endorsement of it – was based on gratitude and appreciation. She was doing so much more than her original job description had asked of her. She was so difficult to read. So diffident. More so with him than with Ruby, who seemed to be inching closer, making inroads. What did they talk about when he wasn't there? Were there the protracted silences, the evident disinclination to be in the same room? He couldn't imagine so.

Tonight, more than ever, he wished that Monica were home. It would be good to come back after work and not feel himself to be treading on eggshells, his voice so cheery it put his own teeth on edge. The eggshells, he reminded himself, were not of Ursula's making. They stemmed from his ill-fated attempts to try and read her better. Perhaps he should stop trying, reconcile himself to the fact that there was actually no need to have any insight at all. He should cut himself some slack; hadn't he got enough on his plate anyway?

39

Peeling the potatoes for the children's supper the next day, Ursula thought about Ruby and Daniel's offer. There were so many reasons why she didn't want to go to the beach, but as usual she had been reserved, perhaps a little prim. Perhaps she should have elaborated, maybe thrown in an antipathy towards sand, an allergy, even. Daniel would probably have countered by saying they could go to a beach with shingle. He had not tried to persuade her, however. He'd been perfectly affable and understanding. She hoped he didn't think she was offended. She was sensitive to the spirit in which it had come about. Ruby's offer was spontaneous, joyful, the child visibly proud of herself for thinking up a collective treat. Ursula, even now, acknowledged the beckoning quality of the lengthening days of May and the appeal of throwing costumes, buckets, spades and Frisbees into a bag and heading for the beach. She resisted the image. She would not go. She bit her lower lip with resolve and began to slice an onion for shepherd's pie.

Gideon had taken her to the beach for the weekend. They'd gone to Salcombe in Devon, and stayed in a cottage overlooking the harbour. Here came the memory, jostling and barging its way into Daniel's kitchen. She'd woken on the Saturday morning after a late arrival the night before, and opened the curtains to see children crouched by the harbour wall fishing for crabs, hauling them up on long lengths of green twine.

They'd sat eating breakfast, outside at a wooden table, and as people walked past Gideon said, *Good morning* and, *What a glorious day!* How expansive he'd been. He'd taken her by the hand and they'd walked the length of Fore Street; he bought coffee in a deli, and they'd sat on a bench watching small yachts tack their way across the estuary. He kept looking at his watch, and caught her noticing.

'You've rumbled me,' he said, laughing. 'I have a surprise at ten o'clock. We can walk down to Whitestrand now; it should be there, ready for us.'

He'd hired a speedboat (what kind was it called, something anatomical, something bony – ah yes, a RIB). It had been brought over from Dartmouth.

'Don't worry,' he said, 'I've driven these things for years. Come, you'll love it out on the water.'

He'd taken a life jacket shaped like a horseshoe, and put it over her head. As he did up the buckle for her, she felt as inept as a child.

Gideon waved jauntily to the boatman as he eased away from the pontoon.

'Eight knots allowed in the estuary,' he said, 'so you can take in the scenery; see that old boathouse there? It's my favourite.'

It was all evidently familiar to him. How often had he been here? Ursula suspected many times, but he offered nothing up, gave her no clue. Had his first wife come from near here? Maybe her family owned a beach house? Ursula resolved not to think about it further. She settled back into the seat, enjoying the crisp breeze that whipped up from the water. She pulled her jacket closer around her. Gideon looked positively carefree.

'This is the Bar,' he said, as they moved over a swathe of water. 'At low tide you can see the rocks. The lifeboat ran aground here once; just before the First World War, I think. Loss of life, frantic bravery; the usual awfulness. Tennyson wrote about it too – the Bar itself, not the lifeboat. See, local history and literature; what a tour guide you've married.'

She smiled, gripping the rail by the seat a little more tightly as she felt him picking up speed. She spotted a white house, isolated, right at the outskirts of the estuary. How solitary it looked, as if keeping some kind of vigil. How glad sailors and fishermen must have been to see it, as they made their way home through a squall. The wind whipped a little more sharply so she zipped up her jacket. It was much colder on the water, which she had not anticipated. Her skirt blew around her legs, and stuck to the splashes of salt spray on her skin.

'Let's see what this can do,' Gideon said, releasing the throttle.

The RIB roared forward, and bounced brutally over each wave it hit.

'It's important,' Gideon shouted, 'to hit them head on, that's how RIBs are designed to take it. Approach a wave sideways and you're done for. Trust me.'

Ursula's hand was now white-knuckled on the rail. The spray was stinging her face, and with the rise and fall of each wave her stomach clenched and flipped.

'Gideon, Gideon,' she said, 'I'm not sure I like this; it's too fast. I'm frightened.' She let out an involuntary scream.

And the most curious thing; he had turned to her and smiled, with a smile that still held its jaunty brightness but also held something else, something she was not sure she could find words for. Was he amused by her fear? They roared past a bay.

'That bay looks so pretty; perhaps we could slow down, take a look?'

The wind whipped the words from her mouth, scattering them into the sea behind her. Gideon went faster. At the crest of one wave, Ursula's necklace flew up and caught her lip and front tooth.

'Ow,' she said, placing her hand to her mouth. She tasted the sweet saltiness of blood.

Gideon turned to face her. 'Had enough?' he called.

She'd nodded, one hand to her mouth, the other still clutching the rail. She feared she might vomit.

He stopped abruptly, the RIB slamming to a halt. He reeled out the anchor. 'Oh my darling,' he said, solicitous now, 'were you afraid?'

He stepped round from the steering column, and took her into his arms. He kissed her blue, bloodied lips, his tongue quick and warm. He licked the blood from her mouth, 'See how I love you,' he said, and decisively lifted her damp, sea-sprayed skirt. How instantly she responded to him, her hand still clutching the rail, but now to steady herself, her face held in his hands, his lips kissing her collarbone. 'Look,' he said afterwards, pointing to a bird wheeling high above a promontory. 'A raven.' The bird's call bounced out across the water to them. Ursula fixed her eyes on the horizon and tongued her swollen lower lip.

When they came alongside the pontoon again, the boatman called out, 'Did you enjoy yourselves?' Gideon laughed and nodded, and made a show of gallantly handing Ursula from the craft and undoing her life jacket with exaggerated care. They walked back across Whitestrand, her legs, her inner ear, still a little shaky from the roll of the water.

'Are you hungry?' Gideon said. 'Shall we go and get some lunch?'

They went to a pub, and Gideon went up to the bar to order some food. Ursula sat very still, her mouth feeling not quite her own. Was she wrong in thinking that out there on the water, the salt spray flying, the enormous speed, the roar and bounce of the RIB, that even if Gideon's initial intent had not been to scare her, he had, upon realising that she was afraid, prolonged it for just a little longer than necessary? Had it made him feel empowered? She had been terrified; and yet she had responded to his touch. Was that what he was savouring, his smile broad, his hands supple, as he raised the anchor?

Afterwards, they'd crossed the estuary on the passenger ferry. They'd walked on the beaches at East Portlemouth, and on around to Mill Bay. Gideon had suggested walking along the coastal path, and they'd reached Seacombe Sands. The gorse was in flower, and the air smelt of coconut, of yellow warmth. He'd taken her hand, kissed her wrist, and carried her over the rocks. She'd resolved to think about the moment on the RIB no further.

'I don't think I have sea legs,' she said to him over dinner.

'Sea legs? Hell, whatever, they're great legs,' he said, momentarily touching her thigh beneath the table.

He fell asleep before she did. All that joviality, she thought, to every single person they encountered, how exhausting that must have been, and how uncharacteristic it had felt to her. How surprising he was; how endlessly surprising.

She lay on her side and looked out through the window. She had not drawn the curtain. She watched, in the moonlight, the suck and swell of the water, and the yellowness of a defiant, plucky lamp in the cabin of a yacht. Across the estuary, she thought she could see the pinprick light of the head torches of two shore fishermen.

What she couldn't escape, lying there, wakeful, Gideon breathing steadily beside her, was the feeling that today, married for less than a year, she had realised how completely he held her in the palm of his hand. Was that how marriage was meant to be?

'*Let me not to the marriage of two minds,*' he'd said to her over dinner recently, '*admit impediments.* I'd like to claim it as my own but it's Shakespeare. One of my favourites, along with the one that says, "Oh stay, and hear; your true love's coming". And I heard you,' he said, 'I heard you.'

And so, lying restlessly, looking out over the water, she'd wondered whether she was up to the force of his mind. Outside, the head torches winked and shone as the fishermen moved around. Most likely they were reeling something in. That thought, and an unwanted, unbidden analogy to herself, made her lip throb further. She lay sleepless in the dark.

Now, in Daniel and Monica's kitchen, she spooned mashed potato onto the pie. She banished the memory by thinking about how much Ruby and Luca would enjoy their supper. When she had finished cooking, she would find where Monica kept their beachwear, their buckets and spades, their sun hats. But no, she would not go the beach.

40

It was the last lesson of the afternoon. Miss Cameron had a large cardboard box on her desk and a face full of surprise-giving.

'I think you're all going to love this,' she said. 'It's science, and a competition, and sort of gardening as well, with a little bit of maths at the same time. I want you to come up to my desk, table by table, and collect your kits.'

Ruby waited. Sometimes, Miss Cameron made things sound more exciting than they actually were.

On this occasion, maybe she wasn't exaggerating; at least, not if they actually grew. Having fetched her kit, Ruby looked at what she had before her: a wide-throated jam jar, a sheet of pink blotting paper, a fat, wrinkled bean and a sticky label on its shiny backing.

Miss Cameron was holding up a piece of the blotting paper.

'What I want you to do is to curl it like this, and pop it into the jam jar, wide enough so that the paper is practically touching the sides. Then I want you to take the bean very carefully in your fingers, and tuck it between the blotting paper and the side of the glass. Don't position it too low, because you need space for the roots to grow down.'

There was a collective in-breath of disbelief from the class. Last year, they'd grown mustard and cress seeds on wet kitchen roll, and that was surprising enough. A bean in a jam jar, seemingly living on fresh air and blotting paper, didn't sound like it would be shooting and rooting anytime soon.

Ruby put the paper in the jam jar and tucked her bean in neatly.

'Now,' said Miss Cameron, 'write your name on your sticky label, and attach it to the other side of the jar. Then open your science books and copy the chart that's on the whiteboard.'

The graph had the number of days running along the bottom, and then measurements along the axis that went up.

'You're going to use two colours of pen,' Miss Cameron was saying. 'A red one to mark how much the shoot is growing, and a green one to mark how much the root is growing. And they may not grow at the same time, or at the same speed; that is what we'll be measuring.'

On this occasion, thought Ruby, Miss Cameron's surprise-giving face was justified. Now the teacher was filling a jug with water from the sink in the corner.

'The last thing we need to do is make the blotting paper wet. Not soaking, just damp, which is why I'm going to show you this first time. When you take it home, it will be your responsibility to water it, to watch it grow and to measure it, and to write down your figures in your book. In three weeks, everyone can bring them back into school, and we'll see whose has grown most, and we can learn a little bit more about what plants need to grow well.'

Ruby watched as the blotting paper swelled and softened in her jam jar, the water trickling from the spout of the jug.

'Carry them home carefully,' said Miss Cameron. 'Let's aim for no breakages.'

When the bell rang, Ruby stared for a little longer at the fat bean in the jar. It looked so full of promise, even though it was wrinkly and didn't smell good. It looked snug, and podged with possibility, nestling between the jar and the pink paper.

Everyone was streaming quickly out of the classroom, and Miss Cameron was packing her cardboard box away. As she lifted it from the table, Ruby heard the clink of other jam jars. Her mind worked quickly. Ursula didn't have a marmalade cat; she didn't even have a drawing of a marmalade cat. She hadn't come to the beach at the weekend. Maybe she could have a bean; a bean growing on her kitchen windowsill, in a team with Ruby's own.

'Miss Cameron,' she said, 'please could I have one extra, if there are some spare, just one extra to take home too? I can measure them both if you'd like.'

'I don't see why not. I've got quite a few spare in case some don't make it home in one piece. Maybe put them on different windowsills at home, then you might learn some things about light and warmth, and how they affect how a plant grows. Let me quickly assemble it for you. Will you be able to carry two home?'

When Ruby came in, Ursula was out in the garden, mowing the lawn. This was unexpected. Daddy mostly did that. Ruby put her two jars down and went out to see her.

'I've run out of things to clean,' Ursula said, tipping the grass cuttings out onto the compost heap. 'I'd be dusting before the dust has even had a chance to resettle.'

'I've got something for you, something else for you to look after, but this time to take home.'

'I'm sorry?'

'Come into the kitchen, I'll show you. I've got something for you to take back to your house.'

Ursula followed her into the kitchen. The two beans sat fatly in their jars, side by side on the island. Ruby had written *Ursula* on the second sticker.

'It's meant to be surnames as well,' she said, 'but I thought that probably didn't matter. We have to dampen the blotting paper, just a little bit, each day, and then the bean will grow, even without any soil, and we can measure the shoot and the root and see whose grows the most. The whole class is doing it and we're putting it in a graph. You don't have to do that bit, but I thought you could just have one to grow, that maybe you'd like that.'

Ursula looked cautiously at the jar, but didn't reach forward to touch it.

'That's so kind of you to think of me,' she said, 'but I don't think the bean should really come to my house. It's far better that it stays here. Why don't we put one on the kitchen windowsill, and the other in your bedroom or the sitting room? Then we can measure the differences. That will be really interesting. We can still have one each, but here.'

'But I got it for you to take home.' Ruby chewed at the inside of her cheek. Miss Cameron's surprise for the class seemed to have gone down better than her own for Ursula.

Ursula paused, and spoke slowly.

'All right. I will take it home, and I'll try to remember to water it. No promises though; I'm really not a gardener.'

Ruby looked out of the kitchen door, to where the lawn was mown very neatly, and the flowerbed newly weeded with the taller plants tied to stakes. She decided not to say anything. Ursula was putting the jam jar by her bag.

As she walked through the front door, the jam jar felt like a bomb, ticking in her bag. Ursula took it out swiftly, and put it on the side, as if just touching it might burn her fingers.

The blotting paper, pink enough in all the colourfulness of Ruby's kitchen, seemed blindingly so in Ursula's. It felt as if it might be necessary to look at it through a pinwheel, as if, like a solar eclipse, staring at it might damage the retina. Ursula squinted at it. The bean was the colour of a walnut shell, and foetal in its curvature. She raised her palm to completely block it from view.

How bold, how defiant it was, here in the bland, empty neutrality of her kitchen. She was at odds over what to do with it. Throwing it away would be simplest. She could tell Ruby, in the morning, that she had dropped it on the doorstep as she fiddled to put the key into the lock. The glass, she could say, flew all over the place. But Ruby would look at her, perhaps raise an eyebrow, and they would both know that the bean would have emerged unscathed, and that the blotting paper would have fluttered softly onto the path. Ruby would point out that a jar would be easy to replace. To claim that it had smashed was not an option. Perhaps it would be better to say nothing. Instead, to give it no water, to wait until it had perished, shrivelled black, and then take it to Ruby, folded in a twist of kitchen paper, and say, *Look, I must have had a dud one, it never grew at all.* And if she chose to do that, she could put it into the cupboard under the stairs, now, where the lack of light would ensure it happened doubly fast. She turned the jar in her fingers. The bean looked snug and cosy. She looked over towards the bin. She could throw it all away right now. She could tell Ruby that she'd over-watered it, that it grew a fuzzy bloom of mould, and then rotted against the indifferent glass. Ruby would never know the truth. Children's minds, anyway, moved on quickly, from one thing to the next. Ruby's perhaps less so, Ursula conceded, her watchfulness sometimes belying her age. She turned her face away and left the jar on the side, pinkly vivid.

Later, rising from bed, she padded softly down into the kitchen. With the glow from the street lamp outside, she could make out the bean. It was implacably *there*. Perhaps it had already begun growing, sucking up water from the blotting paper, preparing to thrust out root or shoot. It would grow; it would grow determinedly, uncompromisingly, the root creamy like milk, the shoot so freshly green it would cause more pain to her eye. Even in the dark, the bean threatened a fierce, calm persistence. She looked at the bin again, and felt a rush of guilt at the thought. Ruby had written her name so neatly on the sticker. She had wanted to give this to her, with an expectation that she would water it, allow it light and warmth. Was it so much to ask?

Ursula stepped over to the tap, filled a glass and drank slowly. A couple of centimetres of water remained when she'd finished. She poured it swiftly onto the blotting paper, seeing the paper darken in the orange half-light of the street lamps.

She put the glass on the draining board, left the kitchen quietly, and climbed the stairs, light of tread, back to her room and to bed. Restless on her pillow, she could not displace the image of the bean. It was imprinted on her retina so that she saw it even with her eyes closed. Maybe it was sucking water up already; summoning life energy, kick-starting all the chaos, scrambling into action. What had she read once, carved into a paving stone? *Water is the source of life and all of life's beginnings.* She turned onto her side, pressed her fingertips against her eyelids. The world exploded blue, vivid and pulsating. She could dispose of the bean tomorrow. She might wake in the morning, resourceful and refreshed, and think of a way to do it that seemed fairer to Ruby. Maybe she could take it outside, thumb it too deep into the soil in a shaded corner of the garden. The bean could lie in the dark, softly choked by the earth. But, she thought, now tossing and turning again, Ruby had asked for an extra one for her. How personal that was. How heart-sweet. How dangerous.

It was six weeks until Monica came home. She must just get through that period with her emotional neutrality preserved. Ruby's little face suffused with expectation, her tangle of curls, her hand, outstretched, proffering the jar. No, Ursula resolved, she would not let herself think of that, nor of the precision it took to take the jar from Ruby's grasp without making any physical contact with her at all.

41

She could hardly believe she'd allowed herself to do it. In an unguarded moment, Ursula had ordered an ice-lolly mould from a catalogue. She unwrapped it tentatively. She'd rationalised to herself that it would be useful; she could make healthy lollies from fruit juice and have them in the freezer for when Ruby came home from school. Now, in the kitchen, she filled them a third full with orange juice and put the mould carefully in the freezer. She looked up at the clock. Nine thirty a.m. She'd add apple juice and the broad, smooth sticks at eleven thirty, and raspberry juice at one thirty. The lollies would look like rockets. How Luca would whoop.

It was not, she reassured herself, very different from cooking the children supper. She made cakes and cookies for after school. An ice lolly didn't ratchet anything up. She folded the packaging from the mould and put it into the bin. Stopping on the way to work to buy the juices was no real stretch either. How often, in the last few weeks, had she stopped for an ingredient for supper, extra milk, stock cubes? It was no different, she assured herself, beginning to unstack the dishwasher.

She reached to open the window. An orange blossom was in flower beyond it, and a rose which scrambled over the sill with vigour. The morning was already warm, and the scent from the flowers washed over her. The sky was an unrelenting blue: it would be hot later. On the windowsill, by the utensils pot, she noticed Ruby's bean was growing, splitting voluptuously, the root boldly emerging. She had watered her own when she left the house this morning. She had resolved to continue doing it only until she'd decided how to dispose of it. Ruby had left her ruler propped next to the jam jar. The root was too small to measure yet, but Ruby's gesture of intent seemed poignantly positive.

Ursula turned to put the fruit juices back into the fridge. Her own mother used to make her lollies. It came back to her now: Ava in the kitchen, reaching into the icebox, banging a metal mould on the worktop until she managed to knock one out.

A blackbird's song drew her out into the garden. It was a day to be outside, a day for picnics, for being beside water, for fishing nets, for blankets to be spread over long grass. As she stood on the terrace and looked out over the garden, such a beating and a pulsing; how it called for a response, for a correlating life energy. Ursula put her face in her hands. Life: its intractable brutality, its indubitable sweetness; its ability to wrestle with one, even standing passive on a terrace, the air heavy with the scent of blossom and roses. How difficult it was to turn away from the beat of a June summer morning.

She went back into the house. There were beds to be stripped, sheets to be laundered and ironed. She could wash down the staircase spindles; they could always be relied on to collect dirt. The blackbird called again, with an urgency, an insistence. Ursula put her hands over her ears, and went into the utility room.

Ruby ran all the way home from school, her plan whirring in her head. Surely Ursula would say yes; it was not far to drive. Luca would love it, and it was so very hot. All afternoon in the classroom, she'd wiped her palms against her checked school uniform dress. Miss Cameron had thrown the windows wide so all the work that was pinned up on the walls fluttered in the breeze.

When she came home, Ursula had made ice lollies. They were perfect. Luca was making his fly like a rocket.

'Ursula, please, please can we go to the water jets in the park? I know where they are because I went to a birthday party there last year. You run on the blue pads and the jets shoot up water from different ones all the time. Luca was too small to run last summer, but he'd love it now. Please can we go, it's so, so hot?'

For a moment the kitchen wavered and shimmered. Ursula put her hand to the back of the chair. Ruby and Luca looked expectantly at her, the lollies in their mouths. What was the harm? She could just sit and watch them, from a blanket. It was not so different from the garden.

'I don't see why not,' she said hesitantly. 'It's the hottest day of the year so far. We'll need sun cream and a blanket. Ruby, can you fetch the checked one from the playroom?'

Ruby darted like a bird, and Ursula stood for a moment, wiping her hands together as if to dry them. She filled a flask with iced squash – the children were bound to be thirsty – then quickly made some sandwiches and cut three slices of gingerbread. An apple each would be a good addition, she thought, and she put it all in a basket. Ruby came back into the kitchen holding the rug and some sunscreen.

'A picnic!' she said delightedly.

'It's just some snacks.'

Ursula knelt on the grass, feeling it criss-cross into the skin of her knees, and undressed Luca until he was wearing only his nappy. She took out the sun cream, squeezed it into her palm and gingerly began applying it, her fingertips attentive but wary. Luca stood patiently, glistening white beneath her hands.

'Ruby, do your arms and legs, then I'll do your back.'

When both children were done, Ruby took Luca's hand and ran towards the jets. All the other children were running between them, screaming and laughing as the water unexpectedly rose up and soaked them.

Ursula stood up, brushed the grass from her knees, and took the blanket from the basket. She held it close to her chest and then rolled it out in a sweeping gesture. How expansive it felt; the blanket flagged out before her, floating momentarily before it settled and sank to the grass. The flamboyance of the gesture was unsettling. She had trained her hands to make only small movements; how habitual it had become to diminish and to fold inwards, until everything she did was as self-contained and unobtrusive as possible. Had there been a time when she would have thrown the rug wide to the sky, clapping with pleasure as it sailed to the ground? She thought that there was.

A woman sat down near her.

'Don't the kids just love this?' she said in a soft Irish accent. 'Mine will run between them for hours. Look at them, falling over each other to be first. There's no more glorious a scent than a child warmed by the sun, with wet hair, is there? Which ones are yours?'

'They're not mine, I just look after them, but they're these two just coming now,' for here was Ruby, holding Luca's hand, both dripping wet and laughing.

'Would you like a sandwich, some sliced apple?' Ursula asked, reaching forward to scoop Luca into a towel, and wrapping him in it, one hand giving a swift dry to his hair, and putting him in a bundle on her lap, and the other giving him a sandwich. The Irish woman, chatty and convivial in the warmth of the sun and the merriment of all the squealing children, smiled and said, 'Well, you're certainly well-practised,' and Ruby bit into her sandwich and thought Ursula must have sun cream in her eye, because she was rubbing it a little at the corner, and it was making the watering worse.

They ran in and out of the jets until it was past five o'clock.

Each time Ruby looked back at the blanket, Ursula was sitting very still, keeping her eye on them both. Some of the mothers were lying back on the grass, their sleeves and trousers rolled up to get the sun to their skin. They lay on their sides watching their children through half-closed eyes. Ursula, meanwhile, Ruby thought, looked like a bird, watching the scatters of children as they ran between the water jets. Each time she looked over, Ursula raised her arm and waved. *I am watching you, I am watching you*, her upright body seemed to say. Ruby felt warm and safe. She clapped her hands as she ran to another jet.

Afterwards, in the kitchen, Ursula folded the blanket carefully, having shaken off the remaining grass outside. She washed up the Tupperware and placed the basket back on the fridge. Luca was sitting on the floor in his nappy, piecing together some Duplo. When Daniel came through the door, Ruby flew to him and told him about the water jets.

'Thank you, Ursula,' he said. 'Completely beyond the call of duty, but they sound as if they had a great time. Little, I'm going to have a cold beer in the garden. Luca, come to Daddy and we'll take that Duplo outside. Ursula, would you like a drink, a glass of wine maybe? After Oakthorpe Park, it's the least I can offer you.'

Ursula shook her head. 'I should be leaving.'

As she stepped into her own house, the hallway felt compressed with heat. She considered walking through each room, flinging the windows wide. She would not. She went into the kitchen, her eye drawn to the bean. The blotting paper was dry. She stood for a moment, the day shifting like sand within her. The feel and scent of Luca as she put sunscreen on him, the weight of him bundled in a towel on her lap, Ruby's eyes seeking her out as she sat on the blanket; the stripy sweetness of the ice lollies, the raspberry juice stain on the children's lips, the orange blossom, the determined rose, the insistent call of the blackbird. Life. Life tugging and tapping and insisting on being allowed in. She resolved not to yield. She would water the bean, but in a desultory fashion.

42

Ruby looked at her bedside clock. It stared back whitely at her. Quarter past nine. It had been hot for days. Outside, a bird was still singing. She could not get to sleep. Her legs were restless and twitchy, her whole body felt hot and bothered. She listened for Ursula moving downstairs. She couldn't hear a thing. Perhaps she was watching television. Maybe she was knitting. Ruby imagined the needles going clickety-click, Ursula's fingers making rows of stitches without even looking. The thought didn't make her feel sleepy. She wriggled her legs, and scratched the skin on her ribcage. In the corner of the room she could hear a fly buzzing. Outside, the bird was still singing. She lifted the edge of the curtain. Still light. Ursula said it was almost the longest day of the year. In next door's garden she could see some clothes left out on the line. A shirt flapped at her forlornly. Now her nose was itchy.

She lay back on her pillow. What would Mummy be doing? She counted back on the clock face. She might be eating lunch. Daddy had gone to a meeting, and then had to go out for dinner with the same people. She listened for his car. It was too early yet. The itchiness seemed to have spread from the tip of her nose upwards to her eyebrows. She scratched those too, and rubbed her heels against the sheet. She turned on her side, and then back to her tummy. Her forehead felt hot. Maybe she'd feel better with a drink of water.

She sat up in bed and thought about calling Ursula. What

could she expect her to do? If Mummy were here, she'd climb into bed with her. They'd lie on their sides, so they were like spoons in the cutlery drawer, and Mummy would sing softly, sometimes just hum if she was tired too, and Ruby never knew at what point she fell asleep, just that when she woke in the morning, spread out like a starfish, Mummy had crept out. Her shoes were often still by the bed. She was properly thirsty now. Maybe she should get a drink. Outside her window the bird had stopped singing. The fly had gone quiet too. Perhaps it was sleeping, tucked up behind the pelmet of the curtain. She looked at the clock again. It was a quarter to ten.

She went out onto the landing and along to the bathroom, where she let the tap run until the water was cooler and pooled some in the palms of her hands. She drank a few scoopfuls and patted the back of her neck for good measure. Maybe that would help. She had just climbed back into bed when she heard Ursula's footfall on the stairs.

'Are you awake, Ruby? Are you out of bed?'

Ursula appeared in her room. There was no need to turn on the light. Ruby could make out her figure, a little fuzzy in the half-light, standing right by the door.

'I can't get to sleep. I've been trying for ages.'

'Do you feel poorly?'

'No, I'm just hot and bothered. I think I'm too tired now, everything feels twitchy.'

'Try and lie still.'

'I tried that. It didn't work. I just had a drink of water.'

Ursula seemed uncertain whether to go or to stay.

'Is there anything I can bring you? Anything I can do to help?'

Ruby shook her head. Ursula peered through the twilight.

'Would you like a night light on? Maybe the window open wider? Although, if you choose both, it will bring in the moths.'

'Why do moths like light?'

'I'm not sure; there must be a scientific reason. Although, if I were a moth, I think I'd like the light too. You can understand how it draws them on through the darkness. It would have a kind of comfort.'

'Are moths the same as butterflies?'

'I think so; one made for the day and one for the night. Most things have a pattern, a balance.'

Ursula's voice seemed lower through the now almost dark.

'If we keep talking, it will keep you awake even longer.'

'Will I be too tired for school tomorrow?'

'Don't think about that. Worrying about whether you will be tired tomorrow is the best way of staying awake.'

The dark, now it had arrived, seemed to be pouring like smoke into the room. Ruby couldn't see Ursula any more, just the smudge of her outline, over by the door. Her voice seemed to float. Ruby suddenly felt anxious. Ursula would go downstairs soon, and she would still be wide awake. All the things of the night-time would be awake alongside her, whilst everything else slept. She imagined an owl swooping low over the garden. The washing line, the prop, her skipping rope, Luca's bike – they were all out in the soft soot of the darkness. It was an unsettling thought.

Ursula cleared her throat softly. Ruby's legs jittered and twitched. She didn't want to be by herself. Sometimes, it would be nice to be Luca, who often got rocked to sleep. Mummy was so far away, and Daddy was out. She strained her ears for his car.

'Ursula,' she said hesitantly, 'please will you sit on my bed? Maybe that would help.'

She listened carefully. For a moment, there was no movement, and then she heard Ursula take a breath, and make five soft steps to the bed. She sat down at the end of it. Ruby tried to make out Ursula's face in the dark. She could still see her outline, but not her nose, her eyes, her mouth. She wished she would sing her a lullaby, even just hum like Mummy did when she was tired. Maybe she didn't know any lullabies; that would be understandable. Why would you know lullabies if you didn't have any children? Ruby turned on her side, her hand close to Ursula's leg. And then, through the darkness, her hand flexing as it lay on the sheet, she felt Ursula's hand first touch the back of her own, and then softly come to rest over it. Ruby's hand felt safe with Ursula's gently curled around it. She relaxed, and let herself drift into sleep.

Later, Ursula lay in the darkness of her own bed, the night air soft through the open window. How still it was. How every sound carried, and amplified.

Gideon was in the room with her. How he could be relied on to come, when sleep was evasive, when her body lay tight as a drum. Whichever way she turned her head, she saw him before her. That first morning in the office, her first glimpse of him, his immaculately polished shoes. Then, in the bar, handing her the peach Bellini, whose sweet stickiness rendered her lips incapable of easy speech. In the rain, by her flat, reaching forward to gently adjust the collar of her pyjamas. Reading E. M. Forster to her in bed in Venice. Taking her photograph opposite the church of Santa Maria della Salute. At her mother's house, in Solihull, a piece of Battenburg held bemusedly in his fingers. She saw him turn to her from the wheel of the RIB, and she recalled, that night, the feeling of a silvery hook invisibly pierced through her lip. The flower shop, before their wedding day, the deep buckets of flowers, and the bouquet he'd chosen for her. Now, at Daniel and Monica's, the same bloom just beyond the kitchen window, the fragrance bringing her to a halt, but with a laundry basket rather than bridal flowers in her hands. The first house he had bought for them, the scarf tied around her eyes, so that she stood on a path in Chalfont St Giles having no idea that she was being shown where her life was headed. How could she ever have conceived? His absolution, he'd called her. How the word rang stark down the years, when any possibility of that, of peace, he had so categorically, so definitively denied her.

And now, tonight, trembling at the outer edges of Ruby's bedroom, so perfectly attuned to the child's increasing anxiety, so familiar with the restlessness of a warm summer night which kept one awake, and feeling stricken about doing what she knew she ought to do; reach forward and comfort the child, stroke her forehead, her cheek, perhaps sing to her softly. And the lullabies were so long buried, and the vigilance, the gentleness, of a woman beside the bed of a child so long denied, that she had stood at the threshold of the bedroom, wanting Ruby to fall asleep without intervention, and the conversation had fluttered between them with the soft beat of moths' wings, and still Ruby was awake, and still Ursula hovered beyond her, until Ruby asked her directly to come and sit on the bed. And she had done so. It seemed such a simple, such an undeniable, request. And she had sat, first so tentatively, Ruby inching hesitantly towards her, and it felt like the culmination of so many moments between them; the child's need for comfort so plain, the darkness swirling about them both. And when Ursula reached forward to take Ruby's hand, containing its smallness, its vulnerability, in her own, it had been all she could do not to weep, because of all the things Gideon had done, and how they paraded before her now, all the things he had done with such unmitigated success. And perhaps his triumph, his complete victory, was most clearly illustrated on this night, because she could still not sit, all these years later, and hold the hand of a child without it causing her heart to break all over again.

Ursula got up from her bed and walked down into the kitchen. She made some camomile tea and sat on a stool, her fingers webbed around her white china mug. On the side, the bean was growing fiercely, defiantly, the shoot parting into two green leaves and the root sprouting additional whiskery tendrils. It had resisted her attempts to deny it, and she had begun watering it as a matter of course.

That was the problem with life. Once let in, it bustled into every available space. Nature abhorred a vacuum, which she'd so diligently tried to become. She touched the tiny green leaves with the very tip of her finger. She hoped Ruby was sleeping peacefully. The feel of her small hand remained with Ursula still.

43

They sat facing Daniel, an auditor, an epidemiologist, and Charlie, who was dispensing courtesies.

'And to stress,' he said, 'this is still at an informal stage.'

Daniel felt resentful. Was Charlie's comment meant to be consoling? It didn't feel like it. They'd eat him alive, given the chance, and he was hardly sitting there feeling compliant. How sanctimonious they looked, the auditor with a greyish pallor. If he marched them down to theatre, showed them a patient strapped down, spine exposed and raw, they'd probably keel over. And yet they sat in judgement upon him. They had the air of a firing squad. He tried to keep his temper from rising.

'What I'd like to do,' he said, 'is to show you an alternative interpretation of the operations listed as contributing to my increased post-operative complication rate. I am confident that, if we examine the figures afresh, I can help you to understand why there might have been subsequent complications. If you'd like to take a look at this chart, it shows how I have resegmented the material.'

He clicked on the slides he had taken hours over, showing which patients had pre-existing conditions, which had other factors to take into account, and which had had subsequent operations, carried out by others, which might have clouded the data. His audience sat silently, scribbling notes onto their tablets. Daniel focused on keeping the bitterness from his voice.

'And here,' he said, 'if we consider Patient D, you can see

from the notes that – prior to my operating on him – he was found to have had a syrinx, which can cause neurological symptoms. The reoccurrence of it was highly likely from the outset. Patient E had a serious heart condition, which made even the fact that she survived the anaesthetic significant. This was achieved, as the case notes show, because of the speed with which the operation was carried out. The post-operative complexities were minor – drop foot, as I believe the notes confirm – and yet, if she had not been operated on, this patient had a significant risk of death from the compression of the thoracic cavity on an already compromised heart.'

He went through every case they had highlighted. Charlie Grace said, at about number twelve, that perhaps they had enough mitigating counter-evidence, but Daniel turned to him coldly and said he would like the opportunity to clear up any misunderstanding about all the operations concerned.

'Especially,' he said, 'in the light of the fact that in the last four weeks you have removed eleven patients from my lists, and in four cases delegated them to far less experienced junior surgeons.'

At the end of the session, the auditor and epidemiologist left. Charlie rubbed his hands together a little awkwardly.

'Good work,' Charlie said. 'That all seemed pretty conclusive. I'm guessing it will come back with your figures completely exonerated. I can see there will be no need to ratchet this up to a Capability Procedure.'

'Lucky me, Charlie. And thanks for the compliment. I'd like to think I always do good work, even when the odds are so heavily stacked against me.'

Afterwards, Daniel returned to his office. He felt oddly deflated. Shouldn't vindication feel sweeter? He could ring Cassie and tell her; he could count on her to be exuberant. He could phone Monica, when she woke up, and run her through it, but garnished with the right outcome so the account could be totally upbeat.

He'd also tell Ursula. He still felt a residual discomfort that she'd glimpsed, that morning, how much he felt himself professionally to be on the line.

When he came into the house, Ursula was clearing away toys and Ruby was throwing a soft ball for Luca, trying to teach him to catch.

'Good news,' he said. 'Successful meeting today. The auditors accepted they were wrong. Drama over. Everything back to as it was. At ease.'

Ursula glanced up, said, 'Oh good', and carried on putting plastic building blocks into a crate. She turned and carried the crate into the playroom.

Good? Daniel lifted his hands in a gesture of confusion. Was that it? Not even a smile? Was the woman made of stone? No, she evidently was not. But you would have thought that she might have summoned up a little more enthusiasm, might at least have given a nod of recognition to all the time he'd spent marshalling his evidence.

He turned towards the children. Cassie would tell him that Ursula's job was to look after them, not him, and she would be correct. But it would have been nice if Ursula had smiled, maybe said, *That's great*, and tried to look as if she'd meant it. Now, in the hallway, she was putting on her coat. He'd been thinking about offering her a glass of wine, to celebrate. Most likely that would have been met with cool neutrality as well.

Later, he called Monica, who seemed blithely nonplussed that he hadn't told her earlier.

'So just to clarify,' she said, 'the national average was two per cent and yours was supposedly five per cent – how much time and money did it take to track the difference of three?'

She sounded very far removed from it all. The way she said it made it all seem a storm in a teacup. It hadn't felt like one. It was hard to explain how infuriating that first meeting with Charlie Grace had been. He didn't elaborate. Perhaps his expectations of both marriage and employee relationships were too high. It was evidently presumptuous to think that your wife and your housekeeper both might take your side.

He refocused his attention to listen to an account of the lead actress's diva tendencies, and then Monica started laughing about an encounter she'd had in a food market. He ended the call feeling disgruntled and irritable, and decided to pour himself a drink. Maybe, he reflected, just as Cassie predicted, instead of keeping the home fires cheerfully burning, he was turning into a needy solipsist who drank grudgingly alone.

44

Sports Day. Daddy would come. He might be late, but he said he would try his absolute best. Often he had to be late, but he still came.

Ruby sat in the row of Year Fours, craning her neck to where the parents' seats were filling up. Claudie's mum was right by the finish line, and she'd saved a whole row. A few minutes earlier she'd come to check that Claudie was 'properly hydrated'. Ruby stretched taller to peer beyond the seats to the area of school field which had been roped off for parking. She couldn't make out Daddy's car. She squinted. Maybe an operation had taken a long time. Maybe it was complicated. That happened often. Maybe Daddy wouldn't be coming, even though he would have tried his absolute best. Claudie's mum would have something to say about it – probably, *Poor Ruby*, said loudly enough for everyone to hear. Ruby resolved to run like the wind, teeth gritted. Daddy would be cheering from theatre; she'd just imagine it like that. She craned her neck again. Was that him? No, it was Sophie's dad. He was tall with dark hair too. Most of the seats were full. It was almost eleven o'clock. She looked back towards the car park. Having somebody watch didn't mean you ran faster.

Ursula answered the phone, casting her eyes to the kitchen clock. It was almost eleven. Phones ringing unexpectedly always had the power to unnerve her. A call in the night was like a jump lead to the heart. Now Daniel spoke hurriedly to her.

'Ursula. I'm caught up in an operation that's much trickier than we anticipated. I'm not going to be able to duck out for Ruby's Sports Day. Is there any way you could pop along? I understand if it doesn't work, but I know it would mean a lot to Rubes.'

'I . . . I . . . I'll do my best.'

'Thanks. Sorry to be abrupt, I have to get back into theatre.'

She stood in the kitchen, and looked down at her empty hands. Sports Day. School. Other parents. Other children. Unbearable. She felt her skin tingle and took a deep breath. *It would mean a lot to Rubes.* Anxiety plucked at her breastbone. She pictured Ruby expectantly looking for Daniel, already accepting that Monica couldn't be there. She pulled back from the thought. Daniel hadn't said she had to go. He'd said he'd understand if it didn't work. He wouldn't ask for an explanation; he'd accept that she just hadn't made it. The clock's tick seemed to get louder. She sat down at the table, closed her eyes, and tried to gather herself. A wave of heat passed through her. She looked at the clock again. She went into the utility room and switched on the iron.

Ruby watched the Year Twos complete their running race. The winners stood on the little podium and the head teacher gave them their medals. The girl who came first kissed it like she'd won the Olympics and waved to the rows of parents like a proper athlete. The Year Threes walked in line from their seats, and stood in rows at the start line. One of the teachers walked along with a tray of cups of water, giving everybody a drink. Mr Stephens, the music teacher, called out the runners' names through the loudspeaker. As the Red Class race began, all the parents were cheering and clapping. Ruby bit her lip and thought of Mummy last year, lying on the blanket with Cassie and Luca. She would be fast asleep now. Maybe she didn't even know it was Sports Day. It would be easy to forget, now her days were so different. The Year Three Red

Class winner ran through the tape. Ruby scanned the rows of parents again. He wasn't there. He definitely wasn't there. She looked down at her feet. Daddy wasn't coming. She took a big swallow and resolved to describe it to him tonight; she'd use her words carefully, remember to tell him that it was hot, especially on her neck in the waiting line, that Mr Griffiths kept telling everyone not racing to keep their sun hats on and make sure they had applied sunscreen, that there were cups of tea and biscuits for the parents, and that the caretaker had painted the white podium with the Olympic rings. If she did all that properly, and remembered all the details, it would make them both feel he'd been there. She decided not to look along the parents' seats again. Instead, she'd focus on feeling determined. That would be more sensible. Miss Cameron called her class forward.

Ruby stood on the start line, and Claudie lined up next to her. She jostled Ruby a little, making sure her elbow was in front.

'Mummy made me special granola this morning for breakfast. Let's see if the almonds work,' she said. 'Oh look, my daddy's here too, and my grandparents. They're right by the finishing line.'

Ruby didn't answer. She watched Miss Cameron with the whistle.

'Year Four, Blue Class, are you on your marks, and getting ready?'

Ruby clenched her fists tightly. In the pause that followed, she felt her stomach flip and turn like a dolphin. And then, in the flicker of hot silence, a voice that was familiar, but which she'd only ever heard speak softly, shouted – really shouted – 'Go Ruby!', the words ringing out from the side of the track and, in a blur, as the whistle blew, and as Ruby's legs pumped fast, faster, fastest down her lane, she saw Ursula, it was definitely Ursula. And when Ruby crossed the line victorious, her arms raised in the air, her heart banging against her vest, Claudie huffing and puffing way back behind her, she turned to see Ursula standing at the side of the track, looking like her usual self, and as if the voice – the massive voice which had shouted so loudly – had been quickly and neatly put away in a drawer.

Later, Ursula sat in her chair, the evening light falling in long shadows beyond her.

When she thought about it, her hands trembled again, a whisper of nerve endings running from her temples to her upper lip.

She reconsidered her morning, the moment, unexpected, seemingly unbidden, when she flicked off the iron, grabbed her car keys and made for the door. The drive to school, her breathing faster, shallower, and getting out of the car, and the walk towards the group of parents gathered on the school field. Her legs felt as if they had been disconnected from her hips, her muscles and tendons jerkily connected like the strings of a puppet. Beneath her, the ground played its familiar tricks. The spraunchy, springy grass rolled away to reveal itself as the bald, spherical surface of the earth, and she was aware of it spinning and turning blackly through space, her feet maintaining their purchase by uncertain means, the inside of her ears rolling and giddy with the vastness of what lay beyond her. Inside her a rushing, a flooding of her blood into each part of her body, so that everything pulsed with fullness. The chatter of the parents buzzed in her head, their laughter ricocheting between the planes of her skull, the sun slapping the back of her neck with a broad fat palm.

She picked her way through the clusters of people, *Excuse me, excuse me, please,* her voice feeling as if it could only just inch its way out of her lips, might be snatched away by the breeze, or sucked up by the intake of the teacher's breath which preceded blowing the whistle. The tape at the end of the track fluttered whitely beyond her, and made all that was above it and below it shimmer and threaten to burst into flames, and the world densely rolled and shifted once more beneath her feet, and she looked at Ruby, lithe and bony-shouldered in her white running vest, her eyes facing resolutely, determinedly ahead.

Where her shout came from, she was still uncertain. It came like a roll of heat, licking up from her bones, from the deep, secret places within her, from the curls and scoops of her joints, from each cell of her being. When it came out of her mouth, it was a roar, it truly felt like a roar, or like something geological which had accumulated invisibly for years, and was now released with an ear-splitting shattering of rock. She registered, for the briefest of split seconds, Ruby's sideways glance and realisation of her presence, and it was as if a wave had burst over her, encasing her in a curl of turquoise water, and she was like a surfer who then emerges triumphant beyond it. But instead she stood quietly, her body softening and calming. Her mouth felt completely empty, as if the two words had been as a catapulted boulder, and she stood utterly still, attempting composure, as Ruby ran over to greet her. They stood a little apart from each other, the medal glinting between them, and a teacher walked past, offering them cups of water. When she swallowed, it felt as if the water, blood-warm from the heat of the sun, coursed straight through her body, spilling out onto the grass through the veins in her feet.

Now, feeling spent with exhaustion, Ursula thought of how she had answered Daniel when he thanked her for going. *I was glad to be there for her*, she'd said. He could not know what those words took.

The twilight gathered around her, and she rubbed her hands on her knees. The image of Ruby's body, breasting the tape, lit by a sharp slice of sunlight, pressed against her eyelids. She would be glad of the darkness when it came. And Monica would be home soon. This was an assuaging thought.

45

Ursula pulled up at the garden centre. This was a step further than buying the lolly mould, and not quite so easily rationalised. She wouldn't ask Daniel to reimburse her, it wouldn't cost much. Yesterday, after school, when they'd all been in the garden, Ruby had said she wished she could grow some vegetables, maybe some flowers. It was such a reasonable, wholesome request.

Ursula sat for a while in the car park. She'd paved over her own garden. It was simpler, tidier. Once a year she sprayed the weeds which struggled up in the cracks between the paving stones. She had intermittently been surprised by the tenacity of flowers. Once, a single stem of lavender, then a scramble of variegated thyme, and a hot pink flower which she was unable to name. One spring, an aquilegia, the colour of Parma violets. She had uprooted them all, her hands, afterwards, fragrant with the lavender and thyme. When the autumn came, she swept up the neighbours' leaves from the paving with a rigid bristle brush. It underlined both the severity of her choice and the absence of the flowers, to be dragging the leaves stiffly across concrete rather than raking them in soft drifts across a lawn.

I'm not a gardener. She'd said that to Ruby, and mostly it was true. Sometimes, she had held the bottom of the ladder for Geoffrey as he trimmed the pleached hornbeams, or the wisteria, or a climbing rose. Once, she'd stood in a shower of blush petals as he pruned something above her. The vegetable patch had been Rose's, and Ursula had helped her with that. It was this

knowledge she drew on now in the garden centre, choosing
tomatoes, strawberries, lettuce and peas. She hesitated by the
pumpkins; Ruby would love them. She could watch them grow
until the autumn and then decorate them for Halloween. Monica
or Daniel could help her to hollow one out; she could put it on
the doorstep, ready for trick or treating. Ursula stayed her hand,
which was hovering over the pumpkin seedlings. She should not
anticipate that. It was no business of hers what Monica's family
might be doing when her contract was long finished. She moved
on from the pumpkins, her eye caught by the jewel colours of
sweet peas. They were surely permissible. She put them into her
trolley.

Ruby walked across the playground, keeping her head low. Claudie
was getting meaner. Now, her smooth words were giving way to
jeers.

'Look at Ruby's funny hair,' she said to Stella at playtime.
'Look at how she walks. Look how ugly her shoes are. No wonder
her mummy has gone away.'

Ruby had ignored her. At least, she'd tried to look like she was
ignoring her, and had played with some of the other girls. But
Claudie came over to where she was in the playground, her group
of friends clustered around her.

'Let's see what Little Miss Not-Perfect is doing now, shall we?'

Ruby had balled up her fist. How satisfying it would be to
push Claudia, or hit her, but that wouldn't solve anything. Claudie
would cry, instantly, loudly, and Ruby would be in trouble; that
was the way it worked. She'd picked up a skipping rope, started
skipping determinedly.

'Let's count how many she can do,' said Claudie. 'I bet hardly
any.'

In English, Claudie had accidentally knocked some water over
Ruby's book.

'Oh, I'm so sorry; oh, it's all wet. Sorry, Miss Cameron. I accidentally knocked my water over Ruby's book.'

Miss Cameron pegged it on the line that was used for drying paintings. She gave Ruby a sheet of paper and told her to carry on working on that.

'What a shame,' Claudie said. 'I feel so awful. I hope it doesn't mean your English book can't be picked for display for the Open afternoon.'

Now, at home time, Ruby watched across the playground. Claudie was whispering something to Stella and Lucy, her mouth covered by her hand. All three girls were looking at her.

Walking home it felt as if someone had put a small stone in her chest. When she took a big breath, it felt like it was blocking where the air came in.

Ursula was not in the kitchen. Ruby called to her, listening at the bottom of the stairs. No sign. She went out into the garden; perhaps she was doing the mowing again. Ruby hoped not. She wasn't sure she wanted to tell Ursula about Claudie, but it would be nice if she could just sit alongside her while Ursula was doing something quietly.

Ursula was digging. That was unexpected. She'd cleared a patch of what had been a tangle of nothingness, down by the fence.

'South facing,' she said, as Ruby approached. 'I think that's the trick. I've been watching where the sun moves, and I think this bit gets the most.'

'What are you doing?' Ruby asked.

'I thought, seeing as you are champion of bean-in-a-jam-jar growing, and you said you were interested, that you could have a little patch in the garden to grow things. Look – look there – I've bought you strawberries and tomatoes and lettuce and peas, all sorts, and sweet pea flowers because they will grow quickly up the canes and the more you cut, the more flowers you get.

You can put them on the table in the kitchen and they will look beautiful.'

Ruby thought she might start to cry. She swallowed a lump in her throat. All Claudie's meanness, and then all Ursula's kindness, clearly laid out on the grass, the plants, and twine and canes and little plastic labels to write on and then push into the ground.

'Do you want to get something to eat – there are biscuits in the tin – and then I should have finished turning over the soil and you can get the trowel and start planting?'

Ruby nodded. Ursula's face had caught the sun. She was flushed, and as she wiped her forehead with the back of her arm she looked stronger than on the first day, when she'd ducked from the possibility of rain as if the drops might actually wound her.

Ruby went inside, ate a biscuit and changed out of her school uniform. Damn Claudie; damn damn damn her. Thinking the word wouldn't make the sky fall in. She wouldn't let Claudie spoil Ursula's kindness. She went back outside, picked up the trowel and did as Ursula showed her.

It was a perfect patch. When she stood back to admire it, an hour and a half later, it was definitely a perfect patch. The tomato plants were tied to green sticks, and the peas and the sweet peas were all set to scramble up a wigwam made from bamboo canes. The lettuces were different colours; some all green, some flecked with purple. She'd dotted bright coloured geraniums and orange Californian poppies between the rows. ('That's for Mummy,' Ursula said, standing back, 'so that when you send her a photo you can show her a part of your patch is American.')

Ursula went into the kitchen and fetched two glasses of squash on a tray. As she walked towards her, Ruby could hear the ice cubes clinking.

'It's very hot work, being a gardener,' Ursula said. 'Here, let's sit and drink these and then we can go and fetch Luca and show him what you've done. I bought him some sunflowers and he can plant them right at the back. If they grow like they should do, they'll be taller than Daddy, with flower heads as big as dinner plates.'

She handed Ruby the squash and looked at her face closely.

'Ruby, is there anything wrong?'

'No, nothing wrong, just . . .'

Ruby trailed her fingers through the grass.

'Just?' Ursula said. She wasn't looking at Ruby now, but instead straight ahead at the patch. That made it easier. Ruby looked straight ahead at it too.

'Just, just Claudie, being mean, saying stuff, not just about Mummy now, but me, how I look, my shoes, how many I skip. All the time today. And she spilt water on my book.'

'I see.'

'But if you tell Daddy, he'll just go and tell Miss Cameron, or send her an e-mail. It's not really important, Claudie's not really important.'

Ursula paused and then said, 'You know everything she says is nonsense and it's just because she's jealous. But she shouldn't be spiteful. Try not to let her bother you. Shall we go and fetch Luca? He's going to be so impressed with your patch.'

Ruby got up to go. Sharing it had made her feel a little bit better, but Ursula couldn't do anything about it. It wouldn't change anything tomorrow, or the day after that.

46

Daniel hadn't seen Cassie since the outcome of his hearing. He'd phoned her to tell her how it had gone and she'd cheered. He wasn't sure in what spirit she meant it, or whether she'd taken the whole thing entirely seriously. Perhaps, like Ursula, she'd questioned whether it was the worst thing that could happen. Regardless, he'd invited her for supper, and as he pulled up in the driveway he smiled when he saw her Fiat 500. No doubt she'd be inside playing the Lord of Misrule with the children. Ursula's car was still there.

When he came in, they were in the kitchen. Ursula was washing up, Cassie was dandling Luca, and he could see Ruby out in the garden, twisting her sweet peas up the wigwams like Ursula had shown her. It would not be long before they were in flower. He resolved to send Monica a photo of Ruby holding the first bunch that she cut. He felt his shoulders relax. The mood in the kitchen felt harmonious, purposeful. Daniel felt a flicker of relief. His family had not been bent out of shape by Monica's absence. He had a sense of it as more pliable, flexible and robust than he had imagined.

Cassie came towards him and gave him an exuberant kiss on the cheek.

'Result!' she said. 'How could they ever have doubted you?'

He smiled.

'And,' she continued, 'now you are so smoothly and predictably off the hook,' – she handed him Luca – 'it's time to support me.' She rustled in her bag. 'Seeing as you are so spectacularly on your lonesome every evening, I thought you might come to this symposium. I'm giving a presentation and could do with the moral support. If nobody applauds my paper, I'll be expecting you to step up to the plate with some actual whooping.'

She handed him a brochure.

'All the great and the good are talking; it's a real step-up for me. The audience will be a combination of barristers, media types, academics. It could take my profile to a whole new level.'

Daniel scanned the contents.

'There's nothing uplifting in the content,' she said. 'If you run down the list of presentations, you can see it's pretty much an account of all the things men do to women when they love them too much, or don't love them at all, or use them as a focal point for all that's actually wrong with themselves. Throw in some sexual violence, the impact of internet porn, and a sprinkling of misogyny, and you've pretty much got the mix. You can be reassured that in comparison, hospital compliance procedures and auditing are mostly tickety-boo. Positively civil. Wouldn't you say so, Ursula?'

Ursula made no comment, and continued to dry up.

'Sounds like a great night,' Daniel said. 'Let me see: rape porn, family annihilators, domestic abuse. One of those nights when I can hold my head high as a man, I'm guessing.'

'As a brother, yes, as a supportive brother, yes indeedy. So you'll come?'

The platter in Ursula's hands crashed to the floor and Cassie jumped, startled. Luca began to wail. From the garden, Ruby turned her head towards the kitchen.

Ursula's hands flew to her mouth.

'I'm sorry. I'm so sorry. How stupid of me. Just butter fingers. I am always so careful. I'm sorry. Obviously I'll pay for it.' Her cheeks flushed red.

She made towards the broom cupboard. 'Sorry, I'll clean it up. The children's bare feet.'

Daniel reached the broom before Ursula did.

'Don't worry, and of course I don't want you to pay for it. It's easily done, and it was just an accident. It's not a problem. Cassie, if you hold on to Luca, I'll sweep it up. Ursula, you have already stayed later than you are meant to. And it looks like I'm going to be asking you to babysit one night next week, so I think going home now is fully deserved. I'd bolt for it while you can.'

'But—'

'No buts, it's been a long day.' And now he called through the window to Ruby, 'Have you got shoes on, Little? Don't come in yet unless you have.'

Ursula, standing marooned in the centre of the floor, twisted her fingers. 'I'm sorry,' she said again. She seemed unable to step over what surrounded her feet.

'Honestly, Ursula, it doesn't matter. Cassie, can you pass me that cardboard box from by the bin? I'll put the pieces in it and then Sellotape it closed. Cassie? Cassie? Can you pass me that box?'

Ursula stepped over the broken pieces and put on her jacket. Cassie, instead of listening to Daniel, seemed to be preoccupied with staring at Ursula hurrying away.

'Please say goodnight to Ruby for me,' she said.

As the front door closed behind her, Cassie turned to Daniel. Her face looked perplexed.

'Horribly familiar; weirdly horribly familiar,' she said. 'She looked on the verge of tears. And the expression on her face, when she'd just dropped it – fleeting, but detectable all the same – was fear. I promise you. I've seen it too many times to be mistaken. The way she apologised, her flushed face, her twisting fingers. God, Daniel, it was awful. I'm shocked. The woman looked terrified that you'd be angry she'd broken a plate.'

Daniel looked up from his sweeping.

'Steady on,' he said mildly. 'I think you might be reading too much into it. She's just a careful person, a very careful person. The crash, it was a hell of a noise, it interrupted our conversation and she's so discreet she'd have hated that, and the mess. I think she was just flustered, and probably tired. I certainly don't think she was scared. We've never had an irritable word, which is pretty remarkable, and completely down to her being so brilliant at what she does.'

'Listen to me, believe me. You were busy making for the broom. You weren't looking at her. I was. There's a man somewhere in her back story, someone abusive; I'd lay money on it. Trust me.'

'But no one's asking you to do that, Cass. It's unnecessary and intrusive to speculate. It's just a broken plate, at the end of a busy day. She's probably had Luca on her hip since five. She was working too quickly, and just trying to get home. Butter fingers, she said it herself. The problem with you being surrounded by so much darkness on a daily basis is that you see it everywhere. Not all women have dysfunctional relationships with men, particularly women over fifty who give no real indication of ever having had any involvement with anyone at all.'

'Okay, dismiss it, even though you've said that she's such a closed book you haven't a clue about her beyond what you see for half an hour at either end of the day.'

'Maybe, but in that short time I see a woman who seems the epitome of calm composure. Can we stop talking about this? If you pass me the box, I can empty the pieces into it, and we can have a glass of wine and put Luca in the bath, and Ruby can come in from the garden before she winds herself up the wigwams.'

Cassie passed him the box.

'I'll go and run the bath,' she said.

Standing by the taps, and swishing the water so that the bubble bath foamed, Cassie bit her lip. Daniel might discount it, but she knew what she'd seen. A woman afraid of how a man might react. Same old, same old, she thought, undressing Luca and lifting him into the water.

'Crash! Crash!' he said, clapping his hands and beaming. The foam flew up beyond him.

'It's all right for you, tiny male child,' she laughed, but with a trace of jaundice in her tone which she instantly regretted. She kissed him apologetically. Maybe Daniel was right; maybe her research, her case studies, made her suspect the worst. She should be more mindful of the good guys. That, and banish the memory of Ursula's fleeting expression, the scribble of some kind of remembered horror. She reached for the soap and began to wash Luca.

Ursula sat parked in her driveway, her head on the steering wheel. She willed herself to stop shaking. It was a plate. It was only a plate. She pressed her palms to her cheeks, which were still burning with heat. It had just slipped from her fingers. One minute she was half listening, the next it crashed to the floor. And Cassie's expression, like a key into a lock. Her eyes were pin-sharp; why had Ursula not noticed that before? Perhaps too busy distracted by the words which flew exuberantly from her mouth. What a smokescreen diversion they were.

Ursula stepped wearily from the car and went inside. In the hallway, the daylight was almost fading. She went to turn on the light, and then paused, her hand hovering over the switch. The twilight was soothing. She stood for a moment longer, trying to steady her breathing. Slowly taking off her coat, she realised she was still wearing her apron. What a panic she'd left in. She reached to untie it, took it off, and began to fold it neatly. In the hem of the fabric, her index finger snagged on a small shard of china. She rolled it between her finger and thumb. If she pressed down hard, it seemed capable of piercing her skin. She waited expectantly for a bead of bright red blood. None came. She held the tip of it carefully and traced a small criss-cross on her fingertip. The smooth elasticity of her skin resisted its fine point. She carried it to the bin, and dropped it in. She could not make herself bleed. How the body stubbornly, robustly, insisted on intactness; chose life, continuity, even when the mind and the spirit were overwhelmed at the prospect. The breath followed its own rhythm, even when the brain willed it to cease in the night.

She summoned up Mizpah. It was a Hebrew term, used in Genesis. 'The Lord watch between me and thee, when we are absent from each other.' The platter had crashed to the floor. Her hands had been unable to catch it.

She walked up the stairs – how tired, how bone-achingly tired she felt. Briefly, at the top of the stairs, she placed her hand flat to a door, and then brought it to her lips. She kissed her fingers softly. Was there consolation in Mizpah? The Lord will watch over the space between us. It was a reasonable extrapolation, even if solace was elusive.

She continued to her room.

47

Ursula sat by Ruby's vegetable patch, drinking a cup of coffee. It was all growing beautifully. Ruby watered it each afternoon when she got back from school, filling the watering can right to the top and then walking back to the patch, her body arced with the effort of carrying it, the muscles in her arm taut, the can knocking against her legs so that she left a trail of splashes where she'd been. Yet she had a cloud over her face – that was the only way Ursula could think of it – each day when she arrived back from school. Yesterday, her mood had been dejected. Ursula had simply said 'Claudie?' and Ruby nodded.

Ursula wound a sweet pea tendril round a cane. It had gone on long enough. Daniel should know, although Ruby had said an e-mail from him could make it worse. Maybe there was something she might do herself. She checked the thought. It wasn't her responsibility. There were channels, protocols. It probably happened all the time, especially in a girls' school. Little girls' words, sharp as tacks and so much harder to duck than the thrown punch of a boy.

At ten to three, Ursula stood agitatedly in the kitchen. Did she need a jacket? The thought of Claudie's mother made her feel sick. How polished she was, with her glossy composure, her considered casual elegance, her hard-edged confidence. Approaching her would be far worse than going to Sports Day. Ursula's legs suddenly felt weak. She stalled and put down her door keys.

Looking out of the window, she was reminded of Ruby's effortful strain as she carried the watering can to her patch. Ruby was dealing with Claudie each day. If Ruby could withstand it, endure it, then Ursula should be able to face her mother. She picked up her keys again, and randomly also an umbrella. The sky was bright blue, it hadn't rained for days. What did she think she was going to do with it?

Ruby looked out of the classroom window. She felt someone's hand slip a folded-up note into her dress pocket. She determined not to read it; it would probably say the same as the others. Glancing again through the window, she thought she could see Ursula. That was surprising, she hadn't expected her to come. Was it Ursula? She looked taller than usual, as if she were stretching her back so that it held her up high. She seemed also to be walking towards Claudie's mum, who was texting on her phone, and didn't seem aware that Ursula was walking towards her.

'Ruby,' said Miss Cameron, 'I'm sure whatever is happening outside isn't as interesting as what is on the page of your book.'

There was perhaps a tone of voice, Ursula thought, as she crossed the playground. A tone of voice that might still be available to her which she had not used for years. Was it nestled in a corner of her voice box, waiting for an occasion when it might be called upon to re-emerge? As she approached Claudie's mother, she cleared her throat.

Claudie's mother was texting, and then rummaging in her handbag for something. There was a flash of diamonds from her finger, a glimpse of a perfectly manicured nail. She looked surprised to see Ursula standing before her.

'Hello,' she said smoothly, 'I don't think we've met.'

How many times had Ursula rehearsed this in her head? She began, speaking quickly, firmly, without stopping to allow the other woman to interject.

'No, we haven't, although I know you are Claudie's mum. I help take care of Ruby. I just wanted to discuss something with you, without having to get school involved. I hope that's okay. The thing is – and Claudie looks a delightful child – but, recently, she's been a little unkind to Ruby, saying things which I know you wouldn't endorse. I'm just hoping you might be able to talk to her, might be able to stop it. As I said, I don't want to involve the school; all their protocols, school records and whatnot. It can so easily escalate. I'm just hoping that you can help Claudie to be as kind to Ruby as she is to the other girls in the class.'

Claudie's mother looked wary and defensive for a moment.

'I'm very surprised to hear this.' Her voice gathered momentum. 'Claudie has always spoken of Ruby with great fondness. She often asks if she can come and play. The fault is perhaps mine in not contacting you to arrange it. These things can sometimes appear more awkward when not dealing with a parent.'

'I understand that, and perhaps some play-dates might have diverted it, but we are where we are. I'm sure you will agree that you have no reason to doubt what I'm sharing with you. I just wanted us to have the opportunity to deal with it in a personal manner without school involvement. Don't you think that's preferable?'

Claudie's mother looked at Ursula sideways and seemed to recognise the opportunity she was being given.

'School protocols, school records; yes, you're right, it can all get terribly complicated very quickly.' She pressed her lips together with studied calm. 'I'm sorry to hear Claudie hasn't been her best self; it happens to us all sometimes, doesn't it? I will talk to her and make it very clear that any unkindness is unacceptable.'

'Thank you, I'm very grateful for your support. I'm sure it will make a very swift difference.'

Ursula looked across the playground.

'Goodness,' she said, 'the girls are out already. Sometimes I don't know where the day goes.'

'What did you say to her?' Ruby asked breathlessly as she ran up to Ursula.

'I asked her to talk to Claudie about being unkind, before it became necessary to let Miss Cameron know. Let's see if that works.'

Ruby glanced across the playground. Claudie's mum had crossed it, swept up Claudie's hand and was walking swiftly to the car. Ruby tried not to stare. She kept pace alongside Ursula.

'Do you know what an air punch is?' she said.

'No, I'm afraid I don't.'

'It's when you punch the air like this, when you've done something that's good and makes you happy.'

'I think that may be beyond me.'

'It doesn't matter, I'll do two, one for each of us.'

At home, when Ruby was watering her garden, Ursula sat in the kitchen. An air punch felt entirely appropriate. What struck her, as she began to prepare supper, was how much easier it was to be brave in the cause of a child than to summon up the same tenacity on her own behalf. Ruby had caused her to be brave. It was good to know her old voice was still in there.

48

He'd committed to going, so he should go. Daniel drove away from the hospital, feeling exhausted after an operation which had taken four hours. The thought of going to listen to presentation after presentation on domestic and sexual abuse wasn't an entertaining prospect. Cassie had texted him twice. *Dress down* said the first one, which was surprising, as he didn't think she'd expect him to arrive dressed as he did for his private practice, and the second said, *Don't be late,* which he hoped he could be relied upon not to be. She was obviously nervous. Cassie nervous was a daunting prospect.

He pulled into the driveway. Obligation was sometimes a kicker. Having said he'd attend, and having organised with Ursula that she would stay late, it would be unfair not to pitch up. His mother, anyway, would be pleased at his display of sibling loyalty and supportiveness. He smiled to himself. How odd to be still thinking of an additional reason why his doughty mother might think he was a good boy.

He opened the door and Ruby greeted him with a hug.

'Look, Daddy; I got my certificate in swimming today.'

'Little mermaid,' he said, and Ruby laughed.

'Daddy, your jokes are so rubbish.'

He lifted her up and kissed her. Ruby was a guaranteed tonic. What he'd give for a night watching television with her, getting fish and chips, eating them from the paper, and allowing her to stay up later than was sensible. When, he thought ruefully, did that start counting as a walk on the wild side? He turned his attention to Ursula, who was holding Luca further down the hallway. Luca, unusually, was grizzling, and Ursula seemed a little agitated.

'How's my champion boy?' he said.

'I've just given him some Calpol. He's a little hot and fretful.'

Daniel put his palm to Luca's forehead.

'The Calpol should kick in quickly. It's probably just a cold or something.'

He made to turn upstairs and Ruby said, 'Daddy, where are you going?'

'I'm going out, so I need to change. I'm going to listen to Cassie speak, at a meeting with all kinds of important people. I'm supposed to clap very loudly after her presentation, so that's what I'll do. Ursula's going to put you to bed and I'll be home soon after. I'll see you for breakfast tomorrow.'

'Can I come too? I could clap for Cassie.'

'It's not really suitable for children; it's about people not behaving well.' He was aware of his inaccuracy. It was not the time, he thought, to share with Ruby that most 'not behaving well' was carried out not by people but by men. What was the statistic Cassie had told him? Men were responsible for 85 per cent of all violent crime. It was baffling. Looking at Luca, restless in Ursula's arms, it was unbearable that boys should somehow grow up to be more disposed to aggression. *Spinal cord looks the same*, he'd told Cassie; *same messaging conduit between the brain and the body.* How did the message get so scrambled? The symposium probably wouldn't have the answer to that.

Ursula reached to take Ruby's hand.

'Not suitable at all,' she said, which Daniel thought was an unusually frank intervention. Although, he suddenly remembered, he'd seen Ursula turn the symposium contents paper face down on the hall table. Evidently, for a grown woman it wasn't exactly edifying reading either.

'Come on,' Ursula continued, 'let's go out into the garden for a little while. Maybe that will distract Luca and make him feel better. Shall you catch a butterfly for him? Where's your butterfly net? When I hung out the washing earlier, there were so many cabbage whites.'

When Daniel arrived at the legal chambers where the symposium was taking place, his first thought was how easy it was to distinguish between the professional tribes. The barristers were mostly in black; the women in well-fitted dresses, the men in expensively tailored suits. QCs' broad pinstripes, he thought, could give private-practice consultants a run for their money, but without the same preponderance of bow ties and silk pocket handkerchiefs. The media people looked sharp, fashionable, the women wearing colours he didn't have names for. The academics looked quirky; most were women with large dangling earrings, wraps, wooden-heeled clogs and complex patterned jackets. Cassie had opted for turquoise and dark brown, with chunky silver jewellery. *You look great,* he told her, knowing that at this point it was probably the best thing to say. Then, glancing down at the presentation titles, he worried if what he had said was an example of everyday sexism. Was telling his sister she looked great a confidence booster or a regrettable emphasis on how she looked over what she was about to say?

It was a minefield, he thought, making his way to his seat while Cassie went to check something with the organisers. Being a considerate man was strewn with all manner of complexities. Being a contemporary father, even more so. God help Ruby and Luca. In Monica's absence, were they feeling loved and secure? Ursula was certainly doing her part. He'd left her in the garden, dandling and soothing Luca. He looked at the agenda again. The fifth talk was entitled, 'Men who use women as the focal point for their own inadequacy'. He wondered if any women managed to do it back.

He looked up to see Cassie making her way towards him.

'The running order's slightly changed,' she said, picking her way through the chairs. 'A last-minute no-show, so I'll be on third, after "Funding Sources for Women's Refuges", and "Family Annihilators".'

'Top spot,' said Daniel, squeezing her arm. 'Bronze, silver, gold.'

Cassie smiled.

'Not tempted by a glass of warmish white wine?' she asked, gesturing towards one of the waitresses.

'No thanks, I've taken to heart what you said about me being a miserable bastard drinking alone.'

'And equally disinclined to be mingling with a bunch of strangers; I anticipated you'd pass on that and duck straight to the seating.'

'Yup. Just mindful there's no networking I could possibly be doing, and that's what everybody else seems mostly intent on. I think talking to me would count as drawing the short straw. I'm just sitting here absorbing what I'm going to be listening to.'

'I reckon you should feel a lot more cheery after you've heard this lot, and a whole lot more chilled about the stresses and strains of your wife working away for three months. In the scheme of what some people can think of to inflict upon their spouses, three months' solo parenting is pretty benign. The paper that precedes mine – it's a colleague who's put it together, it's horrifying. You'll see.'

The conclusion of the first paper was that there was pretty much no funding available for women's refuges. Daniel thought this might be added to the list of geriatric care, drug abuse, prison reform, legal aid, and a whole host of other things which patently needed solving but for which there also appeared to be no money available. It seemed an intractable problem. Tonight, he sensed, might keep him awake later rather than cheering him up about his own situation. How could Cassie steep herself in it and emerge with her sense of humour, her life energy, intact?

A slight woman stepped up to the podium. She put up a slide

which said simply, 'What's the worst thing you could do to someone you once loved?' The audience seemed to take a collective in-breath.

'I'm going to talk about family annihilators,' she said. Her voice was so quiet, even with the microphone, that Daniel felt his whole row was leaning forward to hear her.

'Family annihilators is a term we use for men – and I'm afraid it is overwhelmingly men – who kill their own children in an act of vengeance carried out to punish their estranged wives. This isn't to say that maternal infanticide doesn't happen, but it's usually a manifestation of mental illness, rather than spousal revenge. If you attune your eye, each week in the media you will see another case during a contact weekend, or in half-term, away on holiday; the mother mostly waiting, unsuspecting, for the children to be returned. I want to begin by getting you to think about this in a purely emotional way. It's an inversion, I'm sure you all recognise it as that. Even in this time of less clear paternal role models, there is still the vestige of a notion that a father's key role is to help to protect, to keep safe. Therefore, a father killing his own children to punish the woman who bore them is shocking in a way that demands careful consideration. It is both symptomatic of the most careful, the most meticulous planning and forethought – you will see details of this in the case studies which follow – and yet it is also barbaric beyond any moral coda.

So what turns a man into this kind of sociopath? Are there shared personality traits, shared demographics, shared circumstance? The data I'm about to show you reveals that not to be the case, apart from some commonplaces in being middle-aged and emotionally isolated. What this study reveals is a crime that is unusual because it is on the increase, when all other crimes of extreme violence are in fact decreasing. What deserves special consideration, within the context of this symposium, is that it is also a crime which may be considered a direct reflection of women's increased emancipation. Historically, women did not leave unreasonable husbands, taking their children with them, because they had no jobs, no economic power, and too much social stigma as a single parent. Now, no such barriers exist. The irony behind this most unforgivable of crimes is that it is a direct reflection of women taking control of their lives. The perpetrators feel anger that the woman has left them. They are no longer in control. It all comes back to control.'

Daniel was beginning to feel slightly sick, and still the woman ploughed on, with charts, data figures, lines on graphs that mostly went upwards, horrifying details of the attention to detail achieved by men intent on wreaking the worst possible vengeance.

He was beginning to wish her catalogue of atrocities would stop.

'As a final consideration,' she said (how long had she been talking; the whole room had gone so quiet?), 'I want to think about not just the immediate impact of this most contemporary of crimes, but also its aftermath. I would like to suggest that the whole point of this crime is to achieve something from which recovery is actually impossible; from which there can be no consolation, no softening of the blow. To illustrate this, I have some footage of women who have experienced this loss. This is from 1994.'

She played a short interview with a woman who sat each and every day by the gravesides of her children.

'And then there is this woman, who is interesting because she demonstrates how a sociopath husband manages to implicate his ex-wife in the enormity of his crime. She is tormented, you will see, by the idea that she failed to anticipate it happening; that, in failing to protect her children, she shares some of the blame. This is from an interview in 2002.'

The bolt that shot through Daniel's body nearly jolted him from his chair. Ursula. It was definitely Ursula. Younger, less wiped-smooth, but Ursula, falteringly talking.

'I had gone out running,' she said, 'at what turned out to be the exact time my ex-husband drove to a nearby layby and killed my two children, and himself, by attaching a pipe to the exhaust of his car. I was running along the same road, you see, but in the opposite direction. I wasn't there when my children needed me, when perhaps I might have spotted the car, might have wrenched open the door, might somehow have saved them. I was running in the opposite direction. For this, I can never forgive myself.'

Daniel didn't hear any of the rest of what was said. Ursula. Ursula had had children of her own. Her husband had killed them. She had been a mother; and she had lost two children. Daniel's mind bounced and rattled with things falling into place. Of course she hadn't wanted to look after children, when the memories of her own must have been so painful, so jagged. And hadn't Monica said, *Goodness, Daniel, for a woman who has no children she's unbelievably on the money.* And how standoffish he'd thought her, in her consistent failure to meet his eye; to look at him, to be friendly, to be anything but slightly hesitant at the periphery of his vision. How explicable that was. How difficult it must have been for her to either trust him as a man, or see him father his children. Daniel felt sick to his stomach. He put his head in his hands, and was then distracted by clapping. He looked up. Cassie had just finished speaking. He hadn't heard a word. Someone stood up and said there would now be a break for refreshments. He could see Cassie making her way towards him, her face expectant, animated.

'What did you think, did you think it was well received?' she asked.

'Cassie, didn't you see the presentation before, the family annihilators? For God's sake, Cassie, it was Ursula.'

'Daniel, what are you talking about? I was in a room just out there to the left, just checking through all my slides. I've only seen the raw data before. What are you talking about?'

'Ursula. There was an interview with Ursula, right at the end, where she talked about being out running when her husband murdered both her children. Ursula had children, Cassie, two children, and her husband murdered them when she left him. It was her, on the piece of film. Unmistakably her.'

'So that's why she dropped the plate, not butter fingers at all . . .'

'What?'

'You were reading out the titles of the presentations, don't you remember? She couldn't possibly have known it would include her case history, but I'm guessing just the term "family annihilator" would make her lose her composure. It would have been a knife to her heart. God, how awful. Unspeakable. No wonder she's so reticent.'

'Cassie, I'm sorry, I have to go home. *Is it the worst that can happen?* She asked me that when I told her about the audit. It makes sense now. From her perspective, an audit wouldn't even make it onto the radar. I thought she was being unsympathetic. I feel terrible.'

'Just go home. Go and say whatever words you can cobble together. Just know that nothing you say can make it any better.'

She squeezed his hand hard.

'I don't envy you. I don't know how I'll meet her eyes next time I see her. When I think of me waltzing through the agenda in your kitchen while she stood silently knowing more about it than I could ever conjecture.'

'We didn't know. We didn't know. It's not an excuse, but it's mitigating.'

Cassie looked unconvinced. She watched him leave, and was reminded of him as a child, walking, head down, into their father's study, ready to take the rap for something they'd both done.

49

When Daniel pulled up in the car, Ursula was standing in the window, holding Luca in her arms and pressing a compress, a flannel of some sort, to his head.

When he came through the door, she pre-empted him.

'He's still hot,' she said, 'I've given him a half-dose of infant ibuprofen as well as the Calpol. He's more settled now, but his temperature hasn't gone back to normal. I thought he was going to be sick, but he didn't really eat his supper, so I'm not sure he has anything in his stomach. Ruby was a star; she must have sung him thirty lullabies before she actually sang herself to sleep. She's on the sofa in his room; I've put a quilt over her. I haven't had a chance to carry her through. I didn't want to put Luca down in case he started crying again.'

It was only after she finished speaking that she lifted her eyes from Luca's face and half met Daniel's gaze.

'What's wrong, what else is wrong?' she said with alarm. 'What's happened?'

'Ursula, I saw you tonight. Not you, not you as you are now, obviously, but you as you were about ten years ago, after the night your . . . the night you were out running. In one of the presentations, they played a clip of you talking. I recognised you immediately. Ursula, I had no idea, I'm so sorry. I can't . . .'

She just said, 'Ohhhh' – that was what he told Monica later – but in a way that sounded as if all the breath might have left her body, along with everything that held it upright. Her skin blanched pale, her veins vivid in the turn of her neck. He was reminded of the structure of a leaf. Had even the memory of grief and pain the power to render one translucent? Daniel reached forward to steady her. He placed his hand on her arm, and she flinched from his touch. He understood why. How clear it now was, the way she always chose to remain beyond him. She turned her face from his. Luca was still in her arms. It seemed inappropriate, insensitive, to try to take him from her. He stood before her, his tongue heavy and useless in his mouth, and felt a flicker of self-loathing. All the years that he had prided himself on using language accurately, precisely, and now he was completely at a loss to find the right words to say to the winnowed-out woman who stood before him.

'I'm so sorry,' he said again. 'Ursula, I'm so sorry.' How bald, how ineffectual it sounded.

She was looking beyond him now. Her voice had regained its timbre. She spoke softly and evenly. Luca had hardly stirred. She seemed to be speaking to the room beyond him.

'The truth comes out. Maybe deep down I knew it would. I'd forgotten about the interview; it was from a time when I thought talking might help. I soon realised it didn't. I opted, instead, for some kind of refuge in silence. At least, as much refuge as can be hoped for. I tell no one because there are no words, there is no use or purpose for any words, because there is nothing that can be said to make it any more bearable. I finally mustered the courage to leave my husband when my children were aged twelve and nine after years of bullying. What gave me the courage to leave was the thought that if I stayed they might grow into adults either damaged by his behaviour, or seeing it as an example. Six months after I left him, he killed them both. In my silence I bear witness to my children. It is a last, hopeless resort.'

'And in your daily life, in your actions, your kindness, you've been bearing witness to mine,' Daniel said softly. 'Thank you.'

'I tried to explain to Monica, at the start,' she murmured. 'I told her work is the only dignity. It adds structure to my days. Without it I would be like the other women I met, sitting alone every day by a graveside, or marooned, utterly beached, in a child's empty bedroom.' She handed him Luca. 'I've done nothing with all their things,' she said. 'My children's things. All their things are just as they were.' It was as if the thought had just struck her, the realisation of how many years had passed. 'I should leave. Please can we not speak of this again? I understand that you will want to tell Monica. I'm assuming Cassie knows already.'

Daniel nodded. She was trembling. He struggled with the notion that there was absolutely nothing he could do. When he lifted his eyes again she had silently left the room. He stood by the window and watched her drive away. Should he have offered that she stay?

He held his son closer. How inconceivable, the thought of harming a hair on his head.

He walked up the stairs to where Ruby was sleeping on Luca's sofa, curled contentedly on her side. A year earlier, he remembered, he'd finished reading *The Road* at three in the morning, and he'd found himself ambushed to tears by a book which had articulated so clearly to him what it meant to be a father. He'd gone into Luca's room and taken him, sleeping, from his cot, and carried him into Ruby's room, and he'd sat with them both until the sky turned silver with the dawn, and he had promised them, sitting beside them as they slept, that he would be there for them as long as he had breath in his body. And now, tonight, he renewed that promise, his heart sick at the thought of Ursula, and her children's ghostly bedrooms. He was incapable of understanding a man who could do such a thing. *Daddy loves you*, he said to his sleeping children, and he meant it and felt it with every atom of his being.

50

Ursula lay on her bedroom floor, flat on her back on the carpet, her palms pressed to its softness, her heart still pounding and racing.

Again, again, so familiar, the sensation of the earth spinning and turning dizzily beneath her, rolling through vast blackness, so that she must press the scoop of her spine flat and lie still, absolutely still, to avoid tumbling into the vastness; one bald, shocked cry resonating through space as she fell through the darkness. She dug her nails into the carpet.

Gravity, that night, had not seemed potent enough to hold her; to stop her from falling into an abyss of despair, of hysterical grief, and tonight she felt again the same tipping, the same sliding, the same losing of contact with the certainty, the solidity, of the earth. She saw again Daniel's shocked face before her, his attempt to find some words, any words, to express what he had learned.

Her secret – how long had she buried her secret? – cultivating over the years a kind of invisibility which allowed her to avoid interaction. The gossip had taken a while to peter out; people pointing across a street, *Yes, she's the one, can you imagine, how awful.* She'd held her breath until the words washed over her and away.

On the night it happened, what a run it had been: the air knife-edged with the promise of a silver frost, her breath chilling into clouds before her. How absurd her memory of the detail still seemed. She had new trainers and had taken particular care in tying the laces. The vanity of an unbroken life. She had never run since. When they told her what happened, where it had happened, and she realised she'd been running on the same road in the opposite direction, she had said that to the police officer, aghast, her mouth falling open, her body sinking to the floor, her legs suddenly unable to bear her own weight.

Now, it pushed its way forcefully back. All the years of allowing herself only to think of what preceded it, of her beginnings with Gideon, picking over the detail, the minutiae, as if she might find some clue, some warning. Over and over, her memories like flotsam and jetsam, up to the point where she fell pregnant with Nina where her mind pulled down the shutters; an inability, a refusal, to think beyond that. The unravelling of Gideon's charm and solicitousness, which was replaced, darkly, insidiously, by criticism and control. The afternoon of her children's deaths, she'd been a woman who had walked blithely in a mist of unknowing, living a life that was about to become so altered, so twisted out of shape, that she would never, she was certain, live happily again.

How routinely the evening had begun. She'd showered after her run and wondered about cooking some supper. Would Gideon have fed them? He was always deliberately obstructive about telling her his plans. He would probably have fed them. She settled on making herself some cheese on toast and crouched by the grill, watching the cheese bubble and brown.

They were late. That was how it began; a small, shifting anxiety that they were not home at seven. Her second emotion was impatience: surely he could be mindful that they had school in the morning? There was hair to wash, bags to pack, didn't Joe need his swimming kit? She'd distracted herself, she recalled, searching for his goggles and towel, all the while listening for the sound of Gideon's car outside.

By eight o'clock, when he had still not appeared, she was fretful, unsettled. Where was he? Where had he taken them? Nina said he mainly took them out to restaurants, to movies; or they sat in his flat and watched television while he drank vodka tonics.

He called you a bitch, and a hopeless fool, she had reported once. What nonsense he talks, she'd replied, feeling newly minted then, fresh from the tyranny of his shadow.

He communicated mostly by e-mail – what a relief that had been. She could avoid the whiplash fury of his expression, the snarl of his lip as he spoke. It had taken so much strength, so much resolve, to finally leave him. She'd been terrified. She remembered the feeling of trying to shake awake her limbs as if drowsy from sleep, and to call a halt to what had been years of crushing, manipulative domination. Where was the young woman who'd stood by the water cooler in a navy blue dress? She'd seen, suddenly, clearly, that he'd turned out the lights of her self-esteem one by one, so that the space she lived in was entirely controlled by his censure, his edicts. So, she had willed herself to leave him, to stand in the kitchen, her hands balled to her sides, her voice tremulous but contained, repeating the words she'd practised – over and over – to the mirror, saying, *I cannot bear this any longer, you, your controlling, all these years, so I am leaving you and I am taking the children and don't try to stop me because you can't, I am going.* When she looked up to meet his eyes, he'd slapped her with his wide, flat palm, her cheek blisteringly scarlet, her jawbone throbbing, her ears ringing with the blow.

And do you honestly think you'll achieve even that? he'd responded. *How many years since you have achieved anything other than what I have told you to do?*

And yet she had managed it; tremblingly, fearfully. His power, she'd realised, was like an insidious spider's web, which, over time, had pinned her arms to her sides, laced her lips closed, smothered her skin with a toxic stickiness which made her unable to challenge anything that he demanded. But, then she had steeled herself, answering a sense of injustice which sang out from her bones, and she'd walked out of their home, holding Nina's and Joe's hands.

Nina had been born twelve years previously, Joe three years

later. In their infant years, suffused by the joy of mothering, she'd hoped that family life would strike a different keynote for him. It had not. The three of them, she realised, increasingly spent most of their time alert, vigilant, finely tuned for what Gideon expected of them next. Once, Joe had stumbled and faltered over reading, and Gideon had shouted, giving full vent to his fury. *Just read it, why can't you bloody well read it, the whole world can read.* She'd decided if she couldn't leave him for her own sake, it should be for the children's. Nina's expression, watching Gideon, had begun to mirror her own.

And so, on that day in the kitchen, *You will crawl back,* he'd said, *you're useless without me,* but she had not, buoyed up by a resolute lawyer who told her what she had endured amounted to years of systematic domestic abuse. *He's a sociopath,* she'd said. *He exhibits all the classic character traits, a grandiose sense of self, manipulative, authoritative. The goal,* she explained, *is to exercise control over every aspect of your life, and ultimately to achieve your willing compliance in this.*

How willing she had been, how complicit; gazing at him in front of the church of Santa Maria della Salute, dressed in a pistachio-coloured sweater, her face ardent, responsive. Ready to be bidden. How quickly she'd allowed him to shape her tastes, her preferences. Peggy Guggenheim's bed – *Yes, it is spectacular, isn't it?* In truth, she had been more taken with the row of tomb-stones for Peggy Guggenheim's pug dogs, tucked into a corner of the garden. There was a pathos, she felt, in their implicit intimacy, which was starkly missing from the hard-edged trophy bed. Perhaps Peggy Guggenheim had been kinder to her dogs than to her lovers. How odd that she still remembered so clearly that she had wanted to say this to him. But she had not said any of it; she had demurred to his taste.

I have ordered you a peach Bellini, he'd announced when she walked into the bar. Might her life have been different if she'd said, *Thank you, but I'd prefer a glass of white wine?* How off-putting that might have been for him: an early sign of resistance, an indication that she might not be dominated, moulded. How easily she had swallowed the story of his first wife, a nervous wreck. Perhaps she was not that at all. Maybe she had rumbled him from the off, and laughed with relief at the thought of the ripped-up photograph of her wardrobe, considering herself scot-free, off the hook, restored to her own self.

After the wedding, how compliantly Ursula had agreed to no longer work, to have no independent life or financial means of her own. *Could I have some money for . . .* she'd learned to say, meekly, compliantly.

On the boat, in Salcombe, was it then that she should have known better, or in Chalfont St Giles, as her life was put neatly in a box? When she first found out she was pregnant she had felt a small shiver of fear, a knowledge of a new reliance, of a more complex connection.

She remembered the joy, the lightness which infused her in the months shortly after she left him. Her solicitor had got her enough of a settlement to allow her to buy her new, smaller home. She had shed the feeling of having to always walk very carefully, as if holding a tray stacked high with a pyramid of crystal glasses. *I did it!* she said to the mirror, scooping her hair into a chignon. How she had strode out, after years of planting her feet with timid care.

And yet, how foolish all that premature sense of liberation had been. Gideon, after she left him, had extinguished more light, more life, than she could ever have conceived possible.

And on that night, when the doorbell rang, she saw, outlined in the doorframe, two adult figures, not children aged nine and twelve. And when she opened it, and she saw two police officers, she first paused in her breathing, and then reached out to touch the arm of the younger one who looked so stricken, so shocked, standing there on her doorstep. The irony stayed with her still. Her gesture

had been one that was maternal, reassuring; to lay her hand on the
arm of a young man who looked so distressed. She had been
motherly to the young policeman – it was her default setting – when
what he had arrived to tell her was that she was, in fact, no longer
a mother at all. Gideon had swiftly, cruelly, taken care of that.

They'd driven her to the police station, after they'd lifted her
up from the hall floor and helped her on with her coat. It was
early November, and the sky, as she looked out of the police
car window, was exploding with fireworks. Perhaps it was not
fireworks, perhaps the heavens were rending and falling in,
which felt appropriate, sitting there, clamping her jaw tight to
stop her teeth from chattering, and feeling cold, so very cold,
despite one of the officers wrapping a blanket around her
shoulders.

'But how,' she said, 'but how . . .' when the policewoman had
said, 'I have some dreadful news, there's been . . . not an accident,
but your children, I'm so sorry to have to tell you this but your
children are dead.'

She remembered placing her forehead on the car window, the
indifferent cold of the glass throbbing viciously through her temples.
Beyond, in her peripheral vision, a firework burst scarlet. *Ladybird,
ladybird,* she thought, *fly away home; your house is on fire and your
children are gone.* Her children were gone. How could that be?

They'd talked to her in an interview room in the station – how
bright the fluorescent strip lighting had been. She'd shielded her
eyes from it; the young policeman's face swam greenly before
her. The policewoman sat beside her, and suggested that she
drink some tea. They had loaded it with sugar; her limbs were
shaking with shock.

'What happened,' the young officer said haltingly, 'is that your
ex-husband drove your children out of town, on the road that
goes past the heath. We think they may have dozed off, as there

is no sign of a struggle. He stopped in a layby and threaded a pipe from the exhaust in through the driver's side window. He left the engine running. I'm sorry to say that all three died from carbon monoxide poisoning.'

Ursula stared beyond him, to where a grimy pin-board gave notice of protocol. It reminded occupants that they should behave in a reasonable, ordered fashion. That probably precluded, she thought, standing up and ululating wildly, tearing off her clothes in strips, possibly wrenching her hair out in fisty clumps, and peeling away long, frayed ribbons of red-raw skin. As she looked at the officers, they seemed to be receding into a pinwheel of vision at the centre of her eyes, so that she seemed to be looking at them down a long, narrow tunnel.

'What's curious,' the officer continued, his voice a little quieter, 'is that he had a tape playing in the car, someone reading, *The Wind in the Willows*. Like a bedtime story. The member of the public who found the car thought that they were all asleep, until he saw the pipe, on the other side of the car, the engine still running; that's why he raised the alarm.'

She vomited when he said that, on the station floor; the sugary tea, the cheese on toast she'd eaten earlier. Earlier? A galaxy away when she was still in her kitchen, still a mother, finding swimming kit, waiting for her children to come home.

Joe loved *The Wind in the Willows*. She had bought the audio CD for his birthday. He curled up in her lap and they listened to it together. On Friday evening, he said that he did not want to go to Gideon's. *I want to stay with you*, he'd said; *I don't want to go to Daddy's. I can't ever get to sleep. He just turns out the light and tells me to stop being a girl.*

She had given him the CD; she'd pressed it into his hands along with Nina's mini-CD player. Take this, she had said, put it under your pillow. You can listen to the story; you'll be asleep before you even know it.

But I don't want to go, he replied. *I want to stay here with you. Can't Nina go by herself? Daddy doesn't have to see me.*

But Daddy wants to see you, he very much wants to see you, she'd said. How judicious, how mindful she'd been, remaining scrupulously fair in how she managed her children's contact with their father.

She winced, struck with a searing pain in her head. Joe had not wanted to go. She had persuaded him to go. Her head throbbed. Was it possible, she wondered, cradling her skull, for it to snap off from the stem of her neck and tumble to the floor?

'I'm afraid,' the officer said, 'there is the matter of identifying the bodies. We know from items in the car, and the car itself, that the children fit the ages and description of yours, but it's a formality we have to go through. Is there anyone you would like to identify them for you, or anyone who perhaps you might want to accompany you to the mortuary?'

She had shaken her head, and stood up, still clutching the blanket that she had been given in the car.

'I'd like to see my children now,' she said quietly, 'I will identify them. I am their mother. It is the very least I can do.'

She had limped from the room. She was uncertain why, as she could not recall bruising her leg when she fell in the hall. Loss, she'd decided later, was like a hammer blow to the body, grief incapacitating the muscles, sorrow seizing up the joints. She'd walked out painfully, feeling as if her heart might burst with the effort of beating, might perhaps crash through her ribs and lie puce and shuddering on the tiled floor. And as she had headed towards the car, she had the curious feeling that her feet no longer made contact with the ground, that she was in fact hovering above it, oxygen permeating through her skin rather than being inhaled into her lungs. *In the midst of life we are in death.* The truth of the familiar words struck her forcefully, now buckling her seatbelt, thinking such a safeguard was actually redundant. What did it matter if she flew, star-shaped, through a windscreen, her face frosted with glass? From now on, in life she would not be in death; she would be dead in the midst of life, her heart slammed into stasis, her body emptied of everything but grief.

I'm sorry, the mortuary assistant kept repeating. *I'm very sorry.* Ursula nodded. Any words, any possible response, felt thick and heavy in her mouth. Her jaw ached, her skull throbbed. She had no idea of the time; was it midnight, or later?

I'm sorry, the mortician said again. Was this what people would say to her now, their eyes clouded with awkwardness, or perhaps cross the street to avoid her, to avoid saying anything at all? *Yes, her*, they might whisper, *yes, she is the one; her husband killed her children, terrible, shocking.*

Perhaps if they said it often enough, or if she saw it in people's eyes often enough, maybe it would help her to believe it; to absorb it, to accept it. Otherwise, how might she begin to understand, how could she possibly think her children dead? On that night, walking towards their sheeted bodies on trolleys, it seemed impossible, unfathomable, to believe it was so, when it had seemed as if their bodies could barely contain all their life energy. Each morning they woke and flew up from their beds like small birds, eyes shining.

My children are dead. 'I know, I know,' said the policewoman – who was still by her side. Had she spoken the words out loud? Evidently so. She bit her tongue and drew blood. Its warmth, its immediacy, its iron taste were surprising. Was her children's blood now setting blackly in their veins? Was that what happened, upon death, the flow stopping, coalescing, slowly turning to silt?

The mortician carefully turned back the sheet. It was hard not to cry out; not to scoop up her darling son who looked, surely, as if he were sleeping; a blueness, an unnatural tinge to his lips the only indication that he would not sit up, say, *Hello, Mummy*, and raise his arms to her.

The last intimacy; she could not bear to think of it still. She had reached forward, and smoothed the hair from his forehead. Was it possible that it was still warm, or were her own hands chilled, stiff, beyond reliable sensation? They did not feel like her own. Nothing felt like her own. She stroked his cheekbone and bent forward to kiss his mouth. How cold his lips were. She smoothed her hand along his collarbone, down the length of his upper arm. He felt unbroken, unchanged, his small knot of bicep so known to her touch. His body was so known. How could she think of him, how accept him, dead?

She lifted his hand. How familiar it was; a small blotch of ink on his index finger, a rim of soil under his thumbnail, a tiny callus where he held his pen too tightly, an almost-healed scab where he had grazed his knuckle falling from his skateboard. His hand told the narrative of what had been – but oh, how impossible it seemed – the last few days of his life, his only nine years of life. A noise – was she the one making that noise? A keening, a crying that seemed to razor its way up from somewhere deep in her abdomen. The policewoman had pressed her palms to her ears.

The mortician stepped forward. She turned the second sheet down. The end of Nina's French plait was springing loose from its tie. Ursula reached forward; swiftly made it fast. Each morning, before school, Nina would ask Ursula to tie her French plait tight. She kissed her daughter's lips. Where her T-shirt lay soft to her body, the beginnings of her breasts were evident. Her body, Ursula thought, which was being beckoned towards womanhood; stirrings which, imminently, would have meant she would leave her girlhood body behind. And now she would not. Her father had decreed that she would not. She picked up her daughter's hand and noticed a mark on her wrist. 'Look,' she said (was she gesturing to the policewoman, the mortician?). There were bruises, a pattern of fingertips around Nina's wrist. Had Gideon forced her into the car? Had he prevented her from trying to get out? Had Joe fallen asleep, duped, as they were driving, by the soft timbre of *The Wind in the Willows*? Meanwhile, she, Ursula, had been out running; ridiculously, proudly, neatly tying the laces of her new trainers. The thought made her want to retch again.

The mortician shifted a little restlessly. Was she waiting for Ursula to say something else?

'I'm sorry,' she said again, 'we just need you to confirm identity. Usually, if you want to sit with them, then it is afterwards, at the undertaker's, not here . . .'

The woman was right. The place was cold; all steel, hard-surfaced, the air thick with disinfectant. Bodies were filed away in stacks, reeking of the rawness of death. But how, Ursula thought, suddenly perplexed, could she leave them here?

Now, on her bedroom floor, she remembered contemplating scrambling up beside them, hoping that her heart would combust and drown her body with blood. Might she be killed by her own tsunami of sorrow? The image of the scarlet firework had blazed across her retina. *Your children are gone.* How could that possibly be?

The policewoman placed her hand gently on her arm, and turned her towards the exit.

'One moment, please,' the mortician said suddenly, moving towards a third table, 'I'm not sure who is confirming the identity of the deceased adult. Is that you too?'

The woman's hands hovered over the sheet that covered the third body. The policewoman stepped forward, but Ursula stayed her arm. She stiffened, swallowed hard and walked steadily towards it. She took the edge of the sheet and turned it back herself.

'Yes,' she said flatly, decisively (how distant, how unrecognisable her own voice sounded), 'and this is what a man who has deliberately killed his own children looks like.'

The mortician flinched.

Ursula resisted smashing her fists into Gideon's face. How quickly might it pulp? She turned back towards the door.

'When the undertaker comes,' she said, a sudden fierceness to her tone, 'tell them to do what they like with his body. I want no word of it at all. I don't care what they do.'

'I'm sorry,' the policewoman said when they were back in the car, 'that was not protocol, she shouldn't have asked you to do that, it was an error. I don't think she knew the circumstances . . .' Her voice petered out flatly.

Ursula half-closed her eyes, so that the orange sodium street lights blurred through her lashes. She was glad she had seen his body. In Buddhist practice, wasn't a body carried to the highest place available? Weren't there body carvers who deftly, carefully, sliced the hefts of flesh from the bone, the bones then ground into a paste so that they could be consumed by the birds; the whole body released out into the world beyond it, ready for the cycle to begin again? Given a choice, she thought, a hot, thick fury suddenly choking her throat, she would toss Gideon's body into the fast lane of the motorway, let the cars slam over him, bust the organs right out of him, let the magpies tug at his innards in the early hours of the morning, the ants busy themselves with his eyes, his nostrils, the soft flesh of his mouth, swarms of flies gorge on him, and nights of rain, of merciless wind and sunshine, reduce him to a dark red stain on the tarmac, and then to nothing, absolutely nothing at all. Might there be some comfort in that, some balm for her fury? He would not be released with grace and dignity back into the world, but instead would be smashed from it, pulped by it, obliterated by the force of tyres, of wheel rims, of raw insect hunger. It felt deserved, appropriate, for a man who had turned his hand, his wickedness, his scrupulous rage, against his own offspring.

She closed her eyes completely. How bone-tired she felt.

'I'm not sure you should be alone,' the policewoman said gently, again placing her hand on her arm.

'I am alone,' Ursula replied. For she knew, as she said it, it was a stark truth and that she would be alone for the rest of her life.

When she walked through her door, the first thing she saw was Joe's swimming kit, his goggles and trunks contained neatly within the roll of his towel. On the hall table was a book Nina had been reading; she had turned down the corner of the page she'd reached. Ursula sat on the floor, the book and goggles cradled in her lap. The day grew light around her, and still she did not move.

After the funeral she sat, at a loss, in loss, in her children's bedrooms. What should she do with their things which were scattered around her? Nina's Ugg boots, Joe's neon football, his Fimo plaster animals. A purple rabbit, with red ears and a yellow bobtail, sat forlornly in her palm. Nina's hairbrush, her name painted across it in turquoise nail varnish. A jar of marbles, the most precious ones bound in a twist of clingfilm. A basket of dinosaurs, faded from a summer spent in the garden in a sandpit. A sweater knitted for Joe by her mother not long before she died, the wool scratchy around the neckline, but he chose to wear it anyway. A light-up reindeer made of frosted white glass, a remnant from when they believed it would help guide Santa to their chimney. A notebook, with PRIVATE written in Nina's determined hand. A pair of over-the-knee stripy socks, a Liverpool football scarf. Ursula cradled each item. It was hard not to succumb to a kind of bewilderment. It was the stuff of their lives; lives brought to a halt by their father. How might she absorb that?

To give away, or throw away, their things seemed a further act of betrayal. It would make her complicit in wiping them out. *Perhaps to a charity, or an overseas orphanage*, the grief counsellor had suggested. Ursula had shaken her head. How much easier it was to take refuge in silence. Her words were drying up; mostly, she thought, because there no longer seemed to be anything worth saying at all. *My children are gone*, perhaps she might repeat that over and over, until the words lost their power to repeatedly slay her, and she might emerge somewhere different, somewhere calmer, picked clean like a carrion bone, ready to resume life. It had not happened.

But on that day in their bedrooms, what she said to the grief counsellor (how odd, Ursula still thought, that someone might assume collective sagacity in the individual business of grief) was, *I did not save them, did not see it coming, I was running in the opposite direction.* And the woman nodded, gravely, wordlessly, because there was nothing she could say that was in fact truer, and nothing that would be a balm.

So, she had left all her children's things exactly as they were, their bedrooms completely intact, as if their lives had not slammed to a stop, and as if they might in fact return at 7 p.m. on Sunday evening, to their Cretan money boxes, their favourite hoodies, their slippers, their pencil cases, their toys. And she taped up the window frames to stop the dust eddying softly in, and sealed the doors with thick silver gaffer tape, and each night before she went to bed she placed her palm upon them in a gesture of silent communion with them, which had not lost its intimacy and which bound her to them still. And she wondered if a day might come when she could go into their rooms with equanimity, hold their possessions in her lap and summon each child back without pain. It had not. Once a year she cleaned the rooms painstakingly, and then lay on the floor in her own room, the blinds drawn through the day. *It still fells me*, she might have said to the grief counsellor if they had still been in touch. *It is possible, believe me, for a wound to remain scarlet-raw.*

And she had tried to take solace in Mizpah, the words from Genesis coming to her one citrus-lit spring morning. The Lord watch between me and thee, when we are absent from each other. But the space between them had felt empty of consolation. Her faith – instilled by her mother's Italian Catholic obeisance – dried up like a river's tributary, shrivelled and desiccated with a scattering of remembered psalms and prayers. *I will lift up mine eyes to the hills from whence cometh my help.* But it did not.

The rest of the house she transformed to anonymity, making it a space so neutral as to almost deny the possibility that anyone lived there. Living, she decided, was not a word she would apply to herself. Suspended in life, that would be more accurate. *It will pass*, the grief counsellor had said, *this intense phase will pass*. But it had not; it had ossified around her like a rigid cocoon.

'Do you have children?' a woman had asked her, several years later, queuing for a changing room, her own child impatient, fidgety, at her legs. 'Isn't it impossible trying to shop? Mine can't abide it at all.'

'No,' Ursula had said, 'no, I do not.'

This was much simpler. For to speak the truth, baldly, simply, would be like vomiting, blood-red, all over the shop floor, the scarletness splashing the child's legs, the woman stepping awkwardly away from the puddles of Ursula's pain.

And so she had sustained silence, until tonight, confronted by Daniel's pale, concerned face, his knowledge blurted out, Luca hot and restless between them. And back it came, tumbling relentlessly back, from the police officers visible through the door to the keening which came from within her and seemed both to scald and scar her abdomen so that when she touched her stomach it felt thick with pinked tissue and loss.

51

In the remorseless light of the next morning, Ursula lay on her bedroom floor.

The therapist had called it the most contemporary of crimes, as if a classification might help. Now, her eye alert to it, Ursula read of it all too often in the newspaper: an estranged husband driving his children to a hotel in half-term, to a quiet lane on a Sunday afternoon, to a place where he could invert the natural order in a way that was incomprehensible to most. The brutalities visited upon children – Ursula could not bear to think about it: throats slit, or strangled with pyjama cords, chests stabbed piti-lessly; lungs – like Nina's and Joe's – filled with insidious, invisible carbon monoxide; little bodies hurled from balconies. All carried out by fathers wanting to punish the women who had borne them the children.

It's a control thing, the therapist had patiently explained. *They feel such anger that the woman has left them and that they are no longer in control.* How surely, how swiftly, Ursula reflected, the objective was achieved. How the darkness Gideon had cast would dominate until her dying day. *Recovery is practically impossible*, said the therapist, *and that's the point.*

Now, remembering those sessions, she recalled the parched feel of her lips, the sensation that her hands on her lap were not entirely her own. She had not attended for long. It was hard to keep faith with it. Faith was a word which had lost its density, and Trust another, for how could she ever trust any adult again?

Every avenue is blocked off, that was what she tried to explain to the therapist; every avenue that might lead to something healing or wholesome.

And for Gideon she felt a pure, clear hate, which set to brittleness around her like a toffee-apple shell. 'But hate is so destructive,' the therapist said. 'It's like jealousy and revenge; you dig a grave for your enemy and one for yourself at the same time.'

Her exhortation had made Ursula want to laugh with bitterness. That kind of powdery nonsense could only be spoken by people who had no real cause to hate. They spoke from the luxury of not knowing, or of having no sense of how completely destroyed she already was. To continue to hate felt like proof of not having forgiven. It was the only justice she could mete out for her children.

On the internet, it had been straightforward to find women who had suffered the same thing. Women who wept uncontrollably on the street because a child walked in the same way as their own had, or who could not bear to cross a road because they no longer had a small hand to hold, halting at the kerb, unable to step from the pavement. Women who kept their living room lights blazing at night, so that the casket ashes of their children would never be in the dark. Women who worried whether they had buried their children in enough clothing, mindful of the deep cold of the ground. The small panaceas – light, warmth – which they could no longer gift their children in life and the desperation to still hold intact some scrap of motherhood in their hands.

The other women's experiences had thrown her own finely tuned agony into sharper relief. One father arrived for contact with two identical new footballs. *We will have good sport today*, he said, lifting his sons into the car. Another killed them in his wife's favourite place. What scrupulous attention to detail, to make sure that everything the woman cherished was so completely destroyed.

After a year or so, she had opted for solitude, steeping herself in it like water, allowing it to wash all the attempts at words away. Other people's words, however well-meaning, poked into her ears, made her eardrums tender. She wanted to press her palms to her head. Silence was a muffler, a lint-soft muffler. How speedily it settled on her like thick, blanketing snow.

She had let the words go, other people's attempts at comfort, words other than the practical, the factual; and yet, as she let them slide downstream beyond her, she still struggled for one word that would evoke what he had done to her. And then, one morning, five years ago, as she was unloading the dishwasher, it came to her, gifted, like a bright blue robin's egg in her palm, and finally she had it.

Blindsided. He had blindsided her. She had not conceived of what was coming, and he had embroiled her in his dereliction of duty. She felt she had failed to protect Nina and Joe, because she had not intuited what their father might visit upon them.

He had blinded her too, with pain, and with loss. It was this that she might tell, might share, should she ever decide to haul the word from where it lay, splintering her heart.

Ursula stood up, and made ready to shower. She rubbed her elbows and knees; how stiff they felt from being on the floor all night. She was due back at Daniel's in just over an hour. She turned on the water, allowing it to run scaldingly hot over her skin. Her blood responded, flushing it red. She rolled her shoulders, flexed the vertebrae in her neck.

Before it happened, she had been working part-time as a teaching assistant. It had been part of an optimistic new future, where she gained credits and would then begin to train as a teacher. How foolish, in retrospect, her excitement at the prospect. Afterwards, the thought of a classroom was too much to bear: other people's children; other women who still had their children waiting at the school gate. She'd resigned with immediate effect. *I'm so sorry*, the head teacher said – the phrase was a litany which peppered most of her days – and, *You showed so much potential. I wish I could persuade you to reconsider.* She could not.

Silence was addictive. Its simplicity came back to her now. Had she really contemplated wearing a badge which said, with finality, *I am mute?* She'd stood at too many tills, when the assistant would say, *Oh, this rain, don't you wish it would stop? Call this a summer* . . . and Ursula was aware how dismissive it would sound to reply, *I just couldn't care less.* Her perspective was so altered, she thought, she could never make small talk again.

She watched older women, pausing beside a pushchair, beaming at a baby, asking how much it had weighed at birth. *Oh I had three*, they'd say, *the heaviest was nine pounds eleven*, and then, tapping the younger woman's arm, they might laugh conspiratorially and say, *I truly never thought I'd sleep a night again.* She would not become one of those. At the sight of a pushchair, she quickened her pace. Once, in a shoe shop, a woman turned to her and said, *Aren't school shoes a price?* Had she still looked like a mother then, or had the woman just assumed? Was it a look that gradually blenched from you, worn away by the attrition of empty, childless days? And so she'd just stood there and shrugged, clutching a pair of summer sandals she'd chosen. She could have said, *Aren't they just; my son's feet grew two sizes in just one term*, but she didn't. Or, walking past a woman who was trying to encourage her children to chant their mathematical times tables – *The sevens and nines*, she might have said, *my children hated the sevens and the nines.* Instead, she had quickened her pace. Briskness was best; it prevented overhearing.

For what she might have said, to the woman who asked her about the rain, or to the woman in the shoe shop. *I am a mother and not a mother; is there any way you can help me with that?* She knew that they could not.

Her children came to her in dreams, the smell of them, the sound of them, their laughter trailing like bubbles, their limbs golden, supple, and then she would wake to a hard, bleak-edged, dispassionate morning and find herself doubly bereft, losing them over and over again in a recurring rhythm of loss.

Suicide was surprisingly unachievable. That had been a gradual dawning. Many nights, in the stained dark of her room, self-inflicted death seemed the route to peaceful oblivion. And yet how her body had rebelled, flinched, refused. When she held a razor close to her thigh, wanting to cut a wound which would allow grief to escape, her hand stayed itself, rebellious, suspended above her leg. Her body remained robust. She woke ravenous, walked miles, scrubbed the kitchen floor with strong arcs of her arm.

And her eyes, which surely should have been blinded by grief, were alert, watchful, drawn to the blue of a delphinium, a goldfinch on a branch, a sunset so rosily exquisite she was absorbed into its fractional changes of light.

Eventually she decided that that was her punishment. This body, her body, insisting, defiantly, on continuing to live, refusing oblivion and choosing to pay constant witness to her children's death.

The summer afterwards she had gone back to Salcombe, where they'd holidayed each year as a family. She stifled memories of Gideon fiercely striding beyond them, or dazzling the children with his inventiveness, as he had originally dazzled her

She had spent an afternoon on Seacombe Sands, thinking of Nina and Joe running towards her, holding crabs, seaweed, pails, dripping ice lollies. And each roll and plash of the waves had brought their voices back to her, the companionability of their chatter. She had been infused with her ghosts, and she had sat there with them, on the shoreline, until her feet turned completely blue, her palms pressed flat to the sand alongside her where her children would never again be. And finally, exhausted, she'd had to close her eyes to stop more memories coming: Joe, running to her after school, arms wide, or wheeling triumphant before a goal mouth, or blowing out birthday cake candles. And Nina, wearing Ursula's high-heeled shoes, laughing brightly, sashaying down the landing, or cycling away from her for the first time, whooping, wobbling, when she learned to ride a bike. And Ursula had found herself unable to leave the beach, sitting there stranded when darkness had completely fallen, unable to walk away from the sight of her children, endlessly flipped freshly forward by the impassive sea.

She'd responded to Rose and Geoffrey's advertisement for a housekeeper not long afterwards and had worked mostly in silence. She had polished, waxed, swept, wiped, scrubbed, her countenance unreadable, the surfaces of the house responding to her touch but asking for nothing more. Her face settled into mild stillness. She had moved through the house in a way that was purposeful, contained. It allowed her to exist, and for that she would always be grateful to Rose and Geoffrey. They had not intruded, had asked nothing of her beyond mechanical concentration.

Her decision never to work in a house with children had been part of the same self-protection. She could not face the prospect. The pain of a small pair of pyjamas laid out to be ironed; a sheepskin slipper, retrieved from under a bed, measuring only a hand's length; dirty feet at bath time, stained with grass or soil; tiny hands, cupped, proffering the treasure of a ladybird or a snail. The smell of hair, freshly washed, and the weight of a body, on the lap, cradled softly to sleep. The memory of kissing – fiercely, extravagantly – lithe arms, round cheeks, bony knees. Unbearable.

Now, standing in her dressing gown, her hair wet, her body loofah'd back into sensation, she lifted from the bedside table the

only item in her part of the house that was personal. It was a
poem she had copied out in blue ink and framed by her bed,
written by Emily Dickinson. She read it to herself, the words
familiar, well-worn, her own litany of grief.

> *After great pain, a formal feeling comes –*
> *The Nerves sit ceremonious, like Tombs –*
> *The stiff Heart questions was it He, that bore,*
> *And Yesterday, or Centuries before?*
>
> *The Feet, mechanical, go round –*
> *Of Ground, or Air, or Ought –*
> *A Wooden way*
> *Regardless grown,*
> *A Quartz contentment, like a stone –*
>
> *This is the Hour of Lead –*
> *Remembered, if outlived,*
> *As Freezing persons, recollect the Snow –*
> *First – Chill – then Stupor – then the letting go –*

If there had been anyone who had asked her, anyone she wanted
to tell, she would have said, *This is the story of how it has been,*
and she would have pressed the poem into their hands, so that
Emily Dickinson could tell it as it was. But there was no one she
had ever wanted to tell, and she had slept beside the poem each
night, occasionally holding it to her breast, hoping it might also
give some physical balm. The Hour of Lead, she would have
said, is not in fact an hour, but weeks sewn into months, sewn
into years, with traceless grey thread. And she had, she'd been
surprised to discover, outlived the knowledge, of her children's
deaths; she had felt the feet mechanical, the chill, and the stupor,
but never, never at all, the possibility of letting go.

And now, as she stood in her bedroom, easing a dress from a

hanger and then buttoning it up, she saw clearly that the stupor had lasted for all these years, until this moment.

How hard she had tried over the last ten weeks; how difficult much of it had been. Venturing to the same library where she had always taken her children; the woman, who she thought did not know her, but who may have known of her. The pain, standing in Ruby's classroom before the cake sale, its familiarity piercing, and the panic-struck need to bolt, to escape, to scuttle away across the playground. Going to Sports Day, the storm in her mind as she walked to the track, the memory of Joe's sturdy, athletic body always first over the line, of him running towards her, arms raised, triumphant. And the night Ruby could not sleep, when Ursula had stood beyond her, memories of Nina threatening to up-end her so that she stood, bereft again, remembering her daughter unable to sleep on summer nights, and fighting back tears in the soft darkness of Ruby's room.

She had begun to break her own rules, and she had known she was doing it. Buying the lolly mould, accepting the jam-jar bean, going to the park. She had sung Luca lullabies, stung from her reluctance to do so by her anxiety over his fretfulness; the songs, in her throat, so automatic, so familiar. She felt herself painfully tugged towards her old self. And yet beside the pain jostled new memories, demanding consideration now. Ruby, clutching her spelling sheet triumphantly, making meringue mice with concentration, gazing with perfect happiness at her haber-dasher's shop-in-a-box, and sensing, with a child's unerring instinct, the impossibility of a completely protected world. Ruby twisting sweet peas up the wigwams, Luca filling his bucket with windfall apples, and both of them running, joyfully, between the water jets. The bean sprouting rudely, insistently, forth. So, for the first time, alongside Nina and Joe, and the numbness of their loss, she saw Ruby and Luca, but mostly Ruby. Ruby's bright-eyed face, scrunched with determination, her hand balled into a fist, knocking as if at a window, tap-tap-tapping for her, and for life itself, to finally be let back in.

Ursula went down into the kitchen and boiled the kettle to make tea. She looked at her watch again. It would soon be time to go to work. She had been wrong when she said to Monica that work was the only dignity. This work had been more than that. It had been redemptive in ways she could not have preconceived.

52

Each time Daniel held a spoon of oatmeal to Luca's lips, he pushed it away and continued to grizzle. Luca rubbed his eyes and his cheeks with the back of his hand, then pawed the spoon away. Oatmeal stuck to his fingers and flecked his eyelashes. Daniel patiently wiped his face clean. 'You look miserable, little one. What's wrong? Tell Daddy.'

The night had been difficult. Luca had slept fitfully, waking and crying, and Daniel had lain beside him, equally wakeful.

He rinsed out the flannel and wiped Luca again, pressing its coolness to his temples. The child wailed. He laid his own head on the table, tiredness thrumming at his temples. Ursula's key in the lock, her footfall, were so quiet, he barely had time to lift his eyes to face her. Was it possible for someone to be so deathly pale and to still have blood coursing through their veins? Her eyes were dark as charcoal, the skin beneath them blue-bruised. Daniel took measure of her face. How had he not detected what had always sat there so evidently? Sorrow, implacable and immovable, etched across her even features. He couldn't begin to think of the right words to greet her.

'How was Luca in the night?' she asked.

So this was how it would be. It was Luca they would discuss; Luca who would carry them away from the dreadfulness of last night to talk of temperatures, analgesics, food eaten or not.

'I'm afraid he's no better. We didn't have a good night. He was awake, fretful, and at the same time seemed too exhausted to

have a proper old wail. I've given him more Calpol but he hasn't
perked up. I don't think he can go to nursery. I'd cancel my list
but I have to drive to the hospital in Watford today: they're priority
cases. Please can you take care of him here?'

'Of course. I knew from the schedule on the fridge that it was
Watford today, so I came early on purpose. You've got time for
a shower and some breakfast. Here, let me take him.'

She unbuckled Luca from the high chair and lifted him into
her arms. Luca pressed his face to her, smearing her throat with
silvery threads of saliva. She seemed not to notice. Daniel hesitated about whether to pass her the flannel. It seemed unbearably
intimate. Luca lay in her arms and cried softly, and Ursula stroked
his forehead.

'I'll just take him out into the garden; last night that seemed
to soothe him. There's a robin which sits on the fencepost; it
always catches his eye.'

Ruby came into the kitchen.

'I kept hearing Luca cry in the night,' she said. 'Who carried
me to my bed? Did my singing work?'

'Ursula told me your singing was brilliant,' Daniel said. 'Thank
you.'

'Did you clap your hardest for Cassie?'

'I'm sorry?'

'Last night, did you clap your hardest for Cassie?'

'Yes, yes I did.' Daniel was struck by how uncomplicated the
previous evening now seemed. Life was a past master at that,
rearing up when least expected. Ruby's simple loyalty to Cassie
touched him. He knelt down and gave her a kiss. 'Have I told
you recently that you are quite simply the best girl in the world?'

'All the time. You tell me mostly nearly all the time.'

'See how true it must be then. See how champion you are.'

'Why is Ursula out in the garden?'

'Luca's still hot and bothered. She's trying to settle him.'

'But how come she knows what to do?'

'What do you mean?'

'Well, she's not a nurse or anything and she hasn't got any children but you would think she had. Last night she knew all sorts of things to try and comfort Luca. She kept thinking them up like someone who knew all about poorly children. She even knew lullabies. She sang to him when I didn't know any more.'

'I think she's just very clever, and kind, and we're very lucky to have her while Mummy is in California.'

Ruby had seen it. She had known better, intuited better, Daniel reflected as he walked upstairs. The eyes of his child had seen the truth of things more clearly than his own.

When Ruby had gone to school, Ursula gave Luca a tepid bath and washed his hair. *There, there,* she crooned, pouring water from a jug over his scalp, making sure that none ran in his eyes. *Who's a hot little boy,* she said, *who's a tired little boy?* She took a clean towel, scooped him into its softness and sat on the bathroom floor with him cradled in her lap. Wiping him gently, she rocked forwards and backwards. She towelled his curls and dried carefully between his toes. *Who's fresh and clean as a daisy?* she said. *Luca, little Luca.*

She carried him to his bedroom, put a clean nappy on him and a pair of light cotton pyjamas. Luca was almost asleep in her arms. *Shall I sit with you a while until you are properly asleep?* she said softly, her voice a sing-song. *Shall we sit in the chair and listen to the birds singing outside, and then you can go to sleep and wake up feeling better and I can make you some lunch? Does that sound like a plan to you?*

She sat in the chair with the infant in her lap, and it came to her unbidden how many times she had sat with Nina or Joe poorly in her arms. There had been time for all the conventional childhood illnesses, the ones which she recorded, along with immunisations, in a red, plastic-covered book, given to them at birth. *Your child's health record*, it said in gold letters on the cover, with charts that showed weight gain each week, the circumference of the head, the date of first eating solids. There were line drawings showing situations to be avoided: scalding kettles, chokeable carrot sticks, trailing flexes, plug sockets. She had filled the books out neatly and conscientiously: the dates of vaccinations, of sitting up, crawling, speaking first words. And, in the pages for the illnesses, which ones they had caught when. Chickenpox. They'd had that one after another, one hot July. She'd daubed them with chalky calamine lotion to stop them from scratching the scabs. Joe was only ten months old. She'd put little mittens on him to wear in the night. She remembered, now, the smooth white ribbon she'd tied in a double bow at his wrist. She'd worried, on the first night, that they might be a choking hazard. She'd got up several times to reassure herself that he wasn't sucking the ribbon.

What care she had taken, what constant, vigilant care, taking their hands each time they approached a road. What other illnesses had they had? Parvovirus rose up from her memory. Wasn't it the fifth one of a group of childhood illnesses? She couldn't recall what else it was grouped with, just that the doctor first used its colloquial name. *Slapped cheek virus*, he'd said, when she'd taken Nina to the surgery with a flushed face and a rash which had begun on her hands and feet. But how did it come to be called that, she wanted to ask the doctor. Who on earth would slap a small child on the cheek? Joe had broken his arm falling from a space hopper. That didn't count as an illness, although she'd spent hours in A & E waiting for him to be X-rayed. *He balanced on it,* she told the doctor, *trying to reach a toy on the shelf; it rolled out from under him.* Joe had run around for the next three weeks, his arm in a turquoise plaster cast, held out like a small chicken wing.

Nina, when she was nearly two, had a cough that had become pneumonia. She remembered the effort it took her to draw in a breath, her sternum seeming to touch her spine as she inhaled. Croup. Which one of them had had croup? Joe. He'd been really tiny. She'd called the night doctor, who told her to stand holding him in the shower. And she'd done so, she remembered, shielding him from the actual heat of the water, but enveloped in billowy mists of steam, his breathing becoming clearer, quieter. And where had Gideon been, she thought, when she was taking all this painstaking care? Either in the background, increasingly sardonic and intolerant, or at work, or out entertaining clients. She never asked for details. A young woman had come to their house one day, demanding to see him. He had taken her by the elbow and driven away swiftly in his car.

Luca stirred in her lap. His cry was more like a moan. Ursula startled to full attention, checked his temperature with a thermometer, pressed her lips to his forehead. As she lifted him gently, he vomited violently into her lap. His hands and his feet, she noticed, were suddenly freezing cold. He had a small purplish mark on his stomach; was it the beginning of a rash? Something started to pulse in her brain. In the book, in the red book, what had been the list of dangerous symptoms to check for? A rash, something about a rash that didn't blench when pressed with a glass?

She carried Luca downstairs; his crying had petered out into distressed, laboured breathing. She looked up the number for the hospital in Watford. Daniel would know what to do. 'I'm sorry,' the switchboard advisor said, 'Mr Bailey is in theatre; he won't be available to speak to until after one p.m.' Ursula dialled his mobile, which predictably switched to voicemail. She hung up without leaving a message and looked down at Luca, who seemed to no longer be returning her gaze. His eyes shone glassily, without recognition or focus. Ursula glanced at her vomit-strewn skirt. She spoke quickly, calmly.

'Luca, I'm just going to put you down while I change what

I'm wearing.' Surely something of Monica's would fit? She ran back upstairs, undressed, and opened Monica's wardrobe. She grabbed a skirt and a T-shirt, ran back down the stairs and dressed quickly beside him.

'I'm here, little one, I'm right here,' she said, scooping his limp, hot body back into her arms. 'We're going to the hospital – shall we go to the hospital? – I don't know what's wrong, but I think you need to be there. Let me just call Daddy's voicemail so he will know where we have gone.'

In the car, as she was driving, Luca started to moan softly, and retched a little more. On his tummy, she could see that the rash was maroonly, insidiously spreading. A traffic light turned to red as she approached it. Her heart thumped faster.

53

When she ran into A & E, she was quickly sent to the Resuscitation area. A nurse half walked, half ran beside her, one hand on her shoulder. Another woman, holding a clipboard, asked, *Your relation to the child? Mother?* No, child-minder, mother's help. *Age of the child? Address?* His father, Ursula said, is Mr Bailey, the spinal surgeon. He works in the main hospital, but not today, today he has a list in Watford. Luca felt floppier in her arms. *Please, please focus on him,* she said.

They lay Luca on a bed, and two nurses began to attach leads to him.

'I'm sorry,' the sister said, 'we're going to have to ask you to stand a little to the side just while we get the ECG leads in place. Put the oxygen saturation probe on,' she told one of the nurses, and she clipped it promptly to Luca's index finger. The small screen it was attached to did not flicker into life.

'To his ear; clip it to his ear,' the sister said sharply.

Luca started to wail, a thin, high-pitched cry which reminded Ursula of a rabbit in a snare she'd once come upon in a wild-flower meadow, its femur gleaming whitely where the wire had pulled tight. By the tip of its ear was a perfectly blue chalk milk-wort flower. Why could she remember that now?

'It's all right, little one,' she said, reaching across to try and stroke his forehead.

The sister gently moved her aside, saying to the nurses, 'Put the oxygen mask on.'

As a nurse tried to put on the mask, Luca pawed the elastic away with his fist.

'Hold it to his face,' the sister said calmly.

Luca began to suck in lungfuls of air. The screen attached to the probe started dancing in red lines.

A doctor appeared, and quickly introduced herself to Ursula.

'I'm sorry, this is all a little rushed,' she said. 'You did well to bring him in so promptly. I will examine him now, but first we need to take some blood, for some tests and cultures, so that we know what we are dealing with. Looking at him, it's likely to be some kind of bacterial infection. We just don't know what yet.'

She deftly put a syringe into Luca's arm. It filled quickly with blood. 'Another of my colleagues will be along shortly. We're going to put in a drip, get some fluids and antibiotics into him.' She left with the blood sample.

Luca moaned softly beneath the mask, which a nurse was still gently holding to his face.

'I'm here, Luca. I'm here,' Ursula said, giving the tiny part of his cheek that was not covered by the mask the lightest of touches.

'I'm here,' she said again, suddenly choked, feeling the words carried more import than anyone in the room could know. What a luxury they were. She pressed her palms to her face, and tried not to dissolve into tears.

She watched as a nurse gave Luca some saline – his vein bulged blue beneath the surface of his skin, and then he was connected to a drip, pegged up beside him. Ursula reached out to touch him; his feet and hands were cold and white.

Another doctor came in and introduced himself.

'There's one more thing we'd like to do. It's a lumbar puncture which I'm afraid can be distressing. We just need to check if anything's happening in his spinal fluid. You can wait outside the cubicle if you prefer.'

Ursula shook her head. 'No, no thank you. I'll stay here if that's all right.'

The doctor turned Luca on his side and carried out the procedure. The enormous syringe filled with fluid from his spine. Luca cried the weariest of cries.

'Good boy. Brave boy. All better soon,' Ursula said, massaging his cold little toes, not knowing whether she said it for Luca or for herself.

The first paediatrician reappeared.

'We're done for a little while. He's been really good. He should start to show some signs of improvement. We'll give it fifteen minutes or so, and then we can take him out of Resuscitation and up to the High Dependency Unit on the paediatric ward.' She reached forward and squeezed Ursula's hand. 'You've done really well too. It's not easy, and we see it all the time. Maybe you should take a few minutes to grab a cup of tea, or a sandwich. You look white as a sheet. There's a League of Friends' café just down the corridor on the left.'

'Thank you. I'll just sit with him for a little longer if that's okay. Maybe both our colours will improve.'

A nurse appeared around the curtain.

'They've just paged me from switchboard to tell me that his daddy is on his way. He should be here in about thirty minutes.'

Daniel jabbed his finger on the button for the lift doors to close. For God's sake, could it not work any faster? Perhaps it would have been quicker to sprint up the stairs. He'd got Ursula's message on his mobile when he'd finished his list and had immediately left the hospital in Watford, running across the car park. How instinctive, how hard-wired it felt, to go immediately to one's child if they were in danger. And also, how incomprehensible to be a parent who put them in danger – in mortal danger – by choice. He felt sick to his stomach.

Luca was in the Resus Unit at the hospital. It was evidently serious. At his age, bacterial infections could stampede through the body, inducing organ failure, the whole system collapsing like a sequence of dominoes.

He's in the right place, he'd told himself as he started the car. It was what he frequently said to his patients' parents in an effort to be reassuring. Perhaps, in fact, it wasn't consoling at all. He frequently saw parents mouthing prayers – often unfamiliar, a little rusty on their lips, making the sign of a haphazard cross on their chests as their child was wheeled into theatre – as if God, rather than the NHS, might be the best prospect by which to achieve recovery.

And what, he thought with a sudden jolt, should he tell Monica? Should he be phoning her now, before he knew the full scale of the situation himself? Should she be dashing to the airport? He couldn't bear to think of the guilt that would scythe through her. He thought of Ursula, out running when her children were dying. How unbearable that would be, ricocheting down through the years. He would not tell Monica yet. Luca might speedily rally. Ursula was with him. It was a soothing thought. It was her prompt attention, her intuition that something was seriously wrong, which had meant Luca, in Resus, actually *was* in the right place.

The lift doors opened and Daniel ran into the High Dependency Unit. The first thing that struck him, bizarrely, inexplicably, was that somehow Monica had beaten him there. How on earth had she done that? Maternal instinct, intuition? Surely not. There she stood, by the bedside, familiar in a patterned summer skirt. *Mon*, he started to say, but didn't, puzzled by the fact that her body looked shorter, stockier. When Ursula turned to face him, he was momentarily bewildered. Why was she wearing Monica's things? Seeing his confusion, she gestured to her clothing.

'I'm sorry; Luca was sick all over me just before I brought

him in. I had nothing to change into. I just wanted to get him here as quickly as possible. I'm so relieved you're here.'

He came to the bedside, and picked up the chart pinned to the frame. He touched Luca briefly.

'God, he looks terrible. I can't believe how quickly he's deteriorated. Monica will be beside herself.'

The first paediatrician appeared around the curtain.

'Hi, Daniel, you made it,' she said warmly. 'Bit of an unexpected opportunity to see the ward from a different perspective. I'm guessing that's not something you were actively seeking. The good news is that Ursula's been here for the difficult part. Luca's stabilising relatively quickly and you're probably just in time to see him rally. He should start becoming a little more alert soon.'

'His colour looks awful; and he's so limp.'

The doctor reached over and examined Luca's skin tone, pressing her fingertip to his exposed thigh.

'Rosy by lunchtime, please, little fellow.'

Luca was unresponsive.

Daniel leaned over to kiss him.

'Daddy's here, Daddy's here. What a fright you've given me. You're going to be better soon.'

Ursula slipped from the cubicle.

The doctor picked up Luca's charts.

'The tests are just back,' she said to Daniel. 'It's sepsis. Meningococcal sepsis rather than meningitis so he's lucky. And if Ursula hadn't brought him in when she did, we could have been looking at major organ failure. But I don't need to tell you that. You're looking at one lucky little boy who got the right attention just when he needed it. If I ever need to employ childcare, I'll be coming to you for advice.'

She left and Daniel stood, staring at his infant son.

Ursula had saved him. The irony could not be more dramatic.

He turned to find her standing silently just beyond him, blowing on a cup of tea. She handed him a coffee.

'I thought you could probably do with this.'

'Thank you,' he said. 'Thank you for the coffee, of course, but thank you for Luca, for your quick instincts, for doing exactly the right thing. If you had not acted so promptly . . . Thank you doesn't even begin to cover it.'

He refrained from saying that she'd saved him. It would carry with it too much of a painful inference. Now that what had happened to her children was a knowledge shared, everything else was caught in its potent field of gravity. Every word, every thought, flew to it, like iron filings to a magnet. It was appalling. Was that how her life had been in the yawning years since?

'I'm just so glad we got here in time,' Ursula said.

He hesitated.

'But it's more than that. We both know that. Ursula, if there's ever anything I can do for you, if you need a friend, if you ever need anything, count me in.'

She flushed, and busied herself with tidying the corner of the sheet.

He guessed that she would not answer. Was this how it would now be – both of them mindful of all that would remain unsaid, Ursula opting for neutral, pragmatic ground? He felt united with her in a complex alliance of knowledge, shared purpose, and esteem.

Ursula glanced at her watch.

'I should be going. Hours get swallowed up in here. I've lost all track of time. Ruby will be home soon. She will want to come and visit him. Is that allowed?'

Daniel reached for the notes.

'He has meningococcal sepsis. Caught at this stage, he'll make a speedy recovery, but the public health department of the hospital will want to trace who he's been in contact with in the last couple of days. We'll all be taking antibiotics, just as a safeguard so it's perfectly safe for Ruby to see him if she wants to come. It's likely he'll be here for a couple of days at least, and then it looks like we'll have to bring him in for a daily dose of intravenous anti-biotics until he finishes the course.'

She reached over and touched Luca's forehead briefly.

'When I come back, I'm going to bring in your bunny.'

Daniel looked up from the notes.

'Ursula, do you wear contact lenses?'

She looked perplexed.

'I do. Why?'

'I'm just reading here. The antibiotic they'll give us turns all your bodily fluids orange – temporarily, happily – so if you wear them, you'll stain them orange. Worth mentioning.'

Were they both on the verge of smiling? Daniel wondered if it might be hysteria, delirium. What a twenty-four hours it had been.

'Orange?' Ursula repeated.

'Orange. Everything that comes out of your body – orange.'

She shook her head incredulously.

'Everything? Curiouser and curiouser. I'll leave you to explain it to Ruby.'

54

Ursula folded Monica's clothes neatly in a carrier bag. She smoothed the fabric carefully.

It had been years since she'd worn someone else's clothes; a V-neck sweater of Gideon's, once, when she was pregnant with Nina and they'd walked along a blustery towpath. He'd been terse with her about something, admonished her for another failing. She'd felt herself diminishing, trying to keep pace with his stride. She'd pulled the cuffs of the sweater down over her fingers. He'd glanced at her over his shoulder, scathing, *You look like a child*, he'd said.

Monica's clothes had a fragrance, presumably her perfume, or perhaps it was fabric conditioner, a drawer liner. How awkward she had felt standing in front of Daniel wearing his wife's clothes. It felt curiously intimate, both in relation to Daniel and to Monica herself. Too symbolically close to a notion of stepping into her shoes, which she had not done, and had no intention of trying to do. How scrupulously she had guarded Ruby's connection to Monica.

She dressed in her own clothes, and rummaged in her bedside table drawer for her glasses. If she cried would she weep orange tears? How vivid that would be; maybe even cathartic. Might there be an antibiotic which could achieve tears of scarlet? That would manifest more accurately the grief of a heart that was broken.

But, she reminded herself, there was no need for tears over

Luca, orange or otherwise. He would be get better swiftly, he would be well again. Tragedy was clearly not life's default setting. She should perhaps, for once, try and be mindful of that.

She checked her watch again. If she left now, she would have time to walk to school and meet Ruby in the playground. She could buy her some sweets as a celebratory treat.

She walked out onto the street. It was a glorious June day. After the harsh lighting of the hospital ward, the honey glow of the sunshine was soothing to her eye. *We are here; resolutely, inextinguishably here,* pulsed the roses, the honeysuckle, the alliums she passed. She allowed herself to feel the faintest spring in her step. For years, she'd had the feeling that a street might catastrophically dissolve as she walked along it. But Luca would get better. Maybe tomorrow, he would be well enough to lift onto the rocking horse that was just beyond his bed in the corridor. She was sure he would like that.

Daniel Skyped Monica as soon as he arrived home from the hospital. Aghast, her palms pressed to her face in horror, she started to cry.

'I have to come home, right now. Oh my God, I can't believe you just let me be awake all morning unaware that anything was wrong. I'm coming home right now.'

'Monica, you don't have to. Everything is okay again, he's on the mend. By the time you get here, he'll most likely be home and everything will be back to normal.'

'Yes, because I've been away for nearly twelve weeks and normal doesn't include me any more. Can you imagine how awful that feels? Daniel, I feel like I've woken up from a spell of sleepwalking madness. What on earth was I thinking of? My child could have died and I was out here furthering my stupid career. I put you in an impossible position of having to support me, I've neglected my children, and I wasn't there for my son when he needed me. Daniel, I'm the worst mother in the world.'

'Mon, you're overreacting. This isn't about you. Luca is safe. It was a twenty-four-hour crisis, and now it's over. The person you chose to take care of him in your absence did exactly what you might have hoped of her. Your system is working. The film's going well, and from what you said on Sunday you're going to be finished in three weeks, and all set to come home anyway.'

'But Daniel, Luca could have died, and I wouldn't have been there.'

'Just like any parent, Monica. Ruby could cross a road while I'm at work and I wouldn't be there either.'

'Fantastic, now I'll start worrying about that too. Daniel, I've never felt more distraught in my life.'

'Monica, please don't be. I'm doing the best I can so that you don't have to worry. Ursula's been a star. Ruby is on good form. Finish your film, do a good job and come home to us, but don't bolt now and not bank everything you've achieved so far. Mon, we're nearly there. I swear to you I'd tell you if I thought you should come home.'

'The joke is' – and now she wiped her tear-streaked face with her palms – 'they've made me a job offer for when I get back: a post-production role, full-time, for a couple of months. I was planning on phoning you tonight to tell you. I was so excited. Even though I'd have to commute to London daily, it's a job I'd have given my eye-teeth for three months ago. Coming here has achieved exactly what I hoped it would, and yet now I'm sitting here feeling totally wretched, thinking I should never have come and that I put too much on the line for it.'

'Monica, that's brilliant news. In an all-round pretty horrendous twenty-four hours, that's fantastic news. So, finish up in California and come home and take the next step. I'll ask Ursula if she will stay on. Mon, Luca will be well again soon, with no lasting effects.

Hold on to that thought, give thanks for it, stop berating yourself, and keep doing what you are doing. You have so much to be happy about.'

'Since when did you become so wise and mellow? You're sounding more West Coast than me.'

'It's been a hell of a day. A lot of things have fallen into place; a sense of perspective, primarily, and an idea of what is the worst that can happen.'

'What do you mean? Is there something else? What's given you an idea of the worst that can happen?'

'Now's not the time, but there's something else I need to tell you. I have to shower and change now and get back to the hospital for the night. Ursula and Ruby are waiting for me to swap off with them.'

'I should be doing that, being there at the hospital, swapping off with you. And what can we talk about another time? Why won't you tell me? I'm upset anyway; just tell me and then I can spend the rest of the day crying about that as well.'

'It's not a crying matter, more of a stunned silence kind of thing.'

'What on earth are you talking about?'

'Ursula. I'm talking about Ursula. At Cassie's symposium, which was unbelievably only last night, I found out something about Ursula which explains everything.'

He told her.

She reacted with a stillness, a gravity, a dawning of realisations which froze her completely. 'The lists,' she said first, 'that's why she knew all the details for the lists,' and then, 'Oh God, Daniel, her husband did that to her children, and then she's had to work with you every day, seeing how loving a father can be.' She rocked back on the bed, her hands pressed to her face in shame. 'And what must she have thought of me, when I was choosing to leave my children, choosing to be without my children, when she had hers taken brutally from her. How unbearable it must have all been. No wonder she didn't want to work with children.'

'See what I mean about perspective?' he said. 'She's heroic in ways we can't begin to imagine.'

When he arrived on the ward, Ursula was feeding Luca some supper, and Ruby was making his bunny jump all over the bed and up the drip line.

'I hope you get some sleep,' Ursula said, gesturing to the z-bed which had been set up next to Luca's.

'No problem,' he smiled. 'Years of training as a junior doctor – these beds were what we crashed on. Maybe I'll fall asleep with a comforting sense of déjà vu.'

'Shall we have pizza?' Ursula asked Ruby as they were driving home. 'We could stop at Pizza Express and buy supper there.'

'Are you babysitting me all night if Daddy's not coming home?'

'Yes, I'm going to sleep in the spare bedroom. Look, on the back seat, my overnight bag, all set.'

'Can we eat the pizza even in front of the television?'

'Yes, for a special treat, and you can Skype Mummy afterwards. She'll have missed you and Luca very much today, and it would be good if you told her how much better he is looking.'

55

When Daniel finished his list the next morning, he went straight to the children's ward.

Coming through the swing doors, he saw Ursula, carefully lifting Luca onto the rocking horse in the corridor. Luca was clapping his hands.

'Yes,' he could hear Ursula saying. 'Yes, are you going for a ride on the horse? Let's put your feet in the stirrups, are you all set to giddy up? Hold onto the reins. There's my cowboy boy.'

Daniel came alongside her.

'That's a sight to lift the heart.'

He gave Luca a kiss, and another, saying, 'and that one's from Mummy.'

'How is Monica?' Ursula asked.

'Feeling upset, and wanting to bunk off three weeks early. She's hugely grateful to you. I'm guessing there will be a long letter in the post.'

'She doesn't have to be any of those things. And Mummy will be home soon, won't she, Luca; is your mummy coming home soon?' She looked at the floor. 'I'll miss them. Children creep up on you, make inroads into the heart. Even my scorched one. In this case, especially my scorched one.'

'Well that's good news, as far as I'm concerned, because there's something I need to ask you.'

'What?'

'In the midst of all of this, one thing seems to have gone

smoothly. On the back of her work in LA, Monica's been offered a full-time, short-term contract with the production company here. She got more details through yesterday. The initial contract is for two months, with a view then to an unfixed one. She'll be commuting to London and working in Soho, leaving early, coming back late. We'll be needing an unbelievable childminder, mother's help and housekeeper. Any thoughts?'

Ursula hesitated. What a push–pull in her heart; the instinct to scuttle away or to step forward and take the opportunity he was offering her. She looked him full in the eye, and paused for a second.

'I think I may know someone.'

'Previous experience of the family would obviously be a huge bonus.'

They shook hands in the corridor, by the polka-dot rocking horse.

'Deal done,' said Daniel.

It felt too important an outcome to smile about.

56

Luca tore around the kitchen, laughing and chasing Ruby, who dodged around Ursula and her father.

'Unbelievable,' Daniel said, shaking his head, smiling.

'It's some turnaround,' agreed Ursula, 'when you think, last week, he could barely lift his head from the pillow.'

'Even as a doctor, antibiotics can still seem like some kind of miracle.'

Ursula allowed herself to smile.

'Come here, my boy,' said Daniel to Luca, scooping him up and heartily kissing him. 'Who is Daddy's favourite boy in the whole wide world?'

He turned to Ursula.

'I feel so relieved, so ridiculously joyful; the temptation is to rush out and buy him every pedal car, every toy, every Duplo model an almost-two-year-old might ever have cause to want.'

'Then you'll spoil him, Daddy, and he won't be Luca, he'll be bratty,' Ruby said.

'Point taken.'

'Everything is happy again. Daddy, why don't we go for a day out to celebrate? Or we could stay somewhere, we could go somewhere for a treat for Luca being well again. No more hospital.'

'Hopsital,' Luca echoed.

'Well, hopefully no more hospital until he can say it properly, and then when he's six foot and maybe sustained a minor injury playing rugby,' said Daniel. 'Will you be able to say hospital, not hopsital, when you are eighteen, do you think?'

He kissed Luca's forehead.

'Don't change the subject, Daddy. Ple-ease can we go some-where at the weekend?'

She looked between Daniel and Ursula.

'I'm game,' Daniel said, and then, hesitantly, turning to Ursula, 'no pressure . . .'

Ursula paused.

Ruby looked at her.

'Oh please, Ursula, come with us, it will be such fun. Daddy, why don't you let Ursula choose, that way we know it's somewhere she really wants to go. Ursula, in the whole of England where would you choose to go? There must be somewhere you'd like.'

Daniel looked a little awkward.

'Ursula might be busy this weekend, darling. She might not want to choose, she might not even want to come.'

'You do though, Ursula, don't you? Please say you'll come.'

Ursula looked hesitantly at Daniel.

'Before, once before, you talked about going to the beach. I think I would like to go to the beach; in fact to a particular beach, Seacombe Sands, in Salcombe in Devon. Might that be the sort of place you'd like to go, Ruby?'

'It sounds perfect! Luca, Luca, we are going to the beach because you're not poorly any more. Daddy, let's look on the internet and find a nice place to sleep.'

Daniel booked for them to stay at the Gara Rock Hotel. When Ursula had come to the beach alone in 2002, the old hotel had closed down. Standing in her room when they arrived, she read a leaflet which told her that it had been bought and redevel-oped from 2004. Now, in 2013, it was open again. She looked out of the window. The coastline was still beautifully familiar.

Gara Rock stood sentinel over all she surveyed. Beyond, around the coast, was the lighthouse at Start Point. She didn't think it was manned any more; did anyone light the great lamp? She imagined it prepared for the darkness, steady with its broad stroke of light, lemon across the water.

It was a comforting thought. When the darkness did fall, she didn't know what memories it would bring.

She turned to the door, Ruby's impatient knocking summoning her.

'Ursula, have you unpacked yet? I have. Our room is a little bit bigger than yours, Luca is sleeping in the big bed with Daddy and I have a fold-up one they wheeled in and put by the window. I love it here. Have you seen the swimming pools; there's one inside *and* outside!'

She crossed the room and looked out at the coastline.

'Daddy says it will nearly be dark soon, so it's too late to go down to the beach. And too late for a swim in the pool. Luca just nearly fell asleep in the bath. Daddy says we can just have some quick supper in the restaurant and go to bed and then wake up early and go down there tomorrow. I can still see though, look, can you still see everything? Maybe there's still time.'

'I think wait for the morning; it will still be beautiful in the morning. There will be plenty of time, I promise you. You can explore for hours, all day. Look, see how the coast stretches so far, as far as your eye can see.'

'What's that? That little house, the one that's round and white with a thatched roof?'

'That's the old coastguard lookout. There are rocks, out to sea; it's a dangerous coastline for ships. Even a hundred years ago there was a lookout right there.'

'Where did the coastguard live?'

'Right here, I think. I think there were seven cottages which the coastguards and their families lived in; they had to walk a long way to get anywhere else.'

'Where did the children go to school? After all that walking.'

'East Portlemouth, I'm guessing, which is a village just if you keep walking ri-i-ght round there.' Ursula pointed, and Ruby pressed her face to the glass. 'And maybe for big school across on the little ferry to Salcombe, I don't know.'

'If it was windy, maybe they didn't have to go to school at all. Maybe they'd be blown off the cliffs right into the sea.'

'Do you think that would be a good excuse for missing school on a nice blowy, sunny day, maybe when the waves were a little up and just perfect for jumping in?'

Ruby laughed.

'How do you know all this?' she asked. 'Have you been here before?'

'Not here, not here to this hotel – see how shiny new it all is. But yes, to this place, to this beach, I used to come here every year, for many years.'

'In the morning, will you show me all the best rock pools? Is there a deep one I can sit in just like a bath?'

'From my memory, I think there is. When the tide is right out. And now are you ready for supper? Listen, I can hear Daddy calling you. You must eat and go straight to sleep so that you can wake up bright and early in the morning. That nap in the car doesn't count as proper sleeping. Have you got clean hands? Come, let's go and find Daddy and go to the restaurant. What are you going to choose to eat?'

Ursula pushed the window ajar, and then lay in the darkness, her eyes wide open. She could hear the sea, rolling and crashing on the beach below.

Supper had been merry. That was the right word. How many years since she had sat at a table, with others, with children, and eaten a meal? In a moment of frivolity, encouraged by Ruby's excitement, she'd chosen to drink a Mojito. She hadn't had a drink for years, though Rose occasionally offered her sherry with soup, on cold days in November when the wind swirling around the Great House made it feel bleak. She had always demurred. But when Daniel offered, and said, *Whatever you'd like, I'm sure they can make whatever you'd prefer*, she gave into temptation. Daniel had a scotch. Was he tired, she asked, after all that driving? He'd shaken his head.

'I am really pleased to be here,' he said. 'Great spot.'

He paused.

'And, I'm assuming there's a history, a familiarity that I can only guess at, but if you want to talk – obviously above Ruby's chattering and Luca's babbling because that will be nonstop all weekend . . .' His voice took on a more serious tone. 'If you want to talk, I'm here, if talking, or if I, can be of any help.'

She'd smiled at him. The sincerity of his offer was evident.

In the hospital, he'd said, *If you need a friend, count me in*, and it seemed he was becoming one. How curious, how surprising that was, in a way that was devoid of anything inappropriate, of anything that was not respectful to Monica. They were like allies, she thought, sharing in a common purpose, united in their focus on Ruby and Luca. She had not been aware of the new easiness between them, but she was mindful of it now, the Mojito before her, Luca crawling under the table, fascinated by a dog that was tethered at the next, and Ruby asking, 'Please can we have blue chairs like these ones in our kitchen? I think Mummy would love them.'

And so, when they returned to his room and she helped get Luca ready for bed, brushing his teeth with care, wiping the dribble of toothpaste from his chin with her fingertip, she waited until Ruby had gone into the bathroom to shower, and Daniel was sitting on the bed, stroking Luca's head even though he was already asleep, and she turned to him and said, 'It's the letting go . . . that's what I have never achieved. The chill, and the stupor, those I have felt, all these years, but never the letting go. I need to learn how to do that, how to let Nina and Joe go, without it seeming like a betrayal, without it seeming like I am not there for them again. But how can I let them go when I feel everything I do should bear witness to their death?'

Daniel faced her.

'Ursula, everything you do, everything you are, everything about you, pays homage to them. When I watch you with Ruby and Luca, I see exactly how you must have been as a mother. I know you were a brilliant mother. Until that night, they were very lucky children. And the letting go, maybe it's letting go just the darkness, the pain. Maybe it's not about bearing witness to their death but about bearing witness to their life. Does that make any sense?'

She wept. He had stepped towards her, swiftly, and held her in his arms, fraternally and without awkwardness.

He gave her his handkerchief. She sat on the edge of the bed, and wiped her eyes as Ruby came out of the bathroom.

'Are you all right, Ursula?' she asked, coming out swathed in towels. 'Look how wrapped up I am. I nearly managed to wrap on the bath mat as well.'

'Thank you, I'm fine. In fact, better than in a long time. And yes, that's actually remarkable towel wrapping.'

She nodded her gratitude to Daniel and walked softly to her room.

Now, in her bed, she thought about what he had said. She could honour Nina and Joe in their happiness, in their ready laughter, their joy in things, their constant curiosity, their affection, their open-hearted merriment. She fell asleep and dreamed of them, and they were laughing, out on Seacombe Sands, holding things out to her – a flower, a heart-shaped stone, a thick twist of seaweed, a shorn crab's leg – *Mummy, look, look what I found.*

And when she was woken in the morning – by Ruby knocking,

calling, *Ursula wake up, let's go swimming, do you have your costume? Daddy says we can go in the inside pool but that the outside one will be too cold this early* – she did not feel as bereft as usual. Rather, that she had spent time with her children, allowed herself to luxuriate in the memory of them. Perhaps in her dreams she would allow herself to be their mother still.

They ate breakfast; Luca daubed himself with most of a *pain au chocolat*, and Ursula dipped her napkin in her water glass and wiped him clean. She drank an espresso, felt it jolt through her system. 'All set?' she said to Ruby, who was dancing with impatience at her side.

They walked down the path through the gorse and Ruby ran ahead to the little wooden bridge at the beginning of the path to the beach.

'What's that tumbledown little house?' she called to her father. 'Did anyone live there once, do you think?' She dipped her toes in the small stream which flowed within feet of the ruin.

'I don't know, ask Ursula, I think there was smelting, something to do with iron ore, around here. Maybe it was to do with that. Do you know, Ursula?' He called back to her as she picked her way down the steep path, carrying Luca.

'I have never known what that is,' she confessed. 'It has puzzled me for years.'

'With a roof on, could you live in it?' Ruby asked.

'Anything's possible,' Daniel said.

Ruby leapt off the last part of the rock causeway which led onto the beach. The tide was completely out, and the wide scoop of sand stretched out like a pristine invitation to play.

'There are rock pools, huge rock pools,' Ruby whooped. 'Look, Ursula, look over there by the cliffs.'

Still carrying Luca, Ursula followed Ruby's light tread, her footprints hardly visible in the sand, and stood behind her as

Ruby peered into the long tongues of sand between the contours of the rock face.

'They're like teeth, like huge teeth,' Ruby pronounced, running her fingertips across the grooves of the rock surface.

'Like teef,' shouted Luca, beginning to chatter his teeth, laughing, and pressing his face close to Ursula's.

'Want to get down,' he said, so Ursula took off his plimsolls and pushed them into her pocket, and put him down on the sand. She held onto his upstretched arms, allowing him to paddle between her wide-stepped feet. The sun shone warmly on the back of her neck. How familiar, how known it all felt.

'Daddy, look! Watch me,' squealed Ruby, lying down and wriggling in a rock pool. 'The water's warm,' she shouted. 'Ursula, come and feel, the water's warm.'

'It'll be warmer than the sea is,' Daniel said. 'I'll race you to the edge of the waves.'

Ruby leapt up and ran after him, and they splashed and stamped along the frill of the shoreline.

Ursula followed. How surprising it felt too. In her jaw, the base of her skull, along her lips, she had the curious sensation of wanting to smile broadly. She allowed herself to do so. It felt like an exquisite ripple which began somewhere at her core.

She looked out onto the horizon, at the water dancing and sparkling before her. A bird wheeled high overhead. Out, over towards the estuary, a yacht tacked pluckily on. It was beautiful. She allowed herself to absorb its vitality and to take joy from it; allowed it to wash over and over her with each fresh foray of the waves.

'Ursula, come and sit down here,' Ruby called, now sitting at the water's edge, allowing the incoming waves to scramble up the length of her legs. Nina had loved doing the same. *Oh no!* she would shriek, when an unexpected wave soaked her right through.

'It's not cold, I promise you, come, Ursula, come.'

Ruby patted the sand beside her, and Ursula came and sat as she was asked.

'Look at that rock,' said Ruby, pointing to one which stood isolated, proud on the sand.

Ursula paused. It could only have been that rock Ruby would notice.

'I knew a boy once,' she said, deciding in an instant that Ruby would never know more; she would learn of enough pain in the world without knowing this. She started again. 'I knew a boy once, a boy the same age as you, who could run like the wind too, and he thought that if you looked, really looked at that rock, with your head tipped like this,' and here she used her palms to adjust the tilt of Ruby's head, 'that in fact it looked like an enormous frog, a huge great frog, squatting and watching the tide come racing in.'

And Ruby looked, and considered, her head held as Ursula had shown, her mouth pursed in concentration, her scribble of curls blown by the breeze, and then she turned to Ursula and said, her tone bright and confident, 'Ursula, I think that that boy was completely, exactly right. It's JUST like a frog.'

'Daddy,' she called, turning up the beach to where Daniel was photographing Luca, 'Come and take a picture of this frog rock.'

And it felt to Ursula as if Ruby's words tugged something free. She gave thanks, all these years later, for Joe's image of the rock being validated by a child the same age as he had been when he died. Joe's frog rock went on. She lifted her eyes to the taut horizon, surprised by an unexpected misting of tears.

She saw Ruby glance at her quickly, and then reach out for her hand. The child kissed her wrist fiercely, once, twice, three times, and then followed Ursula's gaze far out to sea. Ursula kissed Ruby's wrist in return and let the moment be, let it be, there on the sand.

Acknowledgements

In researching this book, I'd like to acknowledge Professor Jack Levin, from Northeastern University in Boston, who first coined the term 'family annihilator'. Also, Philip Hodson, Fellow of the British Association for Counselling and Psychotherapy. His observation (expressed in an article written by Sally Williams and published in *The Times*) that 'it is a life sentence from which recovery is well-nigh impossible, and that is the whole point', cuts to the heart of what I was trying to explore in this novel.

I am grateful to Dr Corinne Hayes for advice on medical procedures; to Simeon Maskrey QC for advice on medical negligence; and to Finn Stevenson, whose thesis on scoliosis I plundered for matters spinal. All errors, inaccuracies and embellishments are obviously my own.

All characters in the novel are fictitious, but the hotel at which the story ends is the beautiful Gara Rock, at East Portlemouth, Salcombe. (www.gararock.com)

To early readers Georgia Stevenson, Barbara Bradshaw, Linda Longshaw and Rachel Langdale, many thanks.

Suzie Dooré, my brilliant editor at Hodder and Stoughton, edited this book with precision, perceptiveness and meticulous focus. I am hugely grateful for her input. Thanks also to Francine Toon for skilfully guiding it to press.

In her customary fashion, Helenka Fuglewicz asked all the right questions at its snow-bound beginnings. Thank you. Thanks also to Ros Edwards and Julia Forrest at Edwards Fuglewicz.

Finally, I'd like to acknowledge the women whose heartbreaking accounts of the loss of their children informed my knowledge. It is the cruellest irony that this appalling contemporary crime is usually wrought as a result of women taking back control of their own lives.